III DX □   G.C.

THE GILA WARS

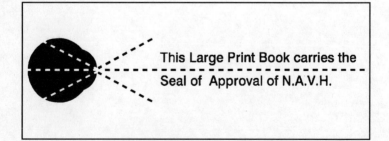

This Large Print Book carries the
Seal of Approval of N.A.V.H.

A JOSIAH WOLFE, TEXAS RANGER NOVEL

THE GILA WARS

LARRY D. SWEAZY

THORNDIKE PRESS
A part of Gale, Cengage Learning

GALE
CENGAGE Learning®

Detroit • New York • San Francisco • New Haven, Conn • Waterville, Maine • London

GALE
CENGAGE Learning®

Copyright © 2013 by Larry D. Sweazy.
Thorndike Press, a part of Gale, Cengage Learning.

Thorndike Press® Large Print Western.
The text of this Large Print edition is unabridged.
Other aspects of the book may vary from the original edition.
Set in 16 pt. Plantin.

LIBRARY OF CONGRESS CATALOGING-IN-PUBLICATION DATA

Sweazy, Larry D.
    The Gila Wars : a Josiah Wolfe, Texas Ranger novel / by Larry D. Sweazy.
    — Large Print edition.
        pages cm. — (Thorndike Press Large Print Western) (A Josiah Wolfe,
    Texas Ranger novel)
    ISBN 978-1-4104-5934-3 (hardcover) — ISBN 1-4104-5934-9 (hardcover)
    1. Texas Rangers—Fiction. 2. Large type books. I. Title.
    PS3619.W438G55 2013
    813'.6—dc23   2013010758

Published in 2013 by arrangement with The Berkley Publishing Group,
a member of Penguin Group (USA) Inc.

Printed in the United States of America
1 2 3 4 5 6 7 17 16 15 14 13

To Loren D. Estleman

ACKNOWLEDGMENTS

I first met Rita Kohn at a book fair. An author and a reviewer, her kindness and enthusiasm toward the Josiah Wolfe series is, and has been, greatly appreciated. Rita edited the book *Full Steam Ahead: Reflections on the Impact of the First Steamboat on the Ohio River, 1811–2011* (Indiana Historical Society Press, 2011), which was helpful when it came to researching steamboats used to transport rustled cattle from Texas to Cuba in 1875. It was more of a happy coincidence than a planned occurrence when a valued source for research turned out to be much closer than I'd anticipated. Thanks again, Rita.

The Indiana Historical Society hosts an author fair every winter, and it has been a great privilege for me to be a participant every year since the Josiah Wolfe series debuted. The Historical Society's support of local authors, and of my books, is greatly appreciated. Becke Bolinger does a fine job organizing this event, and Phil Janes manages the book sales. Thank you to both of you, and to your dedicated staff, for hosting such a fine event. I'm lucky to live in a state with such a vibrant historical society.

I am equally lucky to have the continuing support I do as a writer of this series. My thanks go to the Berkley production team; my editor, Faith Black; my agent, Cherry Weiner; and, of course, to my wife, Rose, whose continued effort and enthusiasm for this series, and my writing aspirations, is unmatched. Thank you all.

AUTHOR'S NOTE

The Red Raid, as it was called, was a violent confrontation to put an end, once and for all, to Juan Cortina's cattle rustling operation. Liberty has been taken with the timeline and the actual events for the purpose of storytelling. For an accurate account of the Texas Rangers' involvement in the raid, I would suggest to readers these two books as good resources: *The Texas Rangers: A Century of Frontier Defense* by Walter Prescott Webb (University of Texas Press, 2008) and *Lone Star Justice: The First Century of the Texas Rangers* by Robert M. Utley (Berkley, 2002).

The following books as good resources may also be of further interest to readers seeking more information about the Texas Rangers and Texas history in general: *The Texas Rangers: Wearing the Cinco Peso, 1821–1900* by Mike Cox (Forge, 2008); *Six*

Years with the Texas Rangers, 1875–1881 by James B. Gillett (Bison Books, 1976); *Lone Star: A History of Texas and The Texans* by T. R. Fehrenbach (Da Capo Press, 2000); and *Frontier Texas: A History of a Borderland to 1880* by Robert F. Pace and Dr. Donald S. Frazier (State House Press, 2004).

PROLOGUE

September 1869

The distant echo of a gunshot stirred Josiah out of a nap. He wasn't sure if the gunshot was real or a remnant of the dream he'd been submerged in. A blink of his eyes told him that he was back in reality, his feet firmly planted on the wood desk in the marshal's office and single cell jail that was his daily domain.

Midday light filtered in through the western-facing window, and the sole street that served the town of Seerville was silent. Weather was of no concern, as far as Josiah could tell. Rain, or the chance of it, had yet to show itself. And any criminal threat that he knew of was miles away the last he'd heard. The sky was calm and as blue as a bird, not skittish at all. There wasn't a cloud to be seen through the dusty window.

There were no prisoners in the jail, at the moment, and no pets, deputies, or mice milling about in the daylight, scavenging for a crumb or two or just lurking about. Rodents, like most prisoners, usually showed up in the night. For the most part, being marshal of Seerville, Texas, was quiet and uneventful. It was as if Josiah were the only person in the world, just sitting around waiting for something to happen.

Josiah sat up in his chair, exhaled, and cleared his eyes. There was nothing of any importance lying in front of him on the desk.

Now he was almost certain the gunshot he'd heard was in his dream, not anywhere outside.

Images flittered in and out of his mind, nothing that he could grab hold of, but he was sure the dream was just a touch of the days and nights from the war coming back to haunt him, or cause him to second-guess his sanity, even four years after the last good man had fallen on Yankee ground.

Josiah had been lucky. He'd come back from the war with all of his limbs and his mind reasonably intact. Most every man he knew who had served the Confederacy, and survived the war, crippled and four-limbed men alike, was burdened with unpleasant dreams and memories. But no one dared speak of them aloud. Conversations with, and about, ghosts held no currency in the daily lives of old soldiers. No use bringing up bad business and defeat, even though the resentment of those feelings lived just beneath the skin of them all, ready to escape in a moment of anger and rage that might just as quickly turn to madness.

Blood, bombs, slow death, and other nightmares rocked the gentlest of souls. Some men were lost, still hankering for morphine, or for the opportunity to kill without consequences. While other men wanted nothing more than a normal, boring life. Josiah Wolfe was one of those men. Boring suited him just fine.

He stood up from the desk then and made his way to the door, just to make sure he was right, that the gunshot he'd heard hadn't been real.

He ignored the three wanted posters on the wall and thought nothing of his own duties as the marshal. The rifles were locked up, and his Colt Army was stuffed in the drawer. His gun belt was empty.

The marshal's job fit Josiah like a well-made set of boots. It offered the security of a place to go every day and a happy alternative to being a farmer, which he had never been any good at, much to his father's disappointment. Josiah had no desire to stock his land with more cows than he needed, or to plant any larger of a garden than it took to feed his growing family. Lily, his wife, was much better at growing things than he was.

As he had assumed, the street was silent, empty.

Seerville was a small town. It was hardly a town at all, really. It was a place on the way to somewhere else for most folks, and so small that it wasn't on any viable maps that Josiah had ever seen. Moscoso's Trail was a good ways off, and it was a half day's ride to Tyler and a little longer to Camp Ford, stuffed right in the heart of the piney woods of East Texas. Most of the locals had cleared some tracts and farmed around the town. There were about twenty frame houses scattered beyond the street in front of the office.

Fall had yet to wrangle away summer, and the air was still hot, thick, and humid. The street was dry, and the hot season had pushed up against being a drought, but relented frequently enough, with storms from the southwest, not to be too much trouble. Still, there had been no rain in the last twenty days, and the stress of no water was starting to show on everything green.

A cloud of dust was pushing its way into

town. Somebody was coming, and they were in a big hurry. The dream was gone, and now Josiah had to reconsider what he'd initially thought.

Another gunshot echoed, cracking through the air like thunder, as foreign and unexpected on this clear late-summer day as a snowflake gliding to the dry ground.

Josiah flinched so deeply he felt it all the way to his bones. His hand slipped to his empty holster, instinctively reaching for equality, for the courage to face whatever was coming his way. He took a deep breath, knowing full well that he didn't have time to rush into the office to grab his gun.

The horse and rider came quickly into view, rushing past the few buildings that made up Seerville: the mercantile that shared a back room, offering the only saloon in a fifteen-mile radius; the bank which had been on its last legs for as long as Josiah could remember; a four-room hotel that was empty most of the time; and Landus Moore's livery and smithy shop, the only viable business in town. Once Josiah recognized the rider, he relaxed a little, but not completely.

There would be no need for a gun, since the horse bore Josiah's deputy, Charlie Langdon.

Charlie was a tall, beefy man, with facial features that always looked like nightfall was right around the corner. He brought his big Palomino mare to a grinding stop right in front of Josiah. The horse kicked up a thick cloud of dust in the process.

An angry look pierced Charlie's almost black eyes, and he held a piece of paper opposite his tight grip of the horse's reins.

Josiah and Charlie had both left Seerville as young men in '61, serving in the First Texas together for the entirety of the war, and like Josiah, Charlie came back whole, at least physically — but more changed, more enraged, and more unsettled, mentally.

Charlie Langdon had learned how to kill in the war. As far as Josiah was concerned, he'd learned to like it, too. Which was one of the reasons why Josiah had hired him as his deputy — so he could keep an eye on him.

"They done went and kilt us, Wolfe. Just done went and cut us off at the gall-durned knees."

"What are you talking about?"

"The train. Nearest curve is planned eight miles out, past the Bullitches' place. Gonna give that old crazy fool a pretty penny to cut his spread in half, while the rest of the town just up and dies. We might as well pack it up and move to Tyler."

"I'm not leaving," Josiah said.

Charlie jumped off the Palomino and stopped a few inches from Josiah. There was a hint of alcohol on his breath, and a week's worth of dirt crusted on his skin. He smelled like the south end of a skunk. "I'm done, Wolfe. I ain't gonna wait for the inevitable." He tore the silver star off his chest and stuck it out, waiting for Josiah to take it with gritted teeth.

"Let me see the paper."

"You don't believe me?"

"Of course I believe you. I just want to read the words for myself."

Josiah knew as much as anyone else what was at stake, what the railroad coming through Seerville would mean to everyone in the town. And more to the point, what it meant if the railroad *didn't* come through town.

A team of surveyors had come through nine months prior, remaining tight-lipped, mumbling to one another, saying only what needed saying to anyone else but themselves. The entire population of townsfolk, including Josiah, watched every move the men made as they went about their business, measuring this and that, eyeing the land like it was a woman who could whisper secrets to them. And there was no doubt, no question, that if the railroad did come through Seerville, like everyone hoped, the Langdons were the ones who would benefit the most. They owned a horseshoe claim of land around the north side of town, the most likely spot for a watering stop. Prosperity, though, would not be the Langdons' alone; everyone who owned a square inch of dirt in Seerville would see their life changed.

Charlie handed the paper to Josiah, still holding out his badge in his other hand. It only took a second for Josiah to see that Charlie was right. The railroad would be too far from Seerville to make a difference. He nodded silently, in agreement.

"Take the badge, Wolfe."

"What're you going to do?"

Charlie dropped the badge, glaring at Josiah. It tumbled to the ground, landing with a thud, disappearing in a poof of dust.

Josiah stared at the ground, at the badge lodged in the dust of the street. "You're really quitting? You're just done? This doesn't mean anything. We're not done. There's still time."

"You always were a slow believer, Wolfe. I thought maybe Chickamauga would have set your head right, but it didn't happen then, and it ain't gonna happen now. The town's dead. You're out of a job; you just don't know it yet. I'm not waitin' around for it to be final. I got time to make up for." Charlie stared at Josiah, the darkness fully set in his face. "I mean what I say, Wolfe. If anybody knows that, it's you."

"What're you going to do?" Josiah repeated, his mouth dry, his own fears about the future creeping up the back up his neck.

"Anything I want to," Charlie said. "Any gall-durned thing I want." He jumped up on the horse, spit into the street, then whipped the reins like he was about to run a race, and sped away from the marshal's office, covering Josiah with a healthy layer of dust and worry.

He knew what Charlie Langdon was capable of. The First Texas was the first regiment into a battle, and the last one out. Josiah had seen Charlie covered in blood from head to toe on more than one occasion, all the while smiling like he was a boy at play. Death didn't scare Charlie Langdon like it did most people. He held no regrets.

Josiah held the paper tight in his hand, not wanting to be the bearer of bad news to anyone he came into contact with. But the town would know soon enough of the decisions they'd have to make, once they knew what he did, and Josiah was betting they'd follow Charlie's lead.

Every man, woman, and child would run out of town as quickly as possible, angry, in search of a new way of life, a new way of looking at the world, rather than staying and building something out of the ruin, turning bad luck into good.

With his shoulders slumped and Charlie's badge in hand, Josiah walked into his office, sat down at the desk, propped his feet back up, and wished he could get the dream back that had slipped away when Charlie fired off the first round into the air, but he knew that was impossible. The past was gone. And now all he could do was wait for the future to catch up to him.

CHAPTER 1

June 1875

The sky pulsed with tiny pokes of silver stars, piercing the black blanket of night for as far as the eye could see. A fire struggled to stay lit in the center of camp, the last bit of mesquite tossed onto it nearly three hours before, when watch duty had changed. Orange coals breathed in and out underneath the fire, almost matching the rhythm of the far-away stars, and the comforting smell of smoke was as noticeable and welcome as the pot of Arbuckle's coffee that had yet to come to a full boil.

A thin line of gray pushed up on the eastern horizon, offering the first glimpse of the new day. It had been a long, warm night, preceded by a hotter than normal day. The expected heat of summer had set in early, and a dry spring had made it seem like mid-August instead of early June.

Some of the Rangers of Company A

stirred about, waking slowly, not making much noise. But mostly, the larger number of men still slept, getting as much rest for the coming day as possible. There was not a one of them that didn't know the night before that the threat of a real fight with Juan Cortina and his men lay at their feet and was likely to be a memorable confrontation. Josiah Wolfe, for one, would be glad to get on with the day; glad it was here, so it could be over with.

"Day's a-comin' on fast, Wolfe," Scrap Elliot said in a low voice. He sat at the edge of the fire pit, his bedroll and belongings already stored away, ready to be packed onto his horse, a trusted blue roan mare he called Missy.

"You sure you're up for it?" Josiah was sitting next to Scrap, watching him roll a cigarette — Scrap called them quirlies — keeping his eye on the coffeepot at the same time.

There was a sweet smell to the coffee, most likely from the egg and sugar coating that had brought roasted coffee to the West. Before 1865, and during the War Between the States, coffee beans were green, less flavorful when they were boiled. Josiah had seen more than one fight break out over the ever-present peppermint stick that came with the package of Arbuckle's.

Josiah's bedroll was still laid out on the hard ground, and the volume of his voice was just above a whisper. He didn't want to get Scrap riled up, and it wouldn't take much. One wrong word could set the boy off.

"Now that's one of the silliest things I've ever heard come out of your mouth, Wolfe," Scrap said, in full voice. "Why would you think I wouldn't be ready for a good fight?"

Scrap was in his early twenties, almost twelve years younger than Josiah. He was fit but thin, lean but strong, and as hot-tempered and opinionated as any man in the company, as far as Josiah was concerned. Even on a good day, Scrap Elliot was unpredictable, but he was a fine horseman, and an even better shot, to boot. He'd saved Josiah's life more than once with his gun skills.

"You haven't been the same since that recent business in Austin," Josiah said.

Scrap finished rolling his quirlie, stuck it in his mouth, then produced a match, seemingly out of nowhere, and lit the cigarette in one swift flick of the wrist. He drew in a hard, deep, breath, and the tip of the tobacco blazed orange, nearly matching the color of the coals at the bottom of the fire.

"That business is over with, Wolfe. I'm a free man." He glared at Josiah as he exhaled, then looked away to the distant horizon.

"I'm just asking. No need to get angry this early in the day. Save it for Cortina. I'll not speak of Austin, or of your time in jail, again."

"I'd appreciate that."

A small bird flittered overhead, distracting both of them with the surprise of its movement. Josiah wasn't sure what kind of bird it was. They'd camped at the edge of a motte, a thick grove of oak trees, not too far from the Arroyo Colorado, a fresh-water inlet that drained out to the Gulf. The spring migration was over with, or nearly so.

The winged spectacle that filled the sky, and ground, in the spring with all kinds of colorful birds was a sight to behold. Some went on north, and some stayed in South Texas. Like Juan Cortina and his legion of cattle rustlers, the birds knew no borders. This one whistled hoarsely, just above them, like it was trying to find its voice, then flew off to the west, seeking out the top of another oak tree, where it started singing in earnest.

The song was soft at first, a series of three or four similar notes. As the gray line on the eastern horizon grew, so did the bird's volume. For the moment, it sang solo.

An uncomfortable silence settled between Josiah and Scrap.

The business Josiah had spoken of involved Scrap getting caught up in a string of murders that had occurred in Austin, being falsely accused, then being thrown in solitary confinement in the county jail. A place that was commonly referred to as the Black Hole of Calcutta because of its dismal environment and the custom of prisoners walking in on two feet only to be sent out flat on their back in a pine box, deader than a doornail. Ultimately, Scrap had been cleared of any wrongdoing because of Josiah and Captain McNelly's efforts, but his freedom had not come easy, or without consequences.

"I don't want you to think I ain't appreciative of what you done for me, Wolfe." Scrap took a long draw on the quirlie, making brief eye contact with Josiah.

The smell of the coffee grew sweeter and cut through the acrid smoke, signaling that the boiling of it was done enough.

Josiah got up, grabbed two porcelain cups, and poured himself and Scrap a healthy dose of morning coffee. It steamed generously, and the smell of it was strong, almost overwhelming, but not too unfriendly.

"I was not right on my feet for a long time after I got home from the war," Josiah said. "I'm just making sure you're not as skittish as that morning bird, that's all. Captain Mc-Nelly's going to need us at our best. This fight's been a long time coming. I just want to make sure you're up to it, that's all."

Scrap nodded, took the last draw off of his quirlie, then stubbed it out on the bottom of his boot. He placed the remaining, half-smoked cigarette in a small white cloth bag, and stuffed it back into his pocket. The comfort and habit of smoking was never too far from his reach.

Josiah, who had never acquired the taste for tobacco, had noticed Scrap reaching for his quirlies more than normal since they'd been on the trail south. And the boy's skin, which was normally a thin shade of unblemished white, seemed even paler than normal. Scrap was a skinny, muscled broomstick, with a dollop of unruly black at the top of his head. He looked like something had been drained out of him. Josiah just wasn't sure what that something was, but there was no mistaking that a deep constitutional change had occurred, something serious, whether Scrap wanted to admit it or not.

"I'm ready for Cortina," Scrap said.

"Don't you worry none about me or my shootin' abilities. We missed him this spring when we came back to Corpus, and you left us to return to Austin when Lyle was sick. But I got a feelin' he's close this time around. The air smells foul, don't it?"

Josiah took a swig of the coffee, glad for the heat from it, pushing away the last remains of sleep. "That past spring seems ages ago." He ignored Scrap's question.

Scrap nodded yes. "I'm glad Lyle's all right. I feared he had the same fevers that took the rest of your family."

Josiah swallowed hard, not wanting to revisit the loss of his wife and three daughters who had died before he joined the Texas Rangers. "Lyle's good for a four-year-old."

"You don't talk about him much."

"It's hard being away, but he's in good hands with Ofelia."

"Says you."

The uncomfortable silence returned between the two men then. This silence was a familiar one. Scrap didn't look kindly on Ofelia, the Mexican woman who cared for Josiah's son while he was on the trail with the Rangers. Josiah's wife, Lily, weakened by the fevers and flu that had taken his three daughters, too, had died in childbirth four years earlier, and eventually, Josiah had moved to Austin from Seerville, just outside of Tyler, bringing Ofelia with him.

Scrap's prejudice was not uncommon, but it was unwelcome. Josiah had no choice in the matter if he was going to continue serving as a Ranger. He was courting a fine woman back in Austin, Pearl Fikes, but they were still a good ways from marriage, if that ever came into being, so as it was, Ofelia was the only woman, the only person in the world, really, that Josiah trusted enough to leave his son with.

The only other alternative was to quit the Rangers for good and find a way to make a living that kept him at home, in the city. It was not a consideration that Josiah was fond of, especially after spending so much time there recently, but he knew the day might come when becoming an Austinite would be a necessity instead of a choice. Luckily, and happily, today was not that day.

"Cortina *is* close," Josiah said, changing the subject. "I heard tell last night, after coming off watch, that there's a Cuban steamer sitting out in the bay, ready to take a load of beeves off Cortina's hands, most of them with American brands."

"King Ranch brands, I'll betchya."

"Likely. It'll take a load of men to see this deal through, and Cortina's not going to let it fall on unwatched shoulders. I'm just sorry we weren't up for the scouting duties. I'da been happy to've been one of the boys Captain McNelly sent out into the night to find out what Cortina's up to, and how many men he's really got on his side."

"You and me both." Scrap drank his coffee and looked away from Josiah again, staring off into the distance. It was like he was looking for something, but knew full well from the beginning that whatever it was wasn't there.

The smell of bacon frying hit Josiah's nose, coming from another fire close by. Soft voices murmured about, drifting up and around him on a slight breeze. Another bird had joined in on the conversation with the one that had flown to the top of the nearby tree. Gray daylight pushed up on the horizon, chasing away the darkness eagerly now, quicker, without regret, or without giving a second thought to turning back. There was no choice in the matter; darkness would lose the battle because it was the way things worked, just how it was. Daylight always won out over night. Always.

If only it were that easy, Josiah thought. *If only it were that easy.*

He stood up then and glanced down a slight rise to the spot in the camp where the captain slept; a white cotton wall tent that was reminiscent of those used in the War Between the States. It glowed from the inside out. Captain McNelly was awake, probably had been moving about before any of them, including Josiah, had stirred. There was no movement to be seen inside the tent, but that meant little. The captain was probably reading, studying, thinking, strategizing about the day ahead of them all. McNelly was a strong, disciplined man, even though he suffered from one of the worst afflictions of consumption that Josiah had ever seen.

Several rows of smaller tents, white as well, that were often referred to as dog tents, spread out past the captain's tent. Josiah, Scrap, and a few of the other boys had chosen to sleep under the stars, with just their bedrolls and an open camp. Josiah and Scrap both liked to be ready to go at a moment's notice if there was no weather to contend with. Some things they agreed on, without question.

The smell of bacon was coming from the fire just outside of McNelly's tent. Josiah was about to scrounge up some breakfast for himself, and the men around their fire, when he heard a low roar of thunder rise up behind him. Scrap heard it, too, and they both turned to face it together.

It was immediately apparent that it wasn't thunder they'd heard; the sky had remained perfectly clear. The sudden rumble was a battery of horse hooves heading their way.

There was a circle of men on night watch duty surrounding the camp, and no alarm had been set off, bringing all of the Rangers to arms, so Josiah knew that the rolling trample of hooves must be the return to camp of Lieutenant Clement Robinson and the eighteen men who had been charged to go out and scout Cortina's position.

The troop of men, led by a bearded, fiercely focused Robinson, a man Josiah knew little about but liked and respected immediately upon meeting him on this trip out, appeared out of the fuzzy grayness of morning, heading straight for the open camp.

Josiah realized that he was standing in the middle of the throughway and jumped back just in time.

Robinson, riding a sweating chestnut gelding, yelled at the top of his lungs, but his words were lost to the unrelenting pace of all of the horses behind him. The ground under Josiah's feet vibrated, and if any man was still asleep in the camp it was because he was either deaf or dead. The message was clear, though: *Move out of the way. We have something urgent to tell the captain.*

It didn't take Josiah but a second to divine what that urgent message was. There were not eighteen scouts. They had picked up an extra man. There were nineteen horses. Robinson had a prisoner, a Mexican bound on a smaller horse than the chestnut gelding, struggling to keep up with the rest, its bit tied to the rider in front of it, the man second to Robinson.

Josiah assumed the Mexican was one of Cortina's men. His clothes were ragged, his eyes defeated, his hands bound tightly, and his face bruised and bloodied. There was no sign of any bullet wound, but the stubby little man leaned forward, like he was in great pain. The lean might have only been one of fear, or part of a plot to escape, but Josiah doubted that. No man was stupid enough to try to break free in a camp of Rangers hungry to quell Juan Cortina. Not if he was in his right mind.

The troop of scouts pushed by, offering no explanation, only a cloud of unsettled dust in their wake. Most of the men had smiles on their faces, though. They knew what waited for them out in the world beyond the camp; a battle, a chance at victory, and now they seemed to have confidence, the upper hand. It would be a good tonic for all of the Rangers to drink before setting out.

Josiah watched, a familiar taste rising from deep inside his throat, as Robinson stopped in front of McNelly's tent, quickly dismounted, and disappeared inside.

"Looks like they found more than they were lookin' for," Scrap said, dusting the dirt off his shoulder.

"Or exactly what Cortina intended them to find," Josiah answered, his hand slipping unconsciously to the grip of his Peacemaker as he scanned the horizon, certain as the sky was gray that they were being watched and scouted themselves.

CHAPTER 2

There were no men in Company A who questioned Captain Leander McNelly's capacity to lead a successful campaign against Juan Cortina — or any outlaw, for that matter.

At first glance, the man looked weak and too racked with consumption to have any kind of productive life at all. He was thin as an arrow, short in stature, his face gaunt and his skin white and pasty. At times, in the sad light of the evening, McNelly looked like a ghost, uncomfortable in this world. His dark brown hair held a natural wave to it, and his goatee was thick and flowed over his chin like a deep fall of dark water. He was neat and tidy about himself, his years of military life evident in every movement and forethought.

Originally from Virginia, McNelly's family had moved to Texas in search of a better life as sheep farmers, and weather that would be more suitable for the young Leander. At the age of seventeen, McNelly enlisted in Company F of the Fifth Regiment of the Texas Mounted Volunteers, serving the Confederacy through the war. He was wounded once, severely, in the Battle of Mansfield in 1864. He took no leave and returned to duty as soon as he was able to stand, leading scouts into Texas, rounding up deserters.

After the war, McNelly returned to Texas, and when he wasn't on his family farm near Burton, he served in the State Police along with another of Josiah's mentors and fellow veterans of the war, Hiram Fikes. Most recently, as the head of the Special Forces, McNelly's memorable outing put an end to the Sutton-Taylor feud in Dewitt County.

The hoots, hollers, and lack of order so early in the morning drew Captain Leander McNelly out of his tent, fully dressed, looking agitated and annoyed by the shenanigans in his camp. Lieutenant Robinson's arrival was not unexpected, but the timing was a surprise.

Josiah and Scrap had followed the troop of scouts and their captive to McNelly's tent, joining the other Rangers in the camp. They were all pressed together, casting an ear toward the tent as Lieutenant Robinson dragged the unwilling Mexican to face McNelly.

"Unhand the man, Robinson," McNelly ordered, running his eyes up and down the Mexican, offering little emotion.

Robinson immediately let go of the Mexican. There was no threat since the man's hands were bound tight with rope, and he had most assuredly been searched and relieved of any weapons, including any knives hidden on his person, before being brought into camp.

The Mexican looked weak and scared as he stumbled forward, stopping inches from McNelly. The captain did not flinch.

"What is your name?"

The Mexican stared at McNelly like he didn't understand a word he'd said.

"Don't play stupid with me, man," McNelly said. "I'd just as soon let my men have a play at you than be cordial. I will succeed whether you cooperate willingly with me or not. Do you understand now?" McNelly said, slipping his hand softly to the hilt of the Bowie knife he wore on his side. "You are on the wrong side of the fence, and my men are anxious for a fight or, at the very least, a smell of enemy blood."

"Rafael," the Mexican said, nodding eagerly. "My name is Rafael Salinas."

"Good," McNelly said. "I'm glad you've decided to make this easy. You speak the Anglo tongue as well as you understand it. This will be easy then."

"Yes, *sí*."

Josiah was squeezed tight in the group of men, about two back from the curve of Rangers that had formed around Robinson, McNelly, and Rafael Salinas. His hand, like Scrap's, and every other man's within earshot, rested within inches of his gun, at the ready, in case something went wrong, or if Salinas was a plant, a distraction.

The feeling of being watched from afar had not left Josiah, but he was more relaxed, surrounded by the boys of the company, all scrunched in like a pack of wolves, ready to pounce on Rafael Salinas at the first opportunity.

Wood smoke mixed with the metallic smell of weapons being readied for battle, and there was a familiar numbness growing deep inside Josiah. He could taste death on his tongue. Kill or be killed. He knew the first steps of the dance, had known it for more than half his life, but it was anything but normal and rarely welcomed. Even the preparations and anticipation were uncomfortable.

"If you tell me of General Cortina's plan

and whereabouts," McNelly said, "I will let you leave here unharmed, let you go free once the dust has settled and there is proof that the information that you are about to give me is, indeed, valuable and correct."

"And what if I don't tell you, señor? What if I fear Juan Nepomuceno Cortina and his rage against a traitor more than I fear you and your bloodthirsty *asesinos*?"

"Then this will be your last day to walk this earth, and your death will be a humiliation to you and your kind. A slow and painful death." McNelly drew in a deep breath, and even from a distance, Josiah could hear the distinct rattle in the captain's chest. But there was no doubt that he spoke the truth. Captain McNelly was not a man who made empty threats about something so serious as death. He said what he meant and meant what he said. If Salinas had any inclination of lying to the captain, then he was a stupid man, playing with his fate like a mouse trying to escape the extended talons of an oncoming hawk.

"I understand," the Mexican said. He spoke English pretty well, but there was still a thick, halting quality to his speech, an accent that revealed the language was learned later in life and was not his original tongue. He hesitated and looked to the sky. Josiah followed the man's gaze as it settled on the rising sun, exposing a pink, cloudless expanse. "There is a party of sixteen of Cortina's best men, set to get a drove of cattle to take to a Cuban steamer that waits in the bay."

"We know this information," McNelly said. And it was true. Every man in the camp knew of Cortina's plans. They just did not know when or where the steamer was coming ashore to load. "That will not save your life, or your dignity. I need something more, Rafael Salinas. Can you feel the ground under your feet?"

"*Sí.*"

"Enjoy it while you still can," McNelly said. "Do you have children?"

Rafael nodded. "*Tres.* I only ride with Cortina to feed them. It is all I have left. The *sequìa,* the dry weather, has left me a poor man, wealthy of nothing more than dust."

"Dust is your children's legacy then, if you offer me nothing more than you have. They will not even know where to mourn you. I will leave your flesh to the coyotes and the buzzards."

"I am in the rear guard sent to remount, señor, under the command of Camillo Lerma and a man known only as *la Aboja,* the Needle. My absence will be noted but will not be of any worry. Another man will be recruited for my place, offered a great reward that I doubt will ever be fully paid. Cortina is a miser with his money, as well as his heart."

"I care little of the man's heart unless it is in my hand, cut from his body. When will they be loading the beeves onto the steamer?"

"I do not know, señor. Honestly, I do not know for certain. Soon, though, in the next week for certain. The ship will not wait forever once it arrives. We were charged to take the cows from La Parra, steal them in the night. The *barco* cannot be far out to sea."

McNelly nodded as he unsheathed his knife. The blade glinted brilliantly as a touch of sunlight bounced off it. "And that is all you can tell me?"

Rafael's face was wet with perspiration. He looked like he had been standing out in the rain. "I swear it, señor, on my *madre*'s grave." He made the sign of the cross from the top of his forehead to his chest, his lip quivering the entire time.

"I believe you. But know this, Rafael Salinas. If you have lied to me, caused me to send my men into any harm, there will be no more questions, no judge to plead to. I will kill you myself. It will be your heart I feed to the buzzards."

Rafael sighed and lowered his head, offering no more words.

"Take him away, Robinson. Get him out of my sight before I change my mind and end this right here and now."

Robinson grabbed Rafael Salinas by the scruff of his shirt collar and pulled him away from the crowd. He hurried south of the captain's tent, where there had already been an enclosure erected with the intention of holding captives. The Ranger camp had been pitched thoughtfully, as a base, not just as a stopping spot for a night or two.

Robinson and Salinas disappeared quickly, leaving McNelly standing alone, facing the crowd of men.

Josiah stood still, not thinking, not consciously breathing, just waiting for whatever was next.

The Mexican had told McNelly where the rustling was going to take place, and that the wait wasn't going to be much longer. The engagement between the Rangers and Cortina's men would be soon, perhaps even on this day. Cortina's men would not give up the rustled beeves without a hard fight.

Scrap remained quiet, as well, standing

41

solemnly by Josiah's side.

It was hard to tell what the boy was thinking, but if Josiah could guess, Scrap was most likely disappointed that the captain hadn't slit Rafael's chest open right then and there. The only thing Scrap Elliot hated more than Mexicans was the Comanche, and for whatever the reason, the only suitable punishment for either brown-skinned man or woman was an unforgiving and painful death.

The hate was one of Scrap's impulses that Josiah feared would lead to trouble, to a bad decision, as had happened in the past. But Scrap was different now, changed somehow on this journey, though Josiah couldn't exactly say he trusted Scrap not to react angrily and without thought. If he was being honest, he'd say the wait for Scrap to release his rage was like a slow-burning fuse. It was just a matter of time before the fire hit the dynamite and exploded.

The captain stood stiffly, looking unaffected and unconcerned by what he had just learned. Instead, he scanned the crowd searching for something, it seemed, to satisfy whatever it was he had in mind now that he knew where the rustling operation was going to occur.

"Wolfe," McNelly demanded, his voice as

loud as it could go. "Come here."

Josiah flinched at the mention of his name. He drew in a deep breath, more than curious why McNelly would want him.

"You, too, Elliot," McNelly said. "The two of you are the perfect pair to find out what Cortina's planning once he leaves La Parra."

CHAPTER 3

The crowd of men parted, allowing Josiah and Scrap through unimpeded and without comment.

It was as silent as a funeral as they made their way to face Captain McNelly. Scrap's shoulders were slumped, and Josiah could feel a hesitation in his step that surprised him. Scrap didn't resist any kind of duty, but being called out in front of the entire company made him uncomfortable.

They stopped in front of McNelly, both at attention, even though a military response wasn't required. Josiah could feel dread working its way to his head all the way from his toes.

"You two have experience as spies. I want you to find the rustlers," McNelly said in as strong a voice as he could muster. "Follow their trail from where Robinson captured Rafael Salinas. See if what he said is true. We'll guard the passes surrounding the Arroyo Colorado and stay concealed there until the beeves are rustled and we can confront Cortina once and for all," McNelly said. "We will stop this shipment of Texas cattle to Cuba if it takes every man in camp, and more if necessary."

Josiah wanted to protest, but he said nothing. He lowered his head, resigned to a duty he didn't want.

It was true; he and Scrap had both served as spies for McNelly. Shortly after Josiah was relieved of his duty in the Frontier Battalion by Captain Pete Feders, they both were sent to Corpus Christi to gather as much information about Cortina's rustling operation as possible. The duty was more a banishment for Josiah than anything else. He'd then been forced to kill Pete Feders in a trek to South Texas, where the captain was going to join forces with Cortina to raise enough money to marry Pearl Fikes and keep her in the manner she was accustomed to — at least that was Feders's excuse for joining forces with the Mexican cattle rustler and an outlaw, Liam O'Reilly, who was set on running the thievery side of the business in Texas. Feders drew his gun on Josiah, giving Josiah no choice but to save himself — and Scrap.

The newspapers in Austin had had a

heyday with the killing, one Ranger killing another. The incident made life difficult for the fledging Ranger organization and the governor himself.

Spy duty had been reason enough to get Josiah out of town, while allowing him to stay in the Rangers, since he'd been cleared of any wrongdoing. Scrap was sent along, but they'd operated separately, with Josiah assuming the identity of Zeb Teter, a hide trader. Scrap pretended to be a down-on-his-luck cowboy looking for work, but he'd had no luck scrounging any worthy information. The Mexicans didn't trust him.

It had been a difficult span of time, and pretending to be a man other than himself didn't suit Josiah well. He had been glad to be back with the company of men, a sergeant among the boys, and nothing more. Being a spy was something he had hoped never to do again.

As the command settled in, Josiah took a deep breath and accepted his fate. Scrap, on the other hand, kicked the dirt — away from McNelly, of course.

"Is there a problem, Elliot?" McNelly demanded, his voice suddenly as sharp as the blade of his Bowie knife that had now found its way back into the sheath on the captain's hip.

"No, sir, it's just that . . . Oh, never mind," Scrap said, not looking at McNelly's face at all, still staring at the ground.

"Spit it out. This is important duty. If there's a problem, speak of it now instead of on the trail, where you could put yourself and Wolfe in danger."

"It's just that I ain't no good at bein' a spy, Captain. That long bit of dusty time I spent in Corpus was as uncomfortable as a Sunday suit in the middle of the week. No offense, but I'd be just as good on the outcrop, hidden with my finger on the trigger, waitin' for Cortina himself to pass by. I'm a better shooter than I am a liar."

"You *are* a good shot, Elliot. One of the best in the company, there's no question of that. But you and Wolfe know the lay of the land, and I'm assuming there might be a contact here or there that was made in your previous trip that could help us find out the final plans of this operation, sooner rather than later. At least confirm what Salinas has told us. I lack faith in his worried words."

"He's right, Scrap," Josiah said in his best sergeant voice. "We're better at this than we think. We can scout and spy, you'll see; the captain's right in sending the two of us." Josiah made eye contact with McNelly and nodded. "We can talk the talk. Folks won't think twice of us being Rangers, if we do this right."

He was not truly as confident as he wanted to be, but Josiah understood McNelly's point in picking them. There was certainly no way Josiah was going to turn down a duty from the captain, not in front of the entire company, and with so much at stake.

Josiah had chosen to ride with the Rangers, to stay on the trail and serve in the best way he could; there was no way he could object — unless he wanted to ride north, back to Austin, and never call himself a Ranger again. That wasn't going to happen. Not anytime soon, anyway. But deep down, what Josiah wanted, more than to serve his duty loyally as a sergeant, was a good measure of redemption that would spread north and restore his reputation as an honorable man. Redemption in the eyes of Governor Richard Coke and the adjunct general, William Steele. Both men had suffered undue attention because of Josiah's actions, and he wanted nothing more than to prove them right for standing by him, believing in him enough to allow a continuation of his service to the Rangers.

Scrap finally nodded, noting that the correctness of the captain's choice was obvious, though his face still showed concern, if not distaste. The same look had been firmly implanted on his every action since the boy had ridden out of Austin. It was more than worrisome for Josiah, but he said nothing. Scrap would be better watched with him on the trail than left behind with the company.

"Well," McNelly said, "what are you waiting for? Daylight's burning."

Josiah tied his bedroll on his horse's saddle and gave it a final tug. Clipper, his Appaloosa, was a good, hearty horse who had seen Josiah through a lot of adventures. He was responsive and easygoing but could be stubborn in situations that were uncomfortable. Clipper would have been a good warhorse. Sudden noise, explosions, and gunfire had no effect on him. The horse wanted nothing more than to do as Josiah asked, or demanded.

Having Clipper along would make it easier to slip into another identity. Hopefully this journey would be far shorter than the last time, when he'd had to walk in Zeb Teter's shoes for four months.

Scrap cinched the saddle on his horse. The mare was fast and, as far as Josiah could tell, just as reliable to Scrap as Clipper was to him.

"What're your plans, Wolfe?" Scrap asked.

The question surprised Josiah. Scrap was usually not so willing to take orders or settle so quickly into second place. "We'll head to Arroyo first. It's a little village not too far from here. It was settled by Mexican herders about the time the war broke out, but last time I was down this way, there were some Anglos there, hide traders as well as agents, working both sides of the border."

"Traitors you mean."

"Call 'em what you want, but it's as good a place to start as any. I'm thinking these *gringos* riding with Cortina must have left some family behind."

Scrap started to say something, then restrained himself. "It'll take me some time to slip out of this skin, Wolfe," he finally said. "You know I ain't got no use for Mexicans, thieves, or *gringos.*"

"I know." The bedroll was firmly in its place, and everything else needed was packed on Clipper, ready to go. Scrap's bedroll was still on the ground, unfurled. "But this duty won't be as long as last time. You don't have as long to put away your own feelings about things. I'd as soon not get killed anytime soon because you're not paying attention to what's in front of us."

"I ain't gonna get you killed, Wolfe. I done saved your life more than once."

"My luck might be running out."

Scrap shot Josiah a hurtful look, his eyes dark with misgivings.

"I'm joshing you, Elliot. Relax."

"Easy for you to say."

Josiah knew it was best to hold his tongue. He'd ridden with Scrap Elliot long enough to know he had a temper set on tinder, looking for a spark. The recent business in Austin had only made matters worse.

He climbed up in the saddle, settled in, and sat staring down at Scrap, waiting. Clipper snorted softly and tossed his head to the right, then to the left, like he was trying to balance himself, readying to go.

There were times like this, Josiah thought to himself, when it would have been useful to have had a younger brother or even a younger sister. But as it was, Josiah had been born an only child to parents who were now dead and gone. He had no natural knowledge when it came to dealing with someone you cared about but had to be firm with. All he had was instinct, lessons learned in the war as he found himself, over and over again, in situations that required him to take charge. And there was also a brief time in his life, after the war, when he came home to Texas and took up the position of marshal of his hometown, Seerville. Along with that duty, he'd had a small, growing family, at the time. Three daughters . . . all who were taken by the fevers, and his wife, Lily, left dead in childbirth. Josiah was left to put his life back together, and he'd found that opportunity in the remaking of the new Rangers, the Frontier Battalion and the Special Forces that McNelly commanded, a little more than a year earlier.

At this age, and with his experience, being able to rise up in the chain of command came just a little easier to him, especially when it came to dealing with some of the boys, none of whom he had known before becoming a Ranger. He didn't consider them friends, like he did Elliot.

"Let's go, Elliot. Like the captain said, 'Daylight's burning.' Taking slow measures won't cause him to change his mind about this outing. The sooner we go, the sooner we get on with it. There's a battle waiting. You have to know that."

"It can't come soon enough," Scrap said. "Not soon enough."

CHAPTER 4

The sun was fully up over the horizon, a white-hot orb rising into the pale sky on a well-traveled path, offering little mystery to its intentions. The day would be hot and cloudless, just like the string of days before it.

Josiah and Scrap were both mounted on their horses, ready to go, but a stir of noise, a wave of notice, flowed over the camp, and caught their attention. Voices grew louder. A few men cheered. And there was a rush of arms and legs, a return to the captain's tent, by all of the men from the company. Knowing they were losing sunlight, and under strict orders from Captain McNelly to depart, Josiah hesitated, then decided to investigate, and see what all the hubbub was about.

Atop Clipper, it was easy to discern if there was a conflict, a reason to draw arms, or a celebration. It was clear there was no threat to the camp. Instead, the mail rider had made his way through the watch ring, set on delivering news from home, or wherever, to men lucky enough to know how to read or write, and to have a letter for them under the rider's charge.

Losing minutes in order to see if there was anything for him didn't seem to matter to Josiah now. He hoped for word about his son, Lyle. Anything concerning the boy would lighten his mood, making the coming days easier to face. The comfort that all was well in Austin, at home, would be a welcome relief from the hidden worry that Josiah carried with him every minute he was away from the boy.

The mail rider was a young man in his early twenties. His smooth face, and all of his clothes, were covered with a thick layer of dust, but cleaning up was not his first concern. He jumped from his horse and started digging in his satchel, pulling out a handful of letters, with little care to their fragility, as a mass of men crowded around him.

"Anson. Wilson. Franks." The mail rider held up three letters, tapping his toe.

The company had gathered at the front of the tent just like they had when Robinson carted Rafael Salinas into the camp. Only this time, there was no sign of McNelly. Or Robinson for that matter. Just a collection of the boys, all as eager and impatient as Josiah for news from the outside world.

Next to Josiah, Scrap sat stiffly on Missy, staring off in the opposite direction from the mail rider, a hard look of disappointment already chiseled on his face. But he said nothing, didn't object to the delay in leaving. He was clearly giving Josiah room and acknowledgment of his need to know if there was a letter for him or not.

They both knew *some* news couldn't wait two or three days. Josiah had been called home from duty before because Lyle had taken ill, and if necessary, he would leave the company again. Orders or no orders. Lyle came first.

The rider spouted off another string of names, and every man ran up to him like he was passing out Christmas presents. Josiah was starting to think there was nothing for him, when the rider finally shouted out his name. "Wolfe!"

Josiah slid off the saddle easily, pushed through the crowd gingerly, and retrieved his letter. The mail rider handed it to him without hesitation, then went back to digging in the mail satchel.

The letter was heavy, more than one page,

and there was no question who the sender was. It was from Pearl Fikes.

Without thinking, Josiah brought the letter gently to his nose and smelled a hint of perfume, a sweet toilet water that tickled distant memories and immediate desires that he had to squelch. It was spring, summer, all of the happy seasons rolled into one. All that was missing was a touch of skin, the satisfaction of Pearl's presence. Words would have to do.

Someone next to him pushed on Josiah's shoulder. "A letter from the sweetheart, huh, Sergeant Wolfe?" It was a boy about Scrap's age, Tom Darkson, new to the Rangers. Darkson had joined up recently, while Josiah was in Austin. New men came and went from the company on a regular basis. Time away from home was hard on a family man, or a man with ambitions of any kind. It was easy to understand. Rangering was not an easy life. Josiah knew little of Darkson except that he seemed like a decent sort, always willing to chip in no matter what the duty was, pitching tents, digging shit holes, or otherwise.

A flush of embarrassment crossed Josiah's face. He felt odd, at his age, courting. But there was no mistaking that he was in the midst of a serious courtship with a woman who had once held a much higher position in society than she did when Josiah last left her.

Pearl Fikes was the daughter of Captain Hiram Fikes, who was killed at the beginning of the Frontier Battalion. Through a series of tragic events of her own making, and some not, like the impact of the Panic of '73, Pearl's mother had managed to lose a fortune, a large estate, and end up in a sanatorium, nearly bankrupt. Pearl's uncle, Captain Fikes's half brother, was her benefactor now, seeing her through normal school so Pearl could support herself as a schoolteacher.

There was a large matter of distance between Pearl and Josiah in regard to their origins, but fate had brought them together, and there was no mistaking the strong attraction they held for each other. Still, Josiah was hesitant to follow his heart, hesitant to put his past behind him, bury Lily and the three girls once and for all, and start a new life, a new love. He knew he needed to give Lyle a family, instead of an absent father and a wet nurse for a mother, but it wasn't as easy for Josiah as he had once thought it might be.

"Enjoy your letter, Sergeant," Tom Darkson said.

Josiah nodded and slipped the letter from Pearl into his pocket. He'd read it when the time was right, when he had a private moment. Now, in front of the company, was obviously not the place. Sharing his personal moments with the boys made him uncomfortable.

He climbed back up on Clipper and looked over to Scrap. The boy's jaw was set hard, and he sat straight as a door frame in his saddle.

"We can wait, see if there's a letter for you, Scrap," Josiah said.

"Ain't gonna be nothin' for me, you know that, Wolfe."

"We can wait five minutes. You don't know that for sure. Not since you left Myra Lynn in Austin."

"With Blanche Dumont."

"She could be under the care, or thumb, of worse people."

Scrap exhaled loudly, then nodded. Myra Lynn was Scrap's sister. Scrap had told Josiah for a long time that his sister was a nun in Fort Worth, sent to a convent after the Comanche had killed their parents. It was an honorable story, except that it was a lie. Myra Lynn had left the convent as soon as she was able and found a life in the saloons, offering her body as her only means

58

of making a living. Scrap was ashamed that his sister was a whore.

Blanche Dumont ran a whorehouse in Austin, a higher class operation than most, and Myra Lynn had been left to her care after being saved by Josiah from certain death. At the house she worked at now, Myra Lynn had regular doctor visits, and a certain number of hours a day were devoted to education. Blanche Dumont knew that the day would come for all of her girls when they would leave the flesh business behind, and she wanted them to be ready.

Scrap was still ashamed of Myra Lynn, but he had seemed glad, at least, to know where she was and that she was getting some kind of care.

"I don't think there's anywhere worse than a whorehouse other than bein' dead, but nobody asked me, did they?" Scrap said. "I can't be no more alone than I am now." He glanced at Josiah's breast pocket. The corner of the letter was sticking out of it in plain sight.

"We'll wait."

"Suit yourself." Scrap shifted himself in the saddle, flicked Missy's reins, pulled her to the right, and headed slowly out of camp, his head down like he was riding into a heavy rainstorm.

Josiah watched Scrap leave, sitting still and staying put, listening closely as the mail rider resumed calling out names.

CHAPTER 5

Josiah caught sight of Scrap from nearly a mile away and did little to encourage Clipper to catch up with the boy. He was riding slow, unassuming, not in a hurry himself to slide back into the life of a spy.

By the time Josiah caught up with Scrap, the sun was nearly at its peak. The terrain surrounding the camp, and the Arroyo Colorado, made for slow going at first, though Josiah was not in a rush to leave the company behind him.

Clipper was no mountain horse, and he didn't need to be, but there were steep rises and wind-cut walls of solid granite and limestone that would have made the journey difficult for any horse. Luckily a good stretch of the ride to the small town of Arroyo was on flat ground — so flat that it was like a giant iron had fallen from the sky, smoothing the ground all of the way to the beaches and, ultimately, to the Gulf of

Mexico. Storm surges and heavy rains made the ground swampy and salty, and the air smelled of rot, stinging inside the nose until it became familiar.

"You should have stayed a little while longer," Josiah said, once he brought Clipper nose to nose with Missy.

"Did I miss a brawl?" Scrap still wore a solid look of disappointment and discontent on his young face.

There were times when Josiah thought Scrap looked ten years younger, like a twelve-year-old instead of a young man in his early twenties. He lacked any kind of facial hair, none that grew on a regular basis to age himself or disguise his true identity. And his deep blue eyes lacked depth, experience, or the ability to hold back the truth of his feelings. Sometimes they looked black and vacant, which worried Josiah more than he liked to admit.

"No, no, there was no fight that I know of. The boys were giddy, glad for the mail, a touch of reality before the real fight with Cortina comes."

The sun beat on the back of Josiah's neck. There was a slight breeze, and the taste of salt in the air was thicker the closer they got to the ocean. There was relief from the discomfort of the ride, of the uncertainty ahead of them, to a small degree.

Spending time some months back on the ocean, learning how to net fish with his friend and Pearl's half uncle, Juan Carlos, had been one of the most calming and relaxing times for Josiah in the last few years. He had no idea where Juan Carlos was now, but since the old Mexican, as Josiah commonly referred to him, also worked in the shadows for Captain Mc-Nelly, he could show up at any time. And usually did.

"Then why in the heck should I have stayed around, Wolfe? So I could ride out with you?" Scrap asked.

"Might not've hurt."

"Are you bein' coy with me, Wolfe?"

Josiah shrugged, then dug into his back pocket, pulled out a letter, and handed it to Scrap. "This came for you."

Scrap stared at the letter, not making any effort to take it from Josiah's hand. He shook his head. "Who's it from? Can't be for me. You must be mistaken, Wolfe. Not many of my people know much about readin', writin', or my whereabouts." he said.

"There's no mistaking it's for you, Scrap. It says Robert Earl Elliot as clear as day on the envelope. That's you, isn't it?"

"To my family."

Josiah dangled the letter from his fingers, offering it further to Scrap. "Take it."

Scrap sighed and took the letter. Missy and Clipper's trot matched pace. Sand flies were starting to pick up at the drop of their hooves. The two horses were accustomed to each other's company, but their tails started to swish with annoyance.

"It can't be good news," Scrap said.

"How do you figure?"

"Because it never is." Scrap let the reins fall from his hand, and Missy came to a stop. He tore the letter open and perused the writing.

Sun beamed through the parchment, and from Josiah's view, the letter looked like elegant chicken scratch. He had no desire to know the contents of the letter if Scrap didn't want him to, so he looked away, to the hazy horizon in the distance.

"It's from Blanche Dumont," Scrap continued. "She says Myra Lynn is doin' good, learnin' her letters, but not good enough to write a full-out letter just yet. She just wants to keep in touch. To let me know she appreciates the new chance at life she has."

A slight smile crossed Josiah's face as he watched Scrap read on, and his body loosen up at the same time. "I'm glad to hear it."

Scrap stopped reading, exhaled loudly, and stuffed the letter inside his breast pocket as gently as he could.

"I ain't got family, outside of Aunt Callie, that cares much about me, Wolfe. I thought I done lost my sister to the sins of the earth. I never figured a woman like Blanche Dumont could be a . . .."

"Good influence?" Josiah asked, finishing the sentence before Scrap could.

Scrap nodded. "Yup. I figured a woman who runs a whorehouse ain't interested in nothing more than money to be made on the backs of the girls she keeps. Why would she give an owl's hoot if a girl can read or better herself? I don't know. It seems that business back in Austin might've turned out for the best. Odd ain't it? Trouble turns out bringin' sunshine. I mean my sister, well, she's still doin' the unthinkable, but at least I know where she is, and that she's cared for."

"Not everything is as it seems."

"I guess not," Scrap said. "I guess not. What about you, Wolfe? Are you going to read your letter?"

Josiah smiled but didn't answer, just urged Clipper to move on like he hadn't heard a word Scrap said. His letter from Pearl was something to savor, read at the right time, and not share — even with Scrap.

There was a glimmer in the distance, and a familiar collection of shadows caught Josiah's eyes. Arroyo beckoned, standing in the flats like an oasis, or a mirage, he wasn't sure which. No matter. He just hoped he'd find what he was looking for, sooner rather than later. Another four-month stint as a spy was unimaginable, more like a prison sentence than an act of duty. It had taken him a long time to see the sunshine himself after that bit of trouble, as Scrap called it. He might not be so lucky this time around.

The cantina was like every other cantina Josiah had seen in South Texas. The walls were made of adobe and shellcrete, ground up seashells formed over a building's frame to give it strength and depth, and the structure had one story and very few windows.

It was dim inside, almost dark, the sunshine cutting into the open front door suspiciously and unwelcome. A water turbine–driven fan whirled overhead, and a lone sconce flickered at the right corner of the dilapidated bar, reflecting off a cracked mirror that cut the small room in half. A slight wisp of coal oil smoke streamed upward to the blackened ceiling.

There was a distinct smell inside the cantina, yeast mixed with a series of spices, that emanated from a pot sitting on a woodstove in the corner that served as the kitchen. Josiah knew they served food at this cantina; he had been here before, passing through, on a mission to establish his name, Zeb Teter, in the territory, as a hide trader, on the lookout for goods. No one bought into his charade then, and he had moved on quickly to Corpus Christi. He hoped he was more successful this time around.

There was no music, no noise, other than the whirl of the fan, and the simmering pot on the stove, bubbling casually like a permanent resident.

Two men sat at the bar, Mexicans, both without hats but each with a full complement of ammunition in his gun belt, their backs to the door. Each man wore a revolver on both hips and carried a sheathed knife. The men looked up at the mirror as Josiah and Scrap entered the bar. They exchanged an unconcerned glance, then stared back down to their beer mugs without saying a word. There was no one else to be seen inside the cantina.

Josiah stopped just inside the door, taking in as much as he could. He knew little about the cantina, who owned it, whether it was friendly to Anglos or not. His assumption, based on his last visit, was that it was not a friendly place at all.

Most places in these parts weren't. Still, if there was a place in Arroyo to gather some information, to stop along the way, this was it. The town, if it could be called that, had been around for less than twenty years, yet it looked old, on the verge of collapse, dying. Any exposed metal, on the hinges of doors and windows, was coated with rust, like it was a rash, bubbling red, breaking open, but so dry there was nothing left inside to seep out.

It was at times like this that Josiah really felt out of his depth. He spoke little Spanish, having picked up what he could from Ofelia and by being exposed to it, never taking the lead and learning the language, making it his own. Scrap wouldn't utter a word understood by Mexicans other than what automatically came out of his mouth. Joining them together as spies made sense to Josiah. Captain McNelly saw the two of them as a pair instead of two individuals — there were skills they were both deficient in. But they had also both saved each other in some fashion. Maybe it was this that showed, and the one thing the captain had counted on to keep them safe and get the information he needed.

Josiah walked into the cantina confidently and pulled up a stool next to the Mexican nearest the stove. *"Hola,"* he said with a nod, then tapped the front brim of his Stetson.

The Mexican was thin-faced, with angry brown eyes, and he didn't flinch when he was spoken to, didn't turn his head toward Josiah at all, just stared into his beer. His face was pockmarked, his dark brown skin ruddy and moist with sweat that looked permanent. His mustache was bushy and unkempt, black as a black cat's tail, and he looked like he had been riding on the trail for a while. There was dust on his shoulders and in every crease of his shirt.

The other Mexican, a bit older than the first, with gray showing in his thick black hair, ignored Josiah with just as much enthusiasm as his friend.

"Is there anyone working here?" Josiah asked. He could see Scrap in the mirror, standing in the center of the room, next to a support beam, between two empty tables, his hands at his sides, his holsters open, wearing a blank, emotionless gaze on his face.

"Anglos aren't welcome here," the Mexican said. His teeth were clenched.

"I'm looking for hides. I deal through

Hector Morales in Corpus Christi."

"Hector Morales is dead. Juan Cortina had his tongue cut out for betraying him to the Rangers." The Mexican turned to face Josiah then, his eyes hard, the muscle under his lip trembling slightly, like he was about to say something else, or erupt in anger.

Josiah took a deep breath, let his hand slip down to his Peacemaker — but he was too slow.

The other Mexican pushed the stool back with a jump, pulling his gun at the same time, swirling around to face Scrap.

Scrap didn't hesitate, didn't blink. Josiah had no time to issue commands, to tell the boy what to do. Thankfully, he didn't have to.

In half a breath, Scrap had pulled his Colt Army .45 from his holster and fired the first round, beating the Mexican on the draw.

The echo of the shot sounded like a cannon going off right behind Josiah's ear. He saw the muzzle flash in the mirror, then heard the bullet rip into flesh and shatter bone as it struck the Mexican in the forehead, sending him spiraling back toward the bar. Blood and cartilage exploded outward, a surprise, but so certain and sudden that the man didn't have the life in him to scream out in pain. Death came quickly, in a sudden flinch, at the hand of a boy with no patience or trust for Mexicans with guns.

To make certain that his aim was on target, Scrap pulled the trigger again, catching the man just under the chin as he fell backward. The Mexican crashed to the floor in a lifeless heap as his own blood rained down on him.

The other man, the one next to Josiah, was not afraid, showed no fear. His hands were out of sight. Time ticked in slow breaths, quickening heartbeats, and eyelids fighting not to blink. The smell of gunpowder overtook every other smell, even conquering the metallic smell of blood.

The outside world had ceased to exist for the three living men inside the cantina.

Josiah stumbled away from the Mexican, out of range of his hands if he chose to go for his knife, but still close enough to see his rage.

Scrap's reflection flinched in the mirror, his attention suddenly drawn away from Josiah and the Mexican, by something near the stove. A shadow of movement caught his eye.

Josiah had not seen it before now, but there was a dark alcove, a pantry to serve the kitchen, and presumably store beer kegs, too, just off to the left of the stove. It would

71

make sense that there was a door there, leading in and out to an alleyway.

The barkeep appeared, a silhouette of a person holding a shotgun, aimed directly at Josiah and the Mexican. The size and shape of the man was inconsequential; his intention was expressed vividly by the direction of the shotgun's barrel.

It was a lot to take in in such a short amount of time. The Mexican had not lost focus, had not been distracted. In another blink of an eye, he had both guns out of his holster, trained on Josiah.

Josiah was a finger-press away from dying. The Mexican's guns were aimed straight at his chest.

Scrap yelled, "Watch out behind you, Wolfe!"

Josiah had no time to react to Scrap's warning. A flash of bright white light, and the loudest explosion Josiah had heard since returning from the war, erupted just out of sight.

It was a gunshot so close to his ear that he couldn't hear anything but the constant reverberation of the blast. He blinked, and felt the first pellet of buckshot pierce his skin. It skidded across his cheek, just under his eye, slicing his skin, and freeing his blood from his flesh. Pain followed, ripping across his face like someone had smashed him into a wall of shattered glass.

Josiah's other eye was wide open — open enough to see the Mexican's face change its expression, writhe in pain, as he dropped his guns and bright red splotches appeared in his throat, his chest, and his forehead, like his partner's. Scrap had unloaded his remaining four shots into the man's body.

The Mexican had got a shot off before dropping the guns.

A bullet glanced across Josiah's shoulder, sending him spinning backward into a graceless dance, peppered as well from the barkeep's shotgun blast.

The floor rose up to meet him, offering nothing but unforgiving stone to greet his falling body.

There was no pain, no feeling in his body as he came to rest on the floor. His mouth filled up with blood, and he could not speak. His vision was blurry, and darkness pushed in from all corners of his sight, aided by the naturally dark surroundings of the cantina.

Josiah heard footsteps, and expected to see Scrap standing over him, but that is not what he saw.

Instead a young Mexican woman hovered over his face, a look of horror and concern set soberly in her deep brown eyes. *"Lo siento,* señor. *Lo siento."*

Josiah knew enough Spanish to know that the woman was saying she was sorry. But he didn't know what for.

The light was fading, and she spoke more words as she squatted down, her face close to his, trying to soothe him, but her words didn't matter anymore.

He was slipping away, more certain than at any other time in his life that he was a dead man, that this was the end of his ride, lost in an unknown cantina hundreds of miles away from home, at the hands of a stranger. His duty to the Rangers, to his son, to Pearl, would forever go unfulfilled.

For some reason, he wasn't surprised.

CHAPTER 6

A candle burned beside the bed. Night had fallen as Josiah struggled to open his eyes. The left side of his face was numb, covered with a large cloth bandage. Another bandage was attached to the top of his shoulder, but there was little pain there. Surprisingly, he felt little pain anywhere.

He took a deep breath as he gained the realization that he was still alive, not dead. He had no idea where he was, what had happened after he had been shot, or how much time had passed. His mouth was dry and he felt weak, hungry, and thirsty. But more than anything, he needed to pee.

Josiah struggled to sit up, and found that he was weaker than he'd thought he was. He fell back down on the thin mattress.

"Hold on there, Wolfe." Scrap appeared out of the dark corner.

Focusing, Josiah saw a chair there and figured Scrap had taken up guard, watching over him. The thought of it made him comfortable, and he instantly relaxed.

"That you, Elliot?" Josiah asked, his voice low and gravelly.

"Who else you think it is? St. Peter?"

"Might be."

"Hardly." Scrap was at his side, offering a glass of water. "You're a lucky man, Wolfe. A few inches to the left, and that girl's mistake would have found your face full on."

Josiah took the water and drank it down hungrily. "Feels that way as it is." He had been wounded in duty before, stabbed in the Lost Valley fight by a Kiowa Indian. That gash took a long time to heal. The scar still itched sometimes, hurt down to the bone at the oddest times, as if to remind him that he was not immortal. Scrap was there then, too. That wound had been his fault, to a degree, moved by anger, but Josiah didn't hold a grudge. Scrap had made up for his impetuous act more than once since. There was no one to blame this time around — though Josiah had no idea what Scrap meant about a girl making a mistake.

Scrap stood over Josiah, eyeing him carefully. "You ought to be fine in a day or so. Well enough to ride back to camp. You just need to get your strength back after losin' as much blood as you did."

Josiah handed the glass back to Scrap.

"More?" Scrap asked.

Josiah nodded yes. He felt the bandage on his shoulder, pushed on it, felt a slight tremor of pain work its way down his arm.

"A good graze," Scrap said. "The buckshot on the side of your face is more worrisome than that if infection sets in."

Josiah nodded. He knew the consequences of infection, of outside poison coursing its way through your insides. He'd seen men shot in the war, grazed, dying a slow, fever-filled, miserable death. A bullet square between the eyes was a surer gift. Take the suffering out of the equation. But that didn't look to be his luck.

"What of the two Mexicans?" Josiah asked.

"I killed 'em both, through and through."

"Too bad. They might've been able to tell us something about Cortina." He took another deep drink of water, then struggled to sit up. He really had to pee.

"It was them or you," Scrap said.

Josiah nodded to the bowl that sat on a table across the room. "I've got to relieve myself."

Scrap fetched the bowl, handed it to Josiah, then turned away.

Only a thin blanket covered him, and until that moment, Josiah hadn't realized that he was naked as the day he was born underneath it. He quickly did his business, glad his functions still worked. Scrap took the pan, disappeared out the door, then quickly returned without it.

"I think you'll be all right here, Wolfe."

"What do you mean? What do you think you're planning?"

"There was a third man. They all were tied together with Cortina and this big sale to Cuba somehow. I'm going after him. He can't be far," Scrap said.

Josiah started to protest, felt the responsibility of his rank and general concern rising to the forefront of his mind, but he allowed it to slip back, stop. "You think you're up to that?"

"What, alone?"

Josiah nodded.

Scrap shrugged. "Don't look like I got much choice. It's either that, or stay here with you for a day or so, or go back to the camp to tell McNelly what's happened. Neither way solves our duty. Besides, I got skills on the trail. I know how to track a man as good as you."

"I didn't say you didn't."

"Then what are you sayin'?"

"I'd just as soon go with you as stay here," Josiah said. "The barkeep shot me if I remember right."

Scrap shook his head no. "The cantina owner's daughter. She was trying to save you, but she ain't much of a shot. They was outside butcherin' a goat when she heard the ruckus and came in to investigate. You'll be safe here. These folks been kind to you and ain't no supporters of Cortina."

"The girl I saw before I blacked out?"

"Yup. This is their house. She feels awful, especially now they know we're Rangers."

"You trust a pair of Mexicans enough to tell them we're Rangers? We were supposed to use our spy names."

"That went out the window once't you got shot. Besides, you know I ain't no good at bein' anything other than myself."

"And you're comfortable enough to just leave me here?"

"Funny, ain't it?"

"You are a curious boy, Scrap Elliot," Josiah said. "A real curious boy."

"Well, I suppose you could think worse of me, but I learned a few things on my own when I was in Corpus a while back. I may not like some Mexicans, but I had to learn there's some good ones, or I woulda been out on a limb most of the time. These two are decent sorts. They gave me information about where to find the third man."

"And you believed them?"

"They believed me when I told 'em I'd come back and kill them both if it was a lie. I ain't got no restrictions to killin' a woman if she's a liar. Besides, you're not that down and out. Your gun's under the mattress, both your arms work, and your legs, too. You can take care of yourself while I track down the third man."

The candle flickered, swaying on an unseen draft, causing the light to become brighter for just a second. Josiah could see Scrap clearly. He was dressed and ready to ride, his gun belt stocked with bullets, his duster sitting on the chair waiting, and his Colt ready in his holster. Scrap's face, so often boyish and wide-eyed, looked hard and chiseled in the dark, his eyes set on a distant horizon that bore no pleasure, offering only the threat of certain danger and the pain of an undeclared war. Somehow, somewhere, and in some time, Scrap Elliot had become a fine soldier, a warrior. But that didn't mean the boy didn't have doubts or fears.

Every man did, Josiah thought, *every man did.* "Go on then," he said. "You're right. I can look after myself."

"I never asked your permission, Wolfe. I know you're my sergeant and all, but I figured with you down on your back, I had to make my decisions."

"Be safe," Josiah said. "I'll be looking forward to your return."

Scrap nodded, spun around, grabbed up his duster, and disappeared through the door, rushing out to meet the darkness that awaited him, eagerly and with anticipation.

CHAPTER 7

Josiah nodded off after Scrap left the room, only to be awakened some time later by the comforting smell of food. The curtains were pulled closed on the only window in the room, and no light burned around the edges, signaling that morning had not come. Darkness of night still prevailed. The same candle burned weakly; it was about half the size it had been when Scrap left the room.

A sudden, unmistakable burst of pain erupted on the side of Josiah's face, reminding him that he had been shot, had caught some buckshot from an uncertain blast of a scattergun. His vision widened, and instinctively he reached to his cheek to soothe the pain he felt.

A warm hand intercepted his. "No, no, señor, please, you'll hurt yourself." It was a soft female voice.

Josiah pulled his hand away and angled his face upward, catching the first sight of the girl he assumed had shot him by mistake. He hadn't gotten a good look at her in the cantina. There was no way to tell then if the shooter had been a man or a woman; everything had happened so quickly.

Even now he could not see the girl clearly. The room was full of shadows, and his movement reaching for the pain had caused the candle to dance, making the light even more unstable. Still, the girl was older than he'd expected. She was a young woman, maybe Scrap's age, in her early twenties, maybe older, not really a girl at all. She had brown skin, saucer plate brown eyes, and neatly combed black hair swept back out of her face, exposing a smooth canvas of concern and caring.

"I am so sorry, Señor Wolfe. I did not mean to harm you. And now you are to be scarred from my carelessness. Can you ever forgive me?"

"I might be dead if you hadn't walked in when you did."

The girl shook her head no. "Señor Elliot put an end to the attack. I am sure he would have conquered the *gringos* without my interference. You, too, from what I understand, are quite capable of protecting yourself." She pulled back then, standing at the side of his bed nervously.

"Call me Josiah." He took a deep breath at the full sight of the girl. She wore a loose-fitting blouse over a long skirt, but even in the faded light, it was easy to see that she was shapely, and her face sweet, like a Spanish angel painted on the ceilings of some of the missions Josiah had been in.

"But, Señor . . ."

". . . I insist."

"As you wish."

"What is your name?"

"Francesca. Francesca Soto."

"That's a fine name."

Silence lingered between them for a long moment. Francesca's English was easy to understand, almost like it was her true language, even though there was still a hint of Mexican from her tongue. It must have been one of the reasons why Scrap was so comfortable in leaving him, that and the need to catch up with the third man.

"*Sí,* it is my mother's name. She died when I was born. It is all I have of her." A veil of sadness fell over Francesca's face, then disappeared as quickly as it had shown itself.

Grief was unmistakable to Josiah, his own losses had been deep, too. He recognized it when he saw it. He shifted in the bed, suddenly uncomfortable, remembering that he was naked underneath the light blanket that covered him. And the smell of the food tempted him, drew him up and away from his modesty. Desire met with weakness.

"I have tamales in the *olla,* Josiah. I take it you like them?"

Josiah nodded yes as his stomach rumbled.

Francesca smiled for the first time. The brightness of her joy and relief crossed her face like a child welcomed into a lap. She opened the *olla,* a ceramic pot that looked like it was as old as time itself, if not older, brown and unglazed, dinged from years of daily use, and a thin cloud of steam spiraled upward in the air. She quickly dished out three tamales, still in the husks, and handed a plate to Josiah.

He had pulled himself up and propped himself against the cool adobe wall with a thin feather pillow, making sure the blanket was securely tucked at his waist. It was uncomfortable, had hurt to move so quickly, annoying his new wounds, and reminding his old ones that they still existed. He took the plate and immediately began to pull off the husks.

The masa melted in his mouth at the first bite, with strings of tender pork following. He ate all three before he stopped to breathe, to take a drink of water from a glass

Francesca had poured and placed on the table next to the bed.

"These are some of the best tamales I've ever had," Josiah said. "But I suppose I shouldn't say that. I might offend Ofelia."

Francesca stood at the side of the bed, close enough to get Josiah anything he might need, but far enough away so there was a still a respectable distance between them. "Who is Ofelia?" There was no expression on her face or inflection in her voice other than curiosity.

"It's hard to explain. She was the wet nurse for my son, but she has stayed on with me. Moved from our home to Austin."

"What became of your wife, if I am not being disrespectful?"

There was a time when it was difficult for Josiah to even mention Lily's name aloud — as it was now, for some reason. Her death had rocked him to the core, brought him to his knees, only to be brought back to his feet by the fact that he had a newborn son to care for.

"She died in childbirth," Josiah whispered.

Francesca's face twisted then, and she looked away. *"Lo siento,"* she said, then made a sign of the cross from the top of her forehead to her chest. "It must be difficult. My papa has been a very lonely man since the death of my mother. It is his cantina, and the visitors that come along pull him from the bed every day. We both feel like half of us is missing, even though Papa says I am a true reflection of my mother. He misses her less when he sees me."

Josiah nodded. "I see my wife, Lily, in Lyle, too. He's like her in a lot of ways. Some days that is hard to see, but I'm glad for it when I'm home."

"I understand. How old is he, your son?"

"Four. Nearly four."

"He is only a *bebé*, then."

"Yes."

"And you leave him for days, weeks at a time?"

"He's in Ofelia's care. She loves him like he is her own."

"But he is not."

"No."

Silence settled between the two of them again. This time it was deeper, more personal. Francesca had touched on the guilt that Josiah carried every day that he rode with the Rangers. He needed little to remind him that his son needed a father in his life.

"I'm sorry," Francesca said, this time in English. "I should not speak of matters that I know nothing about. I have no children of my own. There are more tamales. Would you like some?"

"Sure, yes." It was difficult to be angry with Francesca. She had wandered into an area of his heart that most people usually had no access to. He was vulnerable. Naked. Under a thin blanket, in a house whose rules and comforts he did not know. All matters that made him miss his own home even more.

Francesca dished out three more tamales and handed Josiah the plate. "I will leave you to yourself then."

"You don't have to go. I'm sorry if I was curt with you."

"No, no señor, it is late. I have other chores to finish before I end the day."

"It is only night then? Not morning?"

"*Sí*, Señor Elliot rode out at last light. Papa and I tried to convince him to wait until morning, but he would have nothing of it."

"That would be Scrap."

"I'm sorry?"

"It's a nickname for Señor Elliot."

"I see."

"Please tell your father that I'm grateful for his hospitality."

"*Sí*, I will."

Francesca turned then and walked away from the bed, the light following her gently, allowing Josiah to see the silhouette of her body through the thin linen material of her blouse and skirt.

He turned away once she disappeared out the door, surprised at himself.

He had mentioned Lily, told Francesca of his dead wife, but had not bothered to mention that he was courting a woman in Austin, who had all of the makings of a fine wife and mother for Lyle. It was an omission that made him as uncomfortable as the lumpy foreign mattress he'd woke up and found himself on.

CHAPTER 8

Morning light filtered into the room, shimmering around the closed curtain at the window. The coolness of the night was evaporating, overtaken by the coming heat of the day. A slight breeze pushed under the door, searching for an escape route, finding it in a long crack in the wall adjacent to the window. The window was closed tight. Ugly brown water stains drained down the wall to the floor from the sill, giving a musty smell to the room that Josiah had not noticed before. For a brief moment, he thought he could smell his own sickness, the injury settling under his skin, out to do him harm in an unseen, and unavoidable, attack.

He sat on the edge of the bed, half-awake, still not sure where he was or how he had gotten to the room.

The night had been filled with fits of sleeplessness and of pain and worry. The side of his face felt like he had fallen into a thick patch of prickly pear, itching, stinging, festering inside his skin until it felt like it would explode. If not for the bandage and salve that Francesca had seen to place there, Josiah surely would have gone mad, or succumbed to the wound in total surrender. He was feverish one minute, sweating and wet all over, then dry the next minute, like there was nothing wrong with him at all.

Mostly, though, the night had brought nightmares and dreams, visions of ghosts wafting in and out of his consciousness, untouchable and silent. His voice was vacant, stuck somewhere between the waking world and the sleeping one, not allowing him to speak with the specters. Other faces he did not know, or recognize, visited him as well, until Josiah finally relented and gave up trying to participate in the dream. He woke up then, grasping at the meaning of it all, trying to hang on to the sight of Lily, of friends lost in the war. He wanted nothing more than to hear their voices as he woke, but all he was left with was the whisper of the breeze pushing in under the door and the distant sounds of life stirring just outside it.

A knock came at the door, startling Josiah, pulling him completely out of his dream state and fully into the waking world.

"Are you decent, Señor Josiah?" It was Francesca's voice, certain, sweet, and surprisingly welcome.

"Yes," Josiah said, making sure the blanket was wrapped tightly at his waist. His feet rested on the cool, red tiled floor, and he sat up as straight as he could.

Francesca had seen him bare-chested the night before, but he still felt a bit of real modesty, uncertain if it was proper to be in the company of a strange woman barely covered, even though he was injured and obviously under her care.

The door creaked open, and Francesca peeked inside the room before walking inside.

Josiah's hands tingled, and he was surprised that he was anxious to see the girl. He felt boyishly bashful, then, exposed in a way he was unfamiliar, and uncomfortable, with.

Francesca was dressed similarly to the night before, but in a clean, long burgundy skirt and a loose-fitting white blouse, untucked at the waist. She carried a pail of steaming water and a handful of small white linens. "I am here to change your bandages, señor. Papa is cooking *huevos rancheros,* some breakfast. You like, um, eggs, I hope?"

"Yes, sure, thank you." Josiah shifted uncomfortably on the edge of the bed. "I don't want to be any trouble."

"You are no trouble, señor, I promise you."

"Please, call me Josiah."

"I am sorry, I forgot. It is just habit to be respectful."

"I appreciate that, but I feel like I shouldn't be here, that you're going out of your way unnecessarily. I wasn't expecting to walk into the cantina and get shot right away. I wasn't expecting to get shot at all."

"You do not understand . . ." Francesca hesitated and looked up to the ceiling as she stopped at the end of the bed. "Those men were not nice men." Her eyes were suddenly wet, glazed over with tears threatening to roll down her cheeks, but she fought off the urge to cry with a bite of her bottom lip. Shame replaced the pain on her face, and she hung her head, refusing to show Josiah any more emotion than she already had.

Josiah flexed his fingers and rolled them into a tight fist without thinking about it. "Did they hurt you?"

"No, no. They did not touch me." Francesca's voice was sharp, abrupt, as she looked up, directly into Josiah's eyes. "But it was only a matter of time. Papa is an old man. They were growing tired of waiting for their *amigo,* bored with just looking at me. I am sorry, I should not be telling you this. But please know that not all of us in Arroyo are in agreement with Juan Cortina's desires. We have no quarrel with the Anglos, or the Kings who own the ranch, or with those who rule all of *Tejas.* There are more *banditos* than those two that have visited the cantina in the last few years."

"It has been difficult for you here?"

Francesca nodded. "It is just Papa and I. We do the best we can, but there is nowhere else for us to go. This is all we know to do. So we get up every day and just do what needs to be done, the best we can. Sometimes, we are happy."

"I'm sorry."

Silence fell between them as Francesca looked away and walked to the table next to the bed. She set the bowl and linens down, then pulled open the heavy curtain.

Josiah watched her every move, unable to take his eyes off her. Harsh, bright light cut into the small room, blinding him for a moment.

It was like being inside the dream of the night before, caught in a fire, but feeling no threat, just the warmth and comfort from the light, and the presence of another human being offering nothing but comfort and sustenance.

"How did you sleep?" she asked.

"I dreamed about tamales." It was a lie, but the truth seemed obvious. Josiah didn't want Francesca to think that her care for him was lacking in any way. He did not feel rested at all.

Francesca smiled, then chuckled. "I am not the greatest *cocinero* in the land. No one has ever dreamed of my food before."

"Then I am glad to be the first."

The smile stayed on Francesca's face as she moved to Josiah's side. "I need to remove the *vendajes,* the bandages."

"I understand."

Francesca touched Josiah gently on the shoulder. Her fingers were warm, soft, and skillful as she pulled away the bandage. She drew in a deep breath.

"What's the matter?" Josiah asked.

"You have other scars. I did not notice when I dressed the wounds. I was just concerned about helping you."

Josiah lowered his head then. Each of his scars held a story he'd rather not tell, rather not relive, even to Francesca. So he said nothing.

"Are you a bad man, Josiah Wolfe?" Francesca asked, running her hand over the scar from the Lost Valley fight.

He shook his head no. "I don't think so."

"But like Señor Elliot, you have killed men?"

"Only when I had to," Josiah said. "To save a friend's life, or my own. In battle, or in duty to a cause I signed up for, like this one, to ride with the Rangers. Killing is never easy, at least for me."

The breeze had pushed the door open, and a chicken clucked nervously outside. The first smell of breakfast wafted into the room.

"This wound is red, starting to gape," Francesca said. "I fear infection is setting in. I have a salve, but it may work too slow. If the wound grows worse, we will have to set a hot iron to your skin to stop the infection from growing."

"It's only a graze," Josiah said.

"I have seen men die from simpler wounds, cuts to the hand."

Josiah nodded. He, too, had seen his fair share of deaths in the war caused by grazes, cuts, and wounds that had not seemed life-threatening. Most times, infections were stopped with amputations. He had felt lucky to walk home from the war intact, with all of his arms and legs, while so many of his fellow soldiers had left a piece of themselves behind on the battlefield.

"It is not a worry yet," Francesca said. "I do not want you to have false hope that you are well enough to leave today. You need to rest, give yourself time to heal."

"I fear I have little time to waste," Josiah said. "I'll leave when Scrap returns, whether I'm ready or not."

"I understand, but I hope Señor Elliot takes his time in returning."

Josiah said nothing, just watched Francesca go about tending to his wounds. He could smell her clean scent over the mustiness of the room. She must have already bathed and gotten her chores done for the morning before seeing to him. When she pulled away, it saddened him. He wanted Francesca to stay close to him. There was an energy about her that he felt he needed, that he'd been lacking.

"What is the matter, Josiah?" she asked.

"Nothing," he said, the question snapping him back to reality. The guilt he felt about his rising feelings for Francesca must have crossed his face. He could not forget that he was courting Pearl, that there was a woman in his life, working her way into his heart, but neither could he forget that Pearl was hundreds of miles away, while he was here, being looked after and cared for by a very beautiful woman. "I suppose I'm just missing home."

"You fear never seeing your *hijo,* your son, again?"

Josiah nodded. "It's more than that."

Francesca pulled away and placed the used bandage on the table next to the bed. She was standing, facing him. "What?"

"There is a woman I'm courting. I care about her."

Francesca said nothing. Another chicken clucked outside the door, drawing her attention from him. But there was no mistaking the quick look of disappointment flashing on her face as she turned away. She took a deep breath then, squared her shoulders, and said, "I have warmed a tub of water for you, señor, if you would like to bathe before you eat breakfast."

And with that, Francesca hurried out of the room, leaving behind everything that she had brought in, including her smile and the offer of comfort.

CHAPTER 9

Josiah was sitting outside when Francesca's father brought him a plate of eggs. He was a tall, thin man. His brown skin was lighter than normal, not quite white, more the color of a woven basket, but not as dark and velvety as Francesca's skin. His face was gaunt, wrinkled, with sunken cheeks, and his chestnut eyes flittered about constantly, looking around like a nervous bird's. He had yet to look Josiah directly in the eye.

"Thank you," Josiah said. *Gracias* would have been more appropriate, but speaking another language had always been difficult for Josiah. More to the truth, he was stubborn about talking in the Mexican tongue, refused to on most accounts, unless he absolutely had to. Unless he was undercover as a spy — and that was not the case here, since Scrap had told of their real identities — and even then it was difficult. He was an Anglo. And Anglos spoke Texan, at least his generation of Anglos. His son, Lyle, spoke Mexican more fluently at four years old than Josiah ever would. It was a conflict that was easier to ignore than confront.

"*De nada.* You're welcome, Señor Wolfe," the man said.

A moment of panic ran through Josiah's veins. He already felt weak, but now he felt weaker. Even though Scrap trusted the pair of Mexicans to tell them the truth, Josiah wasn't sure he could trust them both. He had no idea if the father was really a good man. Two Rangers killing two of Cortina's men in a cantina in Arroyo was too good a story not to tell. And with Scrap off chasing one of Cortina's men, Josiah was left to look after himself, weakened by the fight and unsure of everything.

Francesca's father nodded, turned, and started to hurry away.

"Wait," Josiah said. "Please, what is your name? You know my name. I should know yours."

The man stopped and looked to the ground. "Adolfo. Adolfo Soto."

"That is a good name."

"It means noble wolf, but I am just a poor man with a talent for pouring beer and nothing else of value. The Kings are Anglo, owners of more land than I can imagine, noble like the lions who stalk from a distance. Do you know the Kings, señor?"

Josiah flinched at the similarity between his name and the English translation of Adolfo's, but he said nothing to acknowledge it. "No, I don't know any of them. They're a good family, though, undeserving of the thieving that Cortina inflicts on them and their ranch." He hesitated, still unsure if he should fully expose his honest self. "I'm sorry for the intrusion, and I appreciate the hospitality."

"You are hurt, señor. What is a man to do?" Adolfo unconsciously cocked his head over his shoulder, to the right.

Josiah was sitting at a simple table made of mesquite. The roof protected him from the direct sun, and he sat butted up next to the wall, as much in the shadows as possible. He silently followed Adolfo's nod and caught sight of a baked white mission half a block down the street, sitting openly in a field of hard dirt, all by itself, a simple wood cross rising upward from its narrow and short bell tower. The land was flat behind it, stretching out to meet the ocean, too far in the distance to be heard; but it could still be tasted. Salt touched his tongue lightly.

The mission was weathered, streaked with water stains, just like the windowsill in the room he had woken up in. There was a crucifix in the room, but Josiah had paid it no mind, had barely noticed it, thought nothing of its placement. Crosses were as plentiful as roaches in this part of Texas.

Josiah's own religious beliefs were non-existent. His faith was in the moment, in the worry about what lay ahead, as long as he walked on this earth. Beyond that, there was only darkness and the unknown. Death was walking into the night, and never walking out of it.

When Lily, his wife, lay dying, she'd asked for the preacher to come to her bedside from her church in Seerville. Josiah went into town to make the request, and the preacher, a man whose name he could not remember now, refused, fearing for his own life — fearing that he, too, would become infected with the sickness that was eating away inside of Lily, weakening her every breath until she could no longer talk.

Lily was crushed, heartbroken, by the preacher's rejection, by his human fear. She had been a believer all of her life, and in the dire moment when she needed reassurance that her faith was valid and true, that the promises of an afterlife meant something, she was left to face it all on her own. Josiah had never taken another man of God seriously since then — including the ex-monk, turned bounty hunter, who had tried to kill him a few months back.

"Thank you again, Adolfo," Josiah said. "I am in your debt."

Adolfo stood stiffly, fidgeting with the strings of the stained apron he wore. It looked like he had butchered more than one hog while wearing it. "No, no, señor. There is no debt. I have only done what is the right thing to do."

Josiah stared down at the plate of food. Scrap had not told him where their friendship stood, or, at least, it was impossible for Josiah to remember. The fight in the cantina and the pain of the gunshots in his flesh had left him more disoriented than he realized.

The eggs were cooked perfectly, sharing a plate with corn tortillas, mashed up beans, fried more than once, topped with a tomato-chili sauce and some strands of fresh white cheese. The aroma was comforting. He had eaten a similar dish in his own home, from a skillet prepared by Ofelia, many times. But he was not hungry now, and the weakness he had initially felt when he sat down was growing instead of going away, draining what strength he had left. He could barely sit up straight.

"Have you told anyone about us?" Josiah asked. "Who we really are?"

Adolfo shook his head no. "Señor Elliot told us of your mission. He asked me not to spread any more news than I had to." He stopped fidgeting then, dropped his hands to his side, and stiffened.

"He threatened you, didn't he?"

Adolfo shook his head no again.

"He threatened Francesca?"

Adolfo looked away, then back to Josiah quickly, with warm and unflinching eyes. "You are safe here, Señor Wolfe. There is no worry about your story. It is my honor to feed you, to care for you. Now, eat, before your meal gets cold. You need to regain your strength."

"Why? Why would you do this?" Josiah said, pushing away his anger at Scrap, knowing full well the boy wouldn't harm Francesca. He was just young, trying to find any source of power he could. Intimidation was an easy path.

"We are not the enemy, Señor Wolfe," Adolfo answered, his voice finally calm, his eyes settling directly on Josiah, not looking away. "And besides, we have mutual *conocimientos,* um, acquaintances. You will see."

Before Josiah could say anything else, Adolfo hurried away, disappearing inside the cantina.

It wasn't long before a clatter of pots and pans filled the air.

Josiah sat at the table for almost an hour, his appetite as weak as the rest of him. Still, he managed to eat half a plate of the savory food, drinking water more than anything.

The spicy eggs settled easily in his stomach, and he started to feel better, more flushed with energy than without. His face stung as the air caressed his skin. There was no way to attach the bandage, and Francesca had told him that the fresh air would do it good, so the pellet wound was exposed. It was covered with salve and at times burned like it was on fire. When he reached up to touch his face, he could only feel the gooiness of the salve. He didn't dare press harder, fearing the pain. It smelled like the inside of a cactus, broken open for its succulence and nourishment. There would be a scar, but that was the least of his concerns. He only wanted to get better, to be ready to ride back to the Ranger camp when Scrap returned.

Francesca had disappeared. He hadn't seen her since she had left his room. Adolfo ventured in and out of the cantina now and then, checking on him, making sure there was water for him to drink, that he was still in the shade. Josiah didn't ask about Francesca, even though he wanted to. He wanted to see her again. He wanted to know if she was real, or just another vision, a painful response to his need for comfort after being shot. For all he knew, Adolfo was the only one tending to him, and Francesca was only a figment of his imagination. It would have been easier if that were the truth.

CHAPTER 10

A cart pulled by a pair of haggard oxen ambled down the street. Arroyo had little to offer any travelers or its residents; a few adobe buildings along with the mission, a mercantile of sorts, and another building that looked shuttered, closed for business of any kind. For whatever reason, prosperity had overlooked the town and the people who had chosen to call it home.

There had been no horse traffic since Josiah had been sitting on the veranda, so the cart caught his attention, and raised his concern about his own safety, as well as Adolfo's and Francesca's, since he was sitting alone and unarmed.

He stiffened in the chair, knowing he had little energy, or time, to hurry off to his room and find his gun — which he didn't know where to find. Not a good thing since an uncertain need of it had arisen. The realization sat uncomfortably in his stomach, and he knew he'd need to see to rearming himself sooner rather than later. He hoped the man driving the cart was just another Mexican passing through, or arriving home, and nothing more. The sun was in his eyes, and it was difficult to tell much about the driver's features, whether he might be friend or foe.

The breakfast had done little to rid Josiah of the weakness that had greeted him when he'd awoken. It increased instead of fading as he had hoped. Beads of sweat appeared on his forehead as quickly as he could wipe them away, and he shivered unknowingly, thinking it was only a reaction to the fear he felt, the exposure and vulnerability of being alone in an unknown place. Josiah was not accustomed to what he was feeling.

He started to get up and realized he was too weak to stand. His balance was off, and suddenly the world was spinning.

The sky was the ground and the ground was the sky.

If there were clouds, or any weather at all, Josiah couldn't tell. Everything was growing dark. He thought to call out, but his voice caught in his throat, leaving him a prisoner inside his body, any and all control of his functions and fear lost as the darkness quickly turned to black.

■ ■ ■ ■

Josiah awoke in bed, staring at a familiar face.

"It is good to see you, *mi amigo*," Juan Carlos said.

Josiah's mouth was dry. He felt like he had been walking in the desert for months, starved of food and water. He knew it was a great possibility that he was dreaming, that the man hovering over him wasn't really Juan Carlos Montegné, half brother of Hiram Fikes, uncle to his Pearl, as well as a friend and a savior who had stood between him and death on more than one occasion. If *this* was a dream, it would make sense that his mind had conjured Juan Carlos.

A glass full of water appeared at his lips, and Josiah drank it hungrily, slowly accepting the reality that he was still among the living. He flicked his eyes open and closed them as fast as he could, trying to focus, to make sure he was seeing straight. It *was* Juan Carlos he was staring at, and any fear he felt in the recesses of his body dissipated. He knew he was safe now.

After drinking all of the water, he was able to speak, but only softly. His throat was coarse, like his voice box had been dragged through rough sand. "It is good to see you, too. How did you get here?"

"I drove the ox." Juan Carlos smiled, pulled away, and sat the glass gently on the table. "You have a bad infection, señor. I fear for your life."

"No, no, how did you know I was here?" Josiah tried to look past Juan Carlos, but the room was dark, lit by the coal oil sconce on the wall and nothing else. The curtains were drawn, and no other light made its way into the room. Josiah didn't know what time it was, or whether it was night or day. There didn't appear to be anyone else in the room.

"Señor Elliot told me. He is on the hunt for one of Cortina's men?"

Josiah nodded yes. "He is all right?"

"Yes, he was the last time I saw him. He will be fine. It is you that I worry about."

"The tide has turned."

Juan Carlos forced a smile at Josiah's remark, recalling the time not so long ago that he, Juan Carlos, was shot, in bad shape, lost in the in-between world of life and death, fighting the hard battle to live, to take up arms another day.

Juan Carlos was much older than Josiah. His hair was white as snow on a mountaintop, a stark contrast to his wrinkled, brown skin, darkened by many hours in the sun. In the winter, his skin lightened, revealing his Anglo heritage to anyone who noticed that kind of thing. Most people didn't. One drop of Mexican blood made him Mexican through and through to the purists.

There were days when Josiah was among those men who believed that a Texan and an Anglo should be one and the same — but there were other times, simpler times, when the color of a man's skin didn't matter. He had been shown over and over again that a man's character came from his heart and was not a matter of skin color that he had no control over. If all Mexicans were unworthy, Josiah would be long dead and not lying in a sickbed in a cantina, tended to by Mexicans all around. This was one of those moments when differences didn't matter.

"We are going to have to cauterize the wound on your shoulder, Señor Josiah. It is the only way we know to stop the *enfermedad,* the sickness, from spreading," Juan Carlos said. There was deep concern on his face.

Almost as if on command, the door opened and Adolfo walked in, holding a glowing red branding iron. There was no brand, just a strip of metal that had been set under a hot fire for a long time. The tip of the rod smoked and was as red as the sun on the hottest day of the year.

"Here, bite on this." Juan Carlos offered Josiah a rag rolled up from end to end. "Open your mouth." It was an order.

Josiah shook his head no. "Isn't there any other way?" Fear stuck in his vocal cords, and his voice quivered. He felt like a child who had fallen down a well with no way out.

"There is no medicine that will work quickly enough," Juan Carlos said. "You will surely die if we do nothing. The salves have only made the wound worse. I have come a very long way, and I do not wish to bury you on this trip. You will have to trust me, and Adolfo. It is the only way, *mi amigo.*"

Josiah took a deep breath and reluctantly opened his mouth.

Juan Carlos plunged the rag into his mouth then, offering little gentleness. "It will be over before you know it. Bite hard. There will be whiskey on the other side of the pain to ease it and help with the healing."

Adolfo didn't hesitate, didn't give Josiah any more time to protest, to respond to the fear and anticipation that was rising from his toes to the top of his skull. He stepped next to Juan Carlos, who nodded and stepped out of the way but remained close.

The flame in the sconce flickered, causing shadows to dance on the wall and ceiling.

Josiah could smell the hot iron, feel the heat as it came closer to his skin. He tensed, readied himself for the oncoming pain, but was momentarily relieved to see another figure enter the room and stand just inside the door.

He knew it was Francesca, and for whatever the reason, her presence made a difference, calmed him, when Adolfo jammed the hot iron against the throbbing wound.

Josiah screamed as loud as he was able. His voice was muffled, and somehow, with a swiftness he had not seen in a while, Juan Carlos was at his side, anchoring him down as Adolfo continued to grind the iron into his shoulder.

Steam rose from his skin, and the smell of burning flesh filled the room. It was the smell of war, the smell of death. As he struggled to escape, and give in to the treatment at the same time, Josiah felt another hand touch him.

Francesca had moved from the shadows to the opposite side of the bed. She reached out to touch Josiah's face, caressing him, murmuring words that sounded more like a child's lullaby than anything else.

For the second time in a matter of hours, Josiah surrendered to the pain, to the circumstance he'd found himself in, and welcomed the darkness as it came. Only this time, there was a song to accompany him on his journey, a soft touch to see him off.

He could only hope that Francesca was close by when he woke again . . . if that was his luck.

CHAPTER 11

The room was empty. Darkness surrounded Josiah, and for a long moment he listened to see if he could hear anything other than his own breathing and heartbeat. There was nothing, not even the distant cluck of a chicken. A black cloak had fallen over the world, covering him along with it.

He stared at the ceiling, glad that he felt very little pain. His face still stung, but the salve that had been placed there seemed to have worked. The bandage was off, and thankfully, infection hadn't set into that wound. Taking a branding iron to his face was beyond the grasp of his imagination. The pain would last long beyond the initial sizzle, and the scar would ride with him for the rest of his life. A reminder of his failure to see what was coming next with the two unnamed men in the cantina. A closer fight, one with worthier opponents, and the same outcome would have been easier to carry.

But he didn't have to worry about that. The deeper scar he would carry, if he lived on to see another day, would be hidden, like most of his other scars. His face would be changed though, in time. He just didn't know how, nor did he much care at the moment. He was just glad to be breathing, to be awake, and alive.

Josiah had no idea what day it was, how much time he had lost since the red-hot iron had been placed against his skin. All he knew was that it was night, that he'd spent more time in bed in the past few days than he'd ever imagined he would. Not that he wasn't grateful for the care he'd received — he was. More than grateful, was the truth of it. Especially now that he was awake, and had been saved from a trip to the land of the dead.

If that *had been* the outcome, his only regret would have been leaving Lyle behind, an orphan in an unforgiving world. But that was not the case, either. Adolfo and Juan Carlos had saved his life. Francesca, too. He didn't know how he was ever going to repay that debt, but he knew he would try. He had to try — once he was able to get back up on his feet again.

With a deep breath, bracing himself for an onslaught of pain, Josiah pulled himself up against the headboard of the bed from a prone position. He favored his unharmed, strong shoulder, the left one, and there was little pain, just tenderness and weakness that felt familiar to him. Though this wound was not as deep or severe as the Lost Valley knife wound, it was the infection that had threatened him, an unseen foe in league with other invisible enemies trying to snuff out his life — and those of the ones he loved, too.

Losing Lily and the girls to a Comanche attack would have been easier than losing them to influenza. It would have given Josiah something to hate, something to go after, something to never give up on. Revenge was a powerful drug, and it was hard to hold that deep emotion against something he couldn't see, understand, or fight.

As Josiah's eyes adjusted to the darkness, he was able to make out shadows, see the wall, the curtain-clad window, a bit of gray light slipping in under the door. The cloak of black was not as thick as he'd thought, but it was still deep into the night — or he had lost his ability to see clearly, to see colors and light. It was a consideration that left him uncertain, hoping that it was wrong.

He flinched at the recognition that someone was sitting in the corner, a faceless wraith staring straight at him. Not that he could see the person's eyes, he couldn't, but he felt the gaze penetrating into him.

"Who is it? Who's there?" Josiah said, his voice raw, his throat dry and in need of water. He instinctively glanced over to the table for his gun, but could see no sign of it.

No answer came, causing a bit of fear to rise up Josiah's spine.

What if it was the third man looking for his own set of revenge against those who had killed his *amigos*? Or Cortina himself, no less a myth to Josiah at this point, a bedtime story come alive to deliver evil and death in one fell swoop, instead of greedily rustling cattle in the darkness?

Any pain Josiah felt immediately left his body. It was his first clue that the cauterization had stopped the spread of infection, and that some serious time had most assuredly gone by since the procedure had been applied.

"Who's there?" Josiah demanded again, pulling himself higher in the bed, ready to jump out of it and fight if he had to.

"Relax, Josiah, it is me," Francesca said. She stood up then and glided toward him in the darkness, heading straight for the table next to the bed. She poured a glass of water and handed it to him.

Josiah relaxed as soon as he heard Francesca's voice, his visions of an evildoer gone as quickly as they had come. He took the glass and drank the water heartily.

"Slow down. There is plenty more where that came from," Francesca said.

Josiah ignored her. He was parched beyond belief, and hungry, too. He handed the glass to her expectantly. After another glass full of water, he felt a little better, and focused on Francesca.

She was in her nightclothes and barefoot, though she was covered with a heavier shawl than she might have otherwise worn if she were alone, or with someone familiar. The room was comfortable, the air dry, but there was still a hint of the previous day's heat held inside it.

"How long have you been here?" Josiah asked. He was glad she had covered herself appropriately.

"Not long. Juan Carlos watched over you for quite a while. He was very tired from his journey before he arrived here, and I had to argue with him to leave your side."

Josiah nodded. "He is a good friend."

"You have fought together more than once?"

"Yes."

"This battle nearly killed you, Josiah Wolfe."

"I know, I can feel it."

"But you are better?"

Josiah nodded.

"I feared the fever would take you, that we were too late." Francesca hesitated like she wanted to say something else, but she restrained herself. She just stood there, her features barely visible. Still, he could see her silhouette, and feel the softness of compassion in her voice. "You were calling out. Do you remember that?"

Josiah shook his head no. "The last thing I remember is the branding iron burning into my skin, the awful smell of death. I have smelled men burning before. I thought it was my time to die. Who was I calling for?"

"A woman," Francesca said, moving away from the bed, standing next to the window so now he could barely see her at all.

Any hope of seeing her face disappeared. Her motivations and expressions were cloaked by the darkness. Once more, night was the enemy.

Josiah expected to hear Francesca say he had screamed out "Lily" or "Pearl," but she said neither name.

"It sounded like Susie. Like you said Fat

Susie," Francesca said softly, with curiosity in her voice.

CHAPTER 12

Josiah had to digest the meaning of his delirious outcry, the truth of it, if he could. In a flash, he saw the face of a beautiful Mexican woman whom he had known for only one night. He had fallen into her arms in a moment of need and desire, and she into his, he had always believed, for the same reason. She was the first woman he had been intimate with after Lily's death, and she held a special place in his heart. Maybe more special than he knew.

"That is a funny name to call out for," Francesca said. "Who is this Fat Susie, Josiah?"

He drew in a deep breath and turned his head away from Francesca. "She was a woman in Austin I knew briefly."

"Was?"

Josiah turned back to face Francesca, could only see her outline against the wall. Any judgment was still hidden, and he was glad for that, at least. "Yes, she is dead. Killed by her own brother."

"That is sad." Francesca moved away from the window. The gray light under the door was growing brighter. Dawn was obviously rising in the east, the long night almost over. "But you must have cared about her."

"I did care about her, at least as much as was possible in the short time I knew her. This is a hard story to tell a stranger."

"I am no stranger, Josiah. Not now. I have seen you at your worst, and your best. You are a man of character. A decent man, I know that much about you, and it is enough." Francesca's words were halting, like she was searching for the right Anglo word to use to make the most impact. She seemed to have figured out that Josiah was clueless about her language, that she would have to explain every Spanish word she used.

"I don't think you've seen me at my best."

"You are wrong about that. I saw you as a man trying to do the right thing, just trying to do your duty. You didn't come into the cantina with killing on your mind like those *hombres* did."

"No, I didn't."

"I am no stranger, then," Francesca repeated. "You can tell me about this Fat

123

Susie if you like. Or not. It makes no difference to me. You just have an *asombrado,* um, astonished, I think, look on your face every time you say the woman's name."

Josiah lowered his head and sighed. "I'm sure it's a sad look. Right after I joined the Rangers, we were on an assignment to bring an outlaw to trial. We had a history, the outlaw and me. More than a history, really. We went to war together, and came home together, luckily all in one piece. At least physically. Charlie lost the ability to tell right from wrong. The easiness of killing never left him."

"Like it did you?"

"I'm not sure I ever had it. I only killed a man if I had to in the war. That doesn't mean I don't carry my own shame. A man learns a lot about himself on the battlefield. Things he may not like."

"Nothing has changed. Killing is not easy for you now. I could see that in your eyes. It is why I fired the scattergun."

"No, nothing has changed. I may have hesitated, I don't know, I can't remember. If I did, I'm sorry for putting your life in jeopardy."

Francesca sat down gently on the edge of his bed. He could smell her sweet, clean scent, and tried his best to ignore it. "You

124

have nothing to apologize for. You do not mind if I sit?"

"No." Her presence comforted him.

"Stories make us stronger."

"Charlie Langdon, the outlaw, had set up an ambush." Josiah drew in a deep breath, trying to organize the past in his mind and continue where he'd left off. "And my captain was killed in the attack. Charlie escaped, but it was my charge to return Captain Fikes's body back to Austin, back to his family, a wife and a grown daughter, a young widow herself."

"Ah, I see. This widow, she is Fat Susie?"

"No, it's not that simple — she was not Fat Susie. Susie, Suzanne del Toro, ran a whorehouse in Little Mexico." Josiah stumbled on the words, not sure how Francesca would react, if she would become angry when he used the word "whorehouse." When she didn't flinch, didn't offer any judgment, he went on. "She was Captain Fikes's, um, companion when he was off the trail, back in the city. His wife was such in a legal arrangement only, I think, for a lot of years, though I don't know the details of their daily life. The captain spoke little of his home life."

"An Anglo taking up with a Mexican?" Francesca said.

125

"He was a good man. I didn't know about Susie while he was alive. No one did, really, even though it was rumored he had a concubine. He named his horse after her. Whatever the morality of it all was escaped me, and I'm glad for that. He was a good soldier, and the best captain I've ever known."

"I can see you cared for him."

"Captain Fikes is also Juan Carlos's half brother. He had a history, too, with Mexicans, you see. I don't think he could hate his own blood just for the sake of its existence." Josiah could see Francesca nod. It was her turn to look away. "Anyway, one night after I returned the body to Austin, I found my way to the hotel Suzanne ran, *El Paridiso*. I was confused and drunk on my own grief and emotion. It had only been two years since my Lily died, and I was starting to find myself attracted to the captain's daughter. I didn't know what to do, so I ran from her, as far away as I could get."

"You felt that you were betraying your love for your dead wife?"

"Yes," Josiah whispered. "And I ended up in the arms of my captain's woman. Our grief met like two trains crashing head-on on the same track. Somehow, we helped

126

calm each other's sadness, were able to make sense of it for a time. She may have been a tough businesswoman, in a trade that offered women for sale, but Suzanne had a heart, too, and it was broken by the captain's death. They had shared many years together."

Francesca sat silently for a long moment. A rooster crowed in the distance, offering validation to Josiah's earlier assumption that morning was breaking beyond the door.

He could see Francesca's features a little clearer, her own beauty becoming apparent in the soft light. It surprised him that he felt so at ease with her that he could talk about the past so openly. It was something he rarely did. Even Pearl didn't know about his encounter with Fat Susie. It was a secret he wrestled with to this day, but he had reasoned that it was in the past, before he began courting Pearl, and therefore, he was not any more accountable to tell her about Fat Susie than about the women he'd slept with during the war. But there was a link to Suzanne del Toro that did not exist to any other woman, and Josiah knew that Pearl would find the brief episode intolerable, if not a reason to end their relationship entirely.

"And then this Susie was killed by her

brother?" Francesca asked.

"Yes, for her business, her territory, her money. In the end, the Rangers and I went after him. Elliot fired the shot that killed him."

"So revenge was not yours to be had."

"I didn't see it that way."

"Why not?"

"He got what he deserved in the end. It was our duty to defend ourselves, to see justice served. A lot of women were freed to go about their lives after Emilio was killed. I'm just sorry Suzanne wasn't one of them. There was much more to her life than I knew. I wasn't able to help her, to save her, and I will always regret that."

"What of this daughter, the one that sent you running into another woman's arms? Where is she now?"

"Still in Austin." Josiah hesitated. "Waiting for me to return."

CHAPTER 13

Heat shimmered in the distance, rising up from the hard brown dirt like wavy glass curtains, and each minute brought Josiah more energy than the previous one. His recovery seemed expected by everyone around him — Adolfo, Francesca, and Juan Carlos. There had been no sign of Scrap, or of any of Cortina's men, in Arroyo.

Josiah sat on the veranda staring off into the distance, watching a couple of buzzards circle high in the air, uniformly, like hands on an unseen clock. He had eaten a hearty lunch and breakfast, and there was nothing for him to do but sit and wait for Scrap to return, with the hopes that he would be ready to leave when Scrap arrived.

Josiah was not in a hurry to leave Arroyo. He felt comfortable in the cantina, especially with Juan Carlos near.

Clipper was in a stall at the only livery, nearby, looked after nicely while Josiah had been unable to care for the horse himself.

His Peacemaker sat comfortable on his hip, the swing holster snapped closed, allowing Josiah to feel totally whole and safe. Even though he was comfortable, he knew there were still threats about, reasons that he should not completely let his guard down. His mere presence at the cantina had most likely drawn attention from some of the residents in the small town and surrounding area, and it would not have taken much of a bribe, or matter of coin, for them to get word to Cortina.

The news that a Ranger was recuperating in the cantina would surely reach the renowned rustler sooner or later. He had a network of spies that rivaled Captain McNelly's. Hopefully, the news would reach Cortina after Elliot returned and they had left to rejoin the Ranger camp.

Sitting alone, with the afternoon yet to play out before him, Josiah realized, after thinking about his conversation with Francesca about Fat Susie, that he had not read the letter that had arrived from Pearl just as he was leaving camp.

He hesitated, then dug into his jacket pocket and pulled out the letter.

The familiar smell of Pearl's toilet water immediately greeted his nose. It was sweet, springlike, always full of hope, much like Pearl herself. He smiled at the thought of her, though it made him feel a bit melancholy and lonely for home.

The envelope was sealed with a wax stamp, a crest and shield that belonged to her father's family, and one of the few remaining artifacts that noted the Fikes family, and Pearl herself, as people of means and social standing. It was the furthest thing from the truth, at least now.

The captain's widow was in a sanatorium, ailing, her estate lost, and Pearl was seeing her way through normal school to become a teacher, with the help of Juan Carlos, all the while sleeping in a small room in a boardinghouse. The loss of wealth and standing in society had taken a toll on Pearl that neither of them could have imagined, and it was easier for Josiah to be on the trail, at times, than walking through the streets of Austin with Pearl, as she was confronted daily by what she had lost through no effort of her own.

Not being a person of wealth, and knowing it was impossible for him to be such, there were many times that Josiah felt like he was not the right man for Pearl, but she insisted that she wanted a simple life, and she wanted him to be with her on that journey.

Josiah slowly opened the letter, the penmanship perfect and recognizable. He began to read it, and the rest of the world immediately faded away:

My Dearest Josiah,
It is my greatest wish that this letter finds you safe and in good health. The days seem longer than usual in your absence. Summer can be such a miserable time, and I have been lost without your company.

My schooling is nearing its end, and I am certain that by your return, I will have received my first teaching assignment. I am hoping to remain in Austin, but that is as uncertain as everything else at the moment. Mother has taken a turn for the worse, and I fear she is at death's door. She hardly knows I am in the room when I visit, which is not as often as I should. Each time the door chime rings at Miss Amelia's I am most certain that it is Pedro, come to tell me that Mother has passed on to the next life. I know this matters very little to you, as your relationship with Mother was strained and uncomfortable, more so than mine. But when she leaves this world, I will be all alone, especially with you seeing to your duty, out and away from the city. Whatever assignment comes my way, after the completion of my schooling, I will be forced to take it, regardless of the location. I cannot depend on my weary uncle forever.

I have made it a point to stop by and see Lyle at least every other day since you have been away. Ofelia is such a good mother to him that I know it will be impossible to wrestle his heart away from her and ever take her place. I cannot imagine trying, for either of their sakes. Honestly, the two of them seem very settled in their life, and while Ofelia sees to my visits hospitably, I can tell she is very uncertain about my intentions. I wish to hurt no one. I only want to love Lyle, and Ofelia, too, as far as that goes. They are all that remain of your family.

What hurts most is your absence, the long days and even longer nights. I know now what my mother must have faced when my father left her for months at a time, out pursuing Ranger business, or other forms of war and manliness. The loneliness drove her mad, made her angry at every small thing. I fear I see a mirror image of her growing in myself. I am lacking in tolerance since you left. I do not wish to repeat her path, it is too sad to see. As much as I loved my father, I now realize that he put her through more difficulties that I could not, or would not, see. I love her too much to let that knowledge go now.

So it is with certainty and a heavy heart that I must tell you that I do not wish to continue our courtship. I think it is for the best that our lives separate before it is too late and some great harm comes to either of our hearts. I truly hope you can understand why I must do this now, and I hope upon hope that you will not think less of me, and will forgive me, if that is possible.

With great admiration, Pearl N. Fikes

Josiah's hands were trembling. He slowly put the letter back in the envelope and looked up to the sky. The buzzards were gone, and a series of clouds were beginning to build in the distance.

Somewhere from inside the cantina, laughter between a man and a woman, Juan Carlos and Francesca, rang out, shattering the silence, bringing Josiah straight back into the world he had left while reading the letter.

He had no desire to join the merriment, and instead, he got up and walked away from the cantina as silently and stealthily as possible.

CHAPTER 14

The first drop of rain fell just as afternoon began to tilt toward evening. A gray ratty blanket had fallen over the earth, the distance blurry with mist, the sky bumpy and full of roiling clouds. The air was heavy with salt and moisture. If he hadn't known better, Josiah would have thought his eyes were filled with tears. But they weren't. He had cried at Lily's grave and had left his ability to shed any deeper emotion in the ground with her, hundreds of miles away. While he cared greatly about Pearl, he couldn't bring himself to face a broken heart. He was only angry. Angry that she couldn't wait until his return to Austin to end their relationship face-to-face. He would have burned the letter, and placed the moments with Pearl in a locked part of his memory, never to be opened again. But he had neither a match nor the ability to rid himself of such memories, so the effort was futile.

Josiah walked straight into the coming rain. He felt no fear, not until the cold rain finally roused him from his stupor, and he realized that he didn't know where he was. With that, he stopped and looked behind him. There was nothing there but a wall of rain, threatening in its blackness, in its swirls of power. Even lightning seemed to fear it. There was none to be seen. Only the wind seemed to be in cahoots with the rising storm.

From Arroyo, he was coming into a flat area down and away from a low series of limestone outcroppings. The ground was swampy and full of knee-high reeds that grew taller on the distant horizon. A few seabirds scattered about, worried gulls and terns looking to find shelter, struggling in the wind like kites lost without the guiding pressure of a human hand. Other than that, there were no other creatures to been seen or heard. It was like Josiah was the only man in the world, alone at the edge of land, with nowhere else to go. He could not see the ocean, but he could hear the rumble of it in the distance, taste it on his lips, imagine the crashing waves against the rocky beach.

In a matter of minutes, the rain began to steadily fall. The wind gusted up, meeting Josiah in a great thrust, pushing him farther away from the cantina. He wore no coat to protect himself with. He had nothing but the Peacemaker on his hip, his hat, and his wounds, which reminded him that he was not whole, that he was still weak, unable to defend himself fully. The wind nearly blew his hat off, a trusted felt Stetson that was irreplaceable as far he was concerned.

Recognizing that he was alone also brought back the reality of his exposure. He could be walking right into Cortina's camp for all he knew.

Josiah wasn't sure what he'd been thinking. It was a stupid way to react to the letter, running off from an unfamiliar place into an even more unfamiliar place. He should have expected Pearl to toss him aside a long time ago. They were too different. Maybe too desperate to find someone to fill the void left by those who had exited this world, and their lives. Or maybe he was too much of a reminder of her father, a rambling man, her concern more about trust than loss. He didn't care. Not now.

Out of steam, certain that if he kept on walking he'd run into the ocean, or trouble, Josiah decided to turn back and return to Arroyo, if he could find it again. At least he had friends there, a comfortable bed, safety in numbers.

He was defeated and tired, all of the energy that he had gained in his healing almost lost. The unexpected turn of the letter had dulled all of his senses, but they were coming back alive, reminding him of the recent events, of his duty to move forward and be ready for Scrap when he returned. There was no way Josiah was going back to Austin anytime soon. He would rejoin the fight against Cortina no matter what shape he was in. Captain McNelly needed every man he could get, and even at half his normal capabilities, Josiah felt that his years of experience could make up for what he physically lacked.

Putting one foot in front of the other, walking into the wind became difficult as the trail he'd come down jutted upward away from the flat ground. He hadn't noticed the incline coming down it.

Thunder boomed behind him, over the ocean, and the ground shook angrily, nearly toppling Josiah. He needed a walking stick, a cane of some kind to keep his balance, but there were no sticks lying about, only hollow reeds.

Struggling, he made it to the top of the outcropping. The rain grew heavier, and it obscured his vision. He'd hoped to see the village of Arroyo on the horizon, but it had been swallowed up by the gray wall of rain and the raging clouds of the storm. He couldn't see anything. Cold rain peppered his face, and he cowered for a second. But something caught his eye. Movement in the grayness. It only took a blink to realize that what he was looking at was a horse and rider. Heading straight for him, riding hard, like they were on a mission.

If he saw them, they had seen him.

There was no place to hide, no trees to shelter him or give him cover, if the rider was one of Cortina's men. An Anglo standing in the middle of nowhere would be shot outright, no questions asked, especially considering the moment they were standing in. Cortina had to be well aware that the Rangers were looking for him, that they would try to stop the shipment of beeves to Cuba and return the longhorns to their rightful owners. There was no way he couldn't know that. Cortina was a smart man, smarter than most Texans gave him credit for. He was an old man, bent on taking what he felt was his, borders and governments be damned.

Josiah pulled his Peacemaker from the holster, readying himself, then headed back down the trail, cutting off from it at the easiest point where he could try and hide himself against the limestone wall. There were no caves, just wind cuts and indentations in the jagged, wet stone, giving him no place to find shelter from the rain, or bullets.

The temperature of the air dropped with the push of the wind. It was like the storm had sucked all of the heat from the world into the clouds and used it sparingly for the weak streaks of lightning that began to dance over his head. Still, Josiah began to sweat. His heart raced. And he allowed himself to be afraid for a brief moment.

Pearl's letter had reassured Josiah of one thing: Lyle was well cared for, loved, and would not be left an orphan if something happened to him. It was a relief, but he had known this anyway. He wouldn't have ever left Austin again if he hadn't thought Ofelia would care for the boy if something happened to him. They had an unspoken agreement, a trust between each other, that Josiah had with no one else in the world, and now didn't expect to have with anyone else anytime soon.

But Josiah was unwilling to openly surrender if it came to that, if the rider *was* one of Cortina's men. He would die fighting. For himself and for Lyle. If word ever got back to the boy about how his father had died, then Josiah wanted Lyle to know that he had faced death straight on — he was no coward, and there was no coward's blood in Lyle's veins. If nothing else, Lyle would have that pride to carry on. The boy would never have to question what he was made of, and for some reason the thought of that helped Josiah stand up straighter and forget his pain, as he chambered a cartridge in the Peacemaker and prepared himself to face the rider.

The horse was black, or at least it looked black from where Josiah stood, poised, the hammer back, his finger on the trigger. Its rider was small in stature, covered with a duster and a hat, but it was hard to make out any features, or whether the rider wore a gun or was carrying one for that matter.

Josiah's heart rate had slowed. He had been in this situation before. At this very moment, he did not fear death.

Another streak of lightning cracked alive over his head, offering the clarity of vision for a breath or two. In the moment when daylight returned, Josiah saw that the rider was not one of Cortina's men, but a woman.

It was Francesca, come out to look for him.

Unfortunately, what follows lightning is most often a clap of loud thunder. There was no exception this time, and the thunder boomed loudly. It was like a bomb had been set off a few inches over Josiah's head; his eardrums threatened to explode, deafening him forever. If the limestone outcropping had been any higher and more unstable than it was, then an avalanche of rocks and boulders could have been released, trapping or killing Josiah. But as it was, he was safe.

Francesca, on the other hand, had not been prepared for the loud clap of thunder. Either she didn't have a tight hold on the horse's reins or they had slipped out of her hands. The black horse spooked and reared furiously, tossing Francesca to the ground, in a blurry, sudden thrust and then running off — leaving her scream behind as she crashed to the ground, disappearing from Josiah's sight.

CHAPTER 15

Francesca lay on the wet, swampy ground in an unmoving heap. Her eyes were closed tightly; a thin line of blood trickled out of the corner of her mouth. Josiah ran faster than he thought he was able, reaching her side before another finger of lightning streaked over their heads. Thunder erupted again, shaking his whole body from head to toe.

"Francesca," he yelled, bending down to her side, shielding her from the rain as much as he could with his body. "Are you all right?"

He could see that she was still breathing and instantly felt her wrist for a pulse. A strong rhythm met his touch, and that allowed Josiah a moment of relief. He knew better than to move her, at least for the moment. She might have broken bones, a broken back or neck, it was hard to tell, and he was no doctor or expert on the human body.

Francesca's deep brown eyes flickered open. "I knew I'd find you," she said. Her voice was weak, and she tried to force a smile, but pain prevented her from completing the effort.

"It had to be you." It was a whisper. Josiah wasn't sure she'd heard him. He wasn't sure if he'd wanted her to. "Where do you hurt?"

"My back. I think I will be all right. The fall just knocked the air from my lungs." She flexed her fingers and shook both of her feet alive.

The rain fell in buckets. They were both drenched, and there was no sign of Francesca's black filly. The horse had completely disappeared in the enveloping grayness.

"You're sure you're all right?"

Francesca nodded yes. "I was worried about you."

"You shouldn't have come looking for me. I would've come back."

"Juan Carlos is out searching for you, and Papa, too. It is not safe for you to be alone with Cortina's men all around. They will gut you like a stray cat for nothing but the pleasure of it. The Apache, too. They lurk in the shadows, crossing the border to compete with Cortina and steal the *vacas,* too. I

145

could not bear to think of such a thing, of something happening to you. Juan Carlos was worried, too. I could see it on his face, but he did not speak of it, just vanished, in search of you."

"I know."

Francesca's eyes were fully open, staring up at him. Her hat had been tied securely under her chin but had fallen off her head, softening the landing. Rain splattered at her forehead, and she blinked to keep her vision clear from the downpour.

"Do you think you can sit up?" Josiah asked.

"I will try." With a deep heave, Francesca drew in a breath and struggled to lift herself up.

The wind whipped around them, and the sky overhead was black as a burnt stew, bubbling, boiling, threatening to grow worse instead of better. There was no end in sight to the storm clouds. Daylight was a memory, the afternoon taken away by some unseen force, the battle against darkness undefended. If this was a war, all hope was lost.

"There's a bit of cover to be had alongside the rock." Josiah flicked his head behind him, toward the direction he had come from. "Can you walk?"

Francesca sat up, but her face was pale,

and there was no question that she was fighting off some pain. She shook her head no just as another blast of thunder exploded over them. They both drew back, startled by the loud crash.

Rain drove harder against Josiah's face, stinging the buckshot wound. It felt like he was being shot again. He could barely see two feet in front of his nose.

Without a second's hesitation, he scooped up Francesca, picked her up without warning or asking permission, and hurried toward the limestone wall. Josiah ignored the pain, the threat that he might undo all of the healing that had taken place in his shoulder.

He laid Francesca down as gently as he could on the soft, soggy ground.

A thin limestone shelf jutted out above them about six inches, just enough to deter water onto the ground around them and down an easy slope. The wind and rain were coming from the opposite direction — at the moment — protecting them, to a small degree, from the harshest thrust of the downpour.

Francesca sat up and offered her duster to Josiah. He took it and pulled the coat over them, giving them even more shelter to huddle in.

The rain had washed the blood from Francesca's mouth, but her lip still looked slightly swollen. She must have bitten or pinched it in the fall.

Josiah pulled the duster tighter, bringing them closer together than they already were. "Are you all right?"

"I am better now."

"I don't want to be too bold."

"It is better to be here than standing out in the storm." Francesca smiled fully, but briefly, then looked away from Josiah. "Why did you leave? Come out into this *tormenta*?"

He could feel the heat of her body, and he was covered in the smell of her with her coat. She was the only woman in the world he cared about at the moment. "I needed some time to think. I just needed to be away from everyone. I'm sorry. I should've told you I was leaving." His voice wavered. What he'd said was the truth, but not all of it. He never was good at lying. He didn't want to share with her the emotion he'd felt from reading Pearl's letter.

Francesca stared up at him, her brown eyes wide open, platters of warmth searching his face for more than he was willing to offer. "Did I do something to offend you?"

Thunder boomed loudly overhead, and

Josiah had to wait to answer. A curtain of sadness had dropped over Francesca's face as she stared up to him expectantly.

"No, no, not at all. How could you think of such a thing?"

Francesca continued to look into Josiah's eyes, and he was so transfixed he couldn't look away. Without thinking of what he was doing, he leaned in, hesitated, then let his lips touch hers, waiting for her to pull away. She didn't. She met his lips with warmth and desire.

Josiah was glad for the welcome, and lost himself in the moment, his need and desire growing, as he pressed forward, matching her desire heartbeat for heartbeat.

He wasn't surprised, though, when Francesca pulled away, and cupped his face in her hands. "I am no whore like Fat Susie," she said. Her eyes had hardened, grown serious from the duskiness of the moment before.

"Suzanne del Toro was no whore."

Francesca exhaled softly, and nodded. "I am sure she wasn't. Not with you. I can understand that. I just wanted you to know that. I may be Papa's barmaid, but I do not offer myself easily to any man."

"I know that. I know."

The rain continued to beat at the duster,

and the heat and humidity grew underneath it, matched with the rising temperature of both of their clothed bodies.

Without saying another word, Francesca leaned back in and kissed Josiah, deeply and passionately. The world ceased to exist. Any pain that either of them felt was washed away by the medicine of attraction and touch.

It didn't matter that they were caught in the storm, that either of them was less than perfect in health. And the demands of society were far away, lost in a world of manners and expectations. Too far to judge, or care about their age difference, or the colors of their skin, or their heritage. All that mattered was that they had found each other at the moment and chosen to be together in a way that only mattered to them.

Josiah allowed his hand to drift down the side of Francesca's neck, not stopping until he reached the top button of her blouse.

With a flick of his thumb, he popped the button open, followed quickly, but not overly eagerly, by the next one, allowing the material to fall away. When he cupped her breast in his hand, he kissed her more deeply, and in return, Francesca allowed a gentle moan to escape her lips. She arched her back slightly.

Any thought of right or wrong was lost now. Neither of them hesitated, well aware of the ground underneath them and the storm overhead. Still, they managed to touch, kiss, and arouse each other in a respectful, but needful, way. They used their clothes as a quickly made bed, peeling them off while kissing, while tugging at each piece, never losing touch, never hesitating or giving each other the impression that they wanted to stop. Nature had taken over, put them in a private storm of their own. It would only pass as it should, whether violently or with a whimper was yet to be seen.

Josiah thought he was lost in a dream and pushed away any thought of the moments before, the letter from Pearl, the reason why he had fled the cantina in the first place. The past had ceased to exist the moment he recognized Francesca on her horse, knowing only that she had come to look for him.

"Te he querido desde que puse los ojos en usted," Francesca said. Her breathing increased rapidly as they touched, fully naked, body to body, for the first time. "I have wanted you since I first laid eyes on you."

Josiah nuzzled her neck hungrily, touched her wetness, felt her body rise to meet him, then joined her, and lost himself in the

rhythm of the storm and passion as they
became one.

CHAPTER 16

Just as quickly as it had appeared, the storm pushed east, leaving only remnants of thin, gray clouds in its wake. Heat and humidity returned as the day dimmed, promising to subside, if only slightly, once night truly arrived.

Summer nights after a storm could be consumptive — Josiah wondered, sometimes, how Captain McNelly could breathe. The ground was muddy and soft, and there was a clean smell to the heavy air, like the entire world had been cleansed, ready for a fresh start.

He hoisted Francesca up on the saddle of the black filly, who had faithfully returned after the thunder passed, then Josiah climbed up and settled comfortably behind her. "Are you ready to go home?" he asked.

"*Sí,* if we must. Papa will be worried." She settled her head against his chest.

"Yes, I suppose he will be." Josiah took

the horse's reins into his hands, and urged it to get a move on. He didn't look back, didn't feel bad about moving on, though, in more comfortable circumstances, he would've like to have stayed longer.

He could still taste Francesca's desire on his lips, smell her muskiness. It was sweet like nectar, making him want more of whatever she had, but he knew that was impossible, at least at the moment.

"Is something the matter?" Francesca asked.

Josiah kept the horse at an easy gait. The ground was flat, the incline down to the swampy reeds and inlets behind them. "No, it's just . . ."

"Are you having regrets?"

"No. How could I? It's just that I'm uneasy about facing Juan Carlos. He's very wise and will know something happened between us just by looking."

"He is your friend, he should be happy for you."

"Remember, I told you of a woman waiting for me back in Austin?"

"*Sí,* the young widow. The daughter of your captain."

Josiah could only see the side of Francesca's face, could not see directly into her eyes, but when she nodded gently, he knew

154

she understood.

"Juan Carlos," Francesca said, "is this woman's uncle. Or half uncle, as you say, since his brother was Anglo and he is Mexican."

"He is."

"You love her? Is that why you are tense now?"

"Maybe we should've had this discussion an hour ago."

"I am not looking for a husband, Josiah Wolfe. What happened happened only because we wanted it to. We are hundreds of miles away from Austin, and you will leave soon. There are no complications to worry about. This woman will wait, and surely understand that your time away is your own."

Josiah sighed. "It's not that simple. I haven't told you everything. Pearl has decided that our courting is over with, that it won't work. My life and her father's are too much alike, the time apart too much, the distance too far."

"You like the same kind of women as her father, as well." There was no anger in Francesca's voice; she said it almost like she was joking with him, ribbing him about sleeping with Mexican women. She was unflappable, didn't seem invested in any deep emotion or attachment, which surprised Josiah.

"I suppose you're right. It's probably for the best anyway," he said.

"You have nothing to worry about with Juan Carlos. I will make myself scarce on our return."

Josiah scooted up tighter to her, pressed himself against her. "I'd rather you not."

"Make up your mind, Josiah Wolfe."

He smiled, then let it fade away. "I want to keep Juan Carlos as a friend. I'll tell him about Pearl at the right time. He'll understand, I'm sure of it."

"But you were angry about this courtship ending? You do love her."

Josiah shrugged his shoulders. "When I read the letter, yes, I was angry. That's why I left. I needed some time to work things out in my head. I cared about Pearl. I still do. I loved Lily. I know that much. I always will. Lily is dead, though, and I have to accept that I might never love like that again. There are worse things."

"You had the letter with you when you arrived in Arroyo?"

"The mail rider came just as Scrap and I were leaving camp."

Francesca grew quiet and pressed harder against Josiah. "I like how you show love."

There was a smile in her voice.

It didn't take long for Arroyo to come into sight, even at the slowness of the horse's gait, or Josiah's desire to prolong saying good-bye to Francesca for as long as possible.

The only sign left of the storm was deposited on the soggy ground in puddles and fallen limbs from the occasional mesquite tree. Night was still several hours away, allowing Josiah to see ahead of him clearly.

There was a horse tied up in front of the cantina. A familiar horse. A blue roan mare. Scrap had returned.

The sconces on the wall of the cantina burned brightly. The comfortable aroma of slow-cooking meat filled the air, mixing with the bitter-smelling yeast of the ever-present beer. It looked like Adolfo expected business to be brisker than it had been in previous days. Or maybe it was just the first time that Josiah was aware enough, and awake enough, to notice the man's daily routine, and its aftereffects.

Scrap was sitting at the bar, smoking a quirlie. "I heard you'd done up and disappeared. Got everybody around here all riled up about your safety." He took a long drag on the cigarette, held the smoke in his lungs for an even longer second, then exhaled with an exaggerated burst from his lips. "I figured you could take care of yourself. I told that old Mexican that you'd show up sooner or later — and I was right."

Josiah had stopped just inside the door of the cantina. Francesca had gone around to the back entrance with barely a fleeting embrace. They had said their good-byes with a rub and peck before getting off the filly.

There was no one else in the bar except a small Mexican man stuffed into the corner, sitting on the edge of a rickety chair, his head down, his hands bound tightly behind his back with a thick rope. The man didn't look up when Scrap spoke. He didn't even look alive. His torn shirt was splattered with blood, but his chest was heaving, so there was no concern that he was dead.

"I appreciate your concern," Josiah said.

"You're feelin' better, I take it?"

"Better than I thought I would. I see you made a new friend." Josiah walked the rest of the way inside the cantina and made his way uneasily to Scrap's side.

"He calls himself Incuzicon Garcia or some such name. Ain't never heard tell of a name like that. Have you, Wolfe? You'd think all of these durned Mexican's would name themselves somethin' respectful, easy to say."

"Like Robert?" Josiah asked, sitting down on the stool next to Scrap, eyeing him like he was a mad dog tethered at the barn.

"Exactly. Like Robert."

"Incosnasción," the Mexican whispered through gritted teeth. His head still down, staring at the floor. "It is In-cos-nas-ción."

"Shut the hell up, no one asked you nothin'," Scrap said over his shoulder, a snarl on his face.

"You always were good at making new friends," Josiah said.

"That's gonna be some scar on your face. You might scare some people off. We'd be even then."

"If I'm lucky. Where'd you find your friend?"

"He ain't my friend. He's my damn prisoner, thank you very much. I took him on my own, and I expect to hand him over to Captain McNelly just the same way. He's the third man supposed to join up here and go on to fight with Cortina, if'n it comes to that."

Josiah recoiled slightly, threw his hands up palms out. "Whatever you say, Scrap. I would've gone after him with you, but I wasn't able. Looks like you did fine without me."

Adolfo walked in the back door, the same one Francesca had entered when she'd shot Josiah. He was a carrying a bucket of beer. He looked up and instantly made eye contact with Josiah. "It is good to see you again, señor. I was worried about you in the storm. It was a hard one. I feared a tornado, but thankfully, none came. Just your friend, here."

Scrap glared at Adolfo, just as he had Garcia in the corner. There was no mistaking the implication in Adolfo's voice: Scrap had brought as much trouble into the cantina as a storm would have, maybe more.

"Francesca found me," Josiah said.

"I heard." Adolfo looked away and poured the bucket of beer into a ceramic urn under the counter of the bar. "There are all kinds of bad creatures out in the world, Ranger Wolfe. Coyote. *Serpienete,* um, rattlesnake. Gilas. All will do you harm, are at war with you whether you know it or not. Cortina's men, or the Apache, if they are about, are your enemies, too. But you already know that." He hesitated before going on, looked to the open door. "Juan Carlos has yet to return, but he knows this land better than I do. He will be fine, I am sure of it. He could

160

be fifty miles from here by now for all I know."

Josiah nodded. "Sometimes, I think he was born from the land instead of from a human. His wisdom is deep."

Adolfo's face grew tight. "Never forget what I have told you. Enemies under your feet. They will attack when you least expect it." He glanced over at the prisoner, sat the empty bucket down, then turned and walked out the door.

"I think he just threatened you," Scrap said.

"I don't think so. I think he was warning me to look out for myself, not to walk off again into a land that is alien to me."

"If you say so. You got a bad way about makin' friends yourself."

Before Josiah could respond, the Mexican looked up and said, "You are both *demonios.* Cortina will fillet you both, and hand your meat over to *los buitres,* the vultures, free of charge. I will do it myself if I am able. I swear to *Dios,* I will." After that, he spewed a few more words in Spanish that Josiah didn't understand or have anyone to translate for him. He knew he and Scrap had just been cursed; there was no mistaking that.

Scrap jumped backward, causing the stool

to tumble over and bounce off the floor. The loudness and suddenness of his movement, and the crash, were jolting, as if thunder had exploded inside the room.

In a swift, fluid, motion, he flicked the quirlie at the Mexican, surprising him, not giving him enough time to react. The cigarette hit Garcia square in the middle of his forehead. An explosion of orange sparks filled the dim room, followed by a startled scream from the man.

Josiah stood up, but Scrap had already reached the prisoner, and without the offer of a warning, or any words, he punched the man in the jaw as hard as he could.

Spit and blood spewed out of Garcia's mouth, followed by another scream, this one more like a yelp. He cowered from Scrap as best he could, but there was nowhere to go — he was butted up into the corner with nowhere to escape to.

"I said shut the hell up, you greaser. I'll slit your throat right here and now, you threaten us again. You hear me?" Scrap reared back, readying another punch.

Josiah caught his arm before it flew forward. "Stop!"

There was rage in Scrap's eyes, and for a quick second, there was a look on his face like he was considering disobeying Josiah's order. But, with a deep breath, Scrap relented, jerking away from Josiah's grasp.

"Now, go sit down and get hold of yourself, Elliot. You'll not be this man's judge and jury. You'll see him to Captain McNelly safe and sound, alive and in one piece, just like you said."

Scrap's lip trembled, like he really wanted to lash out at Josiah. But he didn't. He turned away silently, his head down, his jaw clenched, his shoulders slumped suddenly in defeat.

The Mexican, Garcia, sat up, and with an amazing amount of accuracy, hocked a healthy stream of bloody spit from his mouth, catching the back of Scrap's boot as he walked away.

CHAPTER 17

Josiah stood his ground, not letting Scrap near Garcia. "If I have to order you outside, Elliot, I will. This is Ranger business no matter who brought this man in, do you understand?"

"If you say so." Scrap was on the other side of the room, back over by the bar.

"I say so."

Adolfo returned almost immediately, his hands empty but eyes focused under the bar. Most likely there was a shotgun hidden away there for troubling times. A shotgun that Francesca was familiar, and handy, with. "Is everything all right in here?"

"Yes," Josiah answered. "Just a little misunderstanding."

"We'll be leaving shortly," Scrap said.

A curious look crossed Adolfo's weathered face, quickly followed by a wash of disappointment. "Is Ranger Wolfe ready to travel?"

164

Scrap pulled out a bag of tobacco from his shirt pocket and began to roll another quirlie. "He looks fit enough to me to make it back to Ranger camp. No use stayin' in this hellhole a minute longer than need be, the way I see it."

Adolfo flinched, tried to ignore Scrap's insult, then stared expectantly at Josiah.

"We need to get Garcia back there as soon as possible," Josiah said. "Elliot's right. There's no quick way to get word to Captain McNelly. We have to leave."

"I see," Adolfo said. "See that there is no more blood spilled here. I do not need the world to think that any Anglo can just walk in and kill two Mexicans one day and whip another one a few days later. I plan to be here after this war with Cortina ends. I plan to be here until the day I die."

"Of course," Josiah said. "Garcia will not be harmed. You have my word."

"But do I have his?" Adolfo asked, nodding toward Scrap.

"Leave him to me," Josiah answered.

Scrap didn't pay either man any direct attention. He lit the thin cigarette and cast a sideways glance to Josiah with a smirk on his face, then looked into the mirror that reflected the open door. "Daylight's burnin'. We ride now or we tie up the greaser and find a hole to throw him into. What say you, Wolfe?"

"I said we were leaving."

"You don't look to be in a big hurry."

"I'm not letting you escort this man back by yourself. One of you won't make it alive."

"Says you."

"Says me. That's all you need to know."

"Yes, sir." Scrap exhaled, and for a brief moment it looked like his entire head had disappeared in a cloud of smoke.

There was very little to pack up, but Josiah returned to the room he'd recuperated in to make sure that there was nothing left behind.

Scrap had been right. Daylight was burning. Dusk was coming on fast, the last of the afternoon light soft and golden. The storm was a memory. Puddles had soaked into the thirsty, arid ground as quickly as they had formed, leaving nothing much behind but an offering of mud and an inch of brown water, if that, in the indentations.

The efforts of the day had drained Josiah of his reserve of energy and the compulsion to make a long journey on horseback — still, he felt compelled, duty-bound, to return to the Ranger camp as quickly as possible.

His injuries were not fully healed. Hardly.

The scabs on his face were still tender, had barely begun to fully form and come to an itch. And the cauterized wound threatened constantly to break free and open up. The burn had been deep and strong, and it had held the skin closed, clearing out the infection in one fell swoop. But his resistance to returning to camp was deeper in his soul, beyond physical capability and the need to do his job. He wasn't sure that he was ready to leave Francesca yet. He had hoped for another night with her, in a proper bed, their time together adventurous and more comfortable. But that was not to be.

Josiah turned when he heard footsteps behind him. Francesca faced him, her expression stoic, her shoulders stiff and thrust as far back as they could go.

In the fading light of the day Francesca looked nearly angelic, only adding to the regret that he already felt.

"So it is true," she said. "You are leaving now?"

Three feet separated them as they stood at the end of the bed where Josiah had regained his strength.

"Yes, it's true. We need to leave now and get Garcia back to camp."

"Another day will make such a big difference?"

"It might. I believe Garcia has information that will be helpful to Captain McNelly as he makes his plans. The steamer that awaits will be expecting the shipment of rustled cattle to arrive at a predetermined time and place. If we can figure out when and where that is, then we can stop the shipment. Maybe put an end to Cortina's operation once and for all. That would make life better here, would it not?"

"There will be something else, or someone else, to make it miserable. It is the way of things in this land. A person. A drought. A great storm. A broken heart," Francesca said.

Josiah stepped back unconsciously. "I'm sorry."

Francesca took a deep breath, then forced a smile. "My heart is fine. It is only tied in knots because I had hoped to get to know you better. But that is not to be. Will you come back?"

"If I can, I'd like to, but . . ."

"There is always a *but,* isn't there?"

"I don't know what's going to happen next."

"None of us do," Francesca said. She stepped forward, never breaking eye contact with Josiah, and slid her arms around his waist. "You are a good man, Josiah Wolfe. I am glad you came here, though I am sorry you will carry scars from the visit for the rest of your life." She reached up and caressed his face gently.

Josiah didn't move, didn't draw back like he once might have, but returned the embrace. He held her as closely as he could, fighting the urge to pull her even tighter. The sweetness of her natural smell only served as an intoxicant, and he knew he could easily lose control of himself — again.

As if she had read his mind, Francesca turned up her head and brushed her lips against his.

Josiah immediately felt a surge of desire vibrating from the back of his neck down to the lower regions of his body. He pulled her closer then, kissed her deeply, knowing full well that it would be for the last time, maybe forever. He was never good at good-byes, and this time was proving to be no exception.

Francesca seemed to know, and accept, the same thing. She responded in kind, snuggling into his chest as far as she could, not grinding with an offer, but pressing next to him like she was trying to drink in the moment so she would never forget it either.

Even though he was transfixed and captivated by Francesca, Josiah was not entirely lost to the outside world. He felt another presence, another set of eyes on him, then heard the soft brush of boots on the step spinning around.

He opened his eyes just in time to see the shadow of a man moving away.

The shadow was familiar, and on most days, most men wouldn't have known who the shadow belonged to, or wouldn't have seen it at all, wouldn't have known what they were looking at. But Josiah did. There was no mistaking that the shadow belonged to Juan Carlos.

Josiah broke free of Francesca and rushed to the door, but when he looked both ways, there was nothing to be seen. Nothing but a pair of fresh boot prints in the mud, hurrying out of sight, slowly filling with water, too late to hide from Josiah's view, or relieve the sinking feeling making its way to his gut.

CHAPTER 18

Josiah settled uncomfortably on Clipper's back. The hard saddle and the prospect of the impending journey were as much an unwelcome development as Scrap's return. Reality had ridden back into Arroyo long before Josiah was ready, but it was too late to lament the hard facts of his circumstances. It was time to leave.

A thin grayness grasped at the golden evening light in the far corners of the sky. Darkness would follow them to camp, quick on their heels. Josiah had thought about trying to waylay Scrap — reasoning it would be best to spend another night in Arroyo, but he knew he was just being selfish, that he was trying to steal away more time with Francesca. Any thought of such a thing was gone, had been gone the moment Josiah walked into the cantina and found Scrap in a surly mood with a prisoner in hand. He still didn't know the details of the capture, but he figured that would come soon enough. Scrap would have to relay the events to Captain McNelly, just like Josiah would have to tell his commanding officer of his new wounds.

Thankfully, there was no question that he was able to make the ride. His strength had returned, though he still felt like his body, head to toe, had been walloped with a big, heavy club. Soreness and stiffness consumed him every time he moved without honoring his injuries, reminding him of the close call he'd had, and of the great care given to him by Adolfo and Francesca. He had been lucky to have fallen on friendly ground, so to speak, in more ways than one.

It was hard to look at Francesca. She was standing next to her father in front of the entrance to the cantina, shoulder to shoulder. Her eyes were vacant, almost hard, staring past Josiah. She showed no sign of tears, or any emotion for that matter. Adolfo wore the same blank look, only he was focused on Scrap, whom he treated like a mad dog, a creature best to be avoided rather than tamed with kindness.

There was no sign of Juan Carlos, and Josiah was certain that the Mexican wouldn't show up to see him off. Disappearing was one of Juan Carlos's greatest skills. It was hard telling when he'd see the man again, but he hoped it would be soon, or at least afford him the opportunity to explain himself when it did occur.

Pearl had ended their relationship, and it was likely that Juan Carlos, who was overly protective of his only niece, didn't know that the relationship was over. Stumbling on Josiah in a romantic embrace with Francesca without knowing the full story could have sent the old man off in a huff. They'd had some problems in the past when it came to matters of the heart, a fissure between them that Josiah thought had been healed. Still, it was hard to tell about Juan Carlos and his whereabouts, and it was little to worry about given the state of things.

What had happened between Josiah and Francesca wasn't any of Juan Carlos's business. Josiah wasn't even sure if he could rationalize their moment together for himself, but it was harder leaving her than he'd thought it would be.

Scrap mounted Missy, the blue roan mare, after securing Garcia on an unknown horse, a shaggy gelding, the color of the muddy road, that Josiah had never seen before. Garcia's hands were bound, the long rope stretched out and tied to the horn of Scrap's saddle.

Josiah and Clipper waited behind Garcia, glad to let Scrap have the lead. At the moment, the farther away Scrap was, the more comfortable Josiah was.

The right side of Garcia's face was swollen from where Scrap had punched him. A mottled bruise, like a thicket of raspberries, protruded under and around his eye. He said nothing, avoided looking at Josiah, too, like he was as evil a man as he thought Scrap to be. What Garcia didn't know, couldn't know, was that Josiah had saved him from a harder beating. Scrap's anger was on a hair trigger, had been since they'd left Austin, and his attitude was getting worse, not better.

Josiah rounded his shoulders and straightened his back, settling in for the ride. There was an odd feeling in the air. Disappointment. Regret. Fear. He knew deep in his heart that it was best that they leave. He had only known Francesca a brief time, but she was mysterious, and a salve to another wound he carried, one that only she knew about, one that had been inflicted by Pearl, whether Josiah wanted to admit it or not.

Scrap clicked his tongue loudly, the sound echoing off the cantina's walls, then began to move forward, pulling Garcia, and his horse, along with him.

Josiah hesitated, held back, then flipped the reins and allowed Clipper to move forward. He questioned leaving so quickly and circled around, stopping in front of Francesca and Adolfo, facing them directly. "Thank you," he said. "I'll always believe that you saved my life."

He was staring directly into Francesca's surprised brown eyes. She nodded and leaned heavily against her father. "I will never see you again, will I?"

Josiah dropped his head. "I don't know. I'll do my best to come back this way."

"But you cannot promise me that you will return?" Francesca demanded.

"I can't. I don't know what's going to happen. I'm a Ranger. I don't have control of where I go. The only way I can know what comes next in my life is if I quit the company, and if I did that, I would live in Austin, with my son. He is the place of my heart, my home."

"You'll have a scar from your time here."

"More than one, I think."

Francesca started to say something else, but restrained herself — at least her tongue. Tears welled up in her eyes, and she fled quickly inside the cantina, taking her disappointment with her.

"You must forgive my Francesca," Adolfo

said. "She pines for the moon and believes in true love. Saying good-bye has never been easy for her. Not even as a girl. Loss is unbearable, but you would know that. She is young in ways of the heart and lonely in her daily chores. Your presence, and injury, took her away from that, gave her something to tend to, to attach to. She will be fine in a day or two, after you've gone. She will heal just as you are. I will see to it."

"I'm sorry. I shouldn't have . . ." Josiah stopped and looked over his shoulder. Scrap and Garcia were completely out of Arroyo, almost on the horizon. He sighed. "I'll return if I can," he said. "She deserves better than to be left behind, but I have no choice. I have my duty to attend to. A life in Austin that I should have thought more of. I failed to think ahead," Josiah said, his voice dropping off softly with regret.

"You are always welcome here, Josiah Wolfe. Remember that." Adolfo nodded toward the horizon. "You better go. I worry about the safety of your charge without your eyes on him."

"I will remember that, and thank you again. I am in your debt." With that, Josiah turned, nudged Clipper gently with his heel, and hurried to catch up with Scrap, pushing down the road with as much speed and restrained heart as he could muster.

For a brief moment, he thought he heard a woman wailing in pain, but he quickly decided that it was only the wind whistling behind him, pushing past him, around him, urging him to move on before he turned back again.

CHAPTER 19

There were no clouds in the black sky, and a fingernail moon rose slowly in the distance, like it was being cranked upward by a weak bit of rope. Silence surrounded Josiah. Any animals who had made their living during the day had found places to rest, unlike the two men he now trailed after.

Traveling at night offered many threats. It was slower, and it was easier to get lost. Stumbling into, or upon, a camp of Apache or Cortina's *desperadoes* was always a possibility. Both had watches of their own. Or they were out, too, in the land, straying from camp, or on a devious mission, rustling cattle or worse.

If a horse stepped into a snake hole, it could be catastrophic. Clipper sustaining an injury traveling at night was not something Josiah wanted to think about. The Appaloosa was like a member of the family to him, the closest thing to a pet he would ever allow himself to possess.

And then there were the snakes themselves, roused from a deep sleep under their rocks, protecting themselves with a strike, no matter the distance or size of the interloper. There were other predators, too, like the big cats known to roam the area that could kill, or seriously maim, a man without warning.

The risk was more than apparent, but Josiah had allowed Scrap to keep the lead, to continue on traveling as the evening fell quickly into night. It was not a decision he was comfortable with, but they were too close to the Ranger camp to stop now.

The trail was clearly defined ahead of them, easy to see, even in the darkness — if they went slowly.

Stopping to make camp was really not an option. If Garcia had any valid information to be gleaned, then the clock was ticking. As it was, the man had offered nothing that Scrap and Josiah didn't already know. Cortina was set on delivering a herd of rustled cattle to an awaiting steamer in the Gulf, but Garcia claimed he didn't know when or where. At least that was his story. Just like Rafael Salinas's when Robinson had captured him and brought him into camp. Josiah wondered if it wasn't a ploy, a command given by Cortina about what to say if they were captured. They both were consistent, and Josiah thought their responses were too much alike for it to be coincidence.

Luckily, the land was relatively flat as they headed away from Arroyo. Josiah kept Clipper at a short, comfortable distance from the rear of Garcia's shaggy mount, close enough to have a conversation with the Mexican if he wanted or needed to, but so far had chosen not to.

Boredom had started to set in, and Josiah decided to take another tack, try and get Garcia to talk more if he could. "You need to get your story in order, Garcia. Captain McNelly will grill you on arrival. You have to know that." He edged up alongside the captive man's horse. The horse smelled like it had rolled in wet cow shit then stood under the full sun to dry.

Scrap cast a nasty glance over his shoulder but held his tongue and turned his attention back to the trail.

"I already told you, Ranger, I was to serve under Camillo Lerma and *la Aboja,* the Needle. We were to steal the cows from La Parra."

"Rafael Salinas told McNelly the same thing. You'll need more than that to save your hide. McNelly is not a fair court jurist.

He's a judge and lawmaker, at least out here. Your life will be in his hands."

The swelling in Garcia's face had subsided a bit, but the raspberry bruise was still evident, even in the darkness. "I do not fear death."

"You're brave," Josiah said.

"I will show you how brave I am once I am free."

"You'll not be free tonight. You'll be hanged, or worse, if you keep it up. Dying doesn't have to be this easy. Tell me what I want to know, and I swear I'll do my best to see you set free, or at least see that you are cared for humanely."

Garcia cocked his head toward Josiah. "You speak with confidence and sugar, señor, while your friend speaks with his fists. Why should I believe you? It is a game you play, pitting me off of him, all the while pretending to be my *amigo.* You think I am *estúpido?*"

"You don't have to believe me, but I'm the closest thing to a friend that you have right now. I've seen enough blood fall in my day for a hundred men. I have no quarrel with you or your like. It's rough terrain here, difficult to make a living."

"You know nothing of the land."

"Suit yourself."

"I am not your *amigo.*"

"You might want to rethink that."

Garcia looked away then and refocused his attention on the back of Scrap's neck, boring into it with hate and anger. His jaw was set hard, and a vein in his forehead pulsed.

The sky was fully black now, and with the moon at just a sliver, it was becoming more and more difficult to see more than five feet ahead of their horses' heads, much less into Garcia's eyes, to see what he was thinking or feeling. Scrap had slowed his pace even more but had given no indication that he was going to abandon the journey and set up a small camp of their own.

A coyote yipped in the distance, quickly followed by a bird sound, a low whine, and then a one-pitch note that sounded like a screech. Josiah knew the bird to be a screech owl, either out for a hunt or calling to its mate. Or maybe neither, if he considered the call more closely. It could've been the watch call, letting them know they were getting close to the perimeter of the Ranger camp. The calls changed nightly, depending on the boys assigned to the posts. It was difficult to know for sure whether he was hearing man or bird. He would find out soon enough. He was sure of it.

"You need to make up your mind, Garcia. We're close."

"I do not trust you. You killed two of my *amigos*. Cortina will want revenge."

"I know all about Cortina and his ways, his revenge. Do you think this is the first time I am on his trail?"

"He hates the Rangers. He will hate you even more for killing his men."

"In self-defense. There wasn't time to talk them out of shooting." Josiah hesitated. "I pulled Elliot off you, doesn't that count for anything? If your welfare wasn't important to me, I would've let him finish you right then and there. We would've buried you in Arroyo, or set you out for the buzzards to pick at. But that didn't happen. You're alive because I saved you."

Garcia glanced over at Josiah, his hard gaze softening. "You are his *sargento,* no?"

"I am."

"Salinas was to be mine."

"He will be happy to see that you are still alive."

"But a captive like him."

"McNelly promised him freedom once this was over . . . if he helped."

"I have no choice, do I?"

"What do you know?" Josiah nudged Clipper closer to Garcia and tried not to show his disgust at the smell of the horse.

"It is tomorrow. The steamer is expected in the bay tomorrow," Garcia said, a sense of resignation in his voice.

CHAPTER 20

The first fires of camp showed on the hill — small orange beacons flickering in the distance, dotted haphazardly on the ground, more akin to a starry sky than the earth.

As Josiah had thought, the owl screech they'd heard earlier had been a watch call. They had encountered the first perimeter guard shortly thereafter and were granted immediate access to McNelly's camp. There had begun to be some worry about their safety and return.

Wood smoke filled the air with its comforting, acrid smell. A guitar strummed softly, and a muffled voice attempted to sing a ballad of some kind. The unknown song rose up slowly into the night, offering a bit of entertainment to any human being within hearing distance, and fear or discomfort to any animal, four-legged or otherwise, far or near.

The wind carried the music like it did a

bird's collection of notes, without judgment or intention. It was good to hear, and calmed Josiah, allowed him to relax and give up the fear for his own safety. He still worried about Garcia's safety though.

A few tents glowed white from the inside out, but they were dim, the lamp flames turned down low.

Darkness had engulfed the world, but Josiah was glad the slow ride back from Arroyo was over. He was tired and sore; his wounds agitated him. His shoulder hurt, and the scattershot scratches on his face continued to itch and burn. The salve Francesca had put on them had started to fade away, just like the vision he held of her. He could still smell her sweet scent, hear her voice whispering in his ear . . . but it was distant, almost like she had died, instead of been left behind.

Even though the camp was relaxed, sure of the guard mounted around the perimeter, their arrival garnered attention, curious and otherwise.

A growing stir could be heard in the camp, a wave of voices rising, spreading the news that Josiah and Scrap had returned with a prisoner in tow, another Mexican. The only disappointment was that it wasn't Juan Cortina himself.

More logs were tossed on the fire, lighting the trail clearer, more thoroughly, leading directly to Captain McNelly's tent. Fresh pots of coffee were set to brew, and a sizzle of meat tossed to the spit caught Josiah's ear.

He was hungry, more than he'd like to admit. A bite or two of jerky had sustained him from Arroyo. He'd lost his appetite the second he'd recognized Scrap's horse waiting outside the cantina.

The guitar faded away, and the singing stopped once they crested a rise in the hill and the trail descended fully into the camp.

Scrap sat stiffly in his saddle, his back straight, shoulders squared, and his proud, hairless chin thrust forward. Josiah could only see the back of his head and body, but he knew the look that was on the boy's face. He was sure Scrap was gloating, proud of himself and the injuries he'd inflicted on Garcia — not to mention the blood that had been drawn in the cantina.

Scrap had taken a liking to killing and inflicting pain, and the development more than worried Josiah. Not that Scrap had ever been reluctant on the trigger, he hadn't, but in the past the boy had shown some restraint, some respect for human life. Ever since he'd walked out of the jail in Austin, though, he shot first and didn't bother to ask questions.

The world might not have been at war like it was when Josiah was Scrap's age, but there was a battle raging under the boy's skin. One that Josiah recognized and knew, no matter what he said or did, wouldn't end until it was time. That might happen soon, or never at all. It could go either way with Scrap, and that's what made him so dangerous. He was carrying a load of dynamite, just waiting for it to explode.

Garcia, on the other hand, was demoralized.

His head was hung deep to his chest, and even his horse seemed to sense defeat, that they were on enemy ground with no possible escape to be had. Its head was dropped nearly nose to the ground, and the bushy tail had lost its sway.

The Mexican was going to have to speak up to save his neck, even though Josiah knew now when Cortina was planning on transferring the cattle to the steamer.

Regardless, Josiah was just glad to be back among the Rangers, home for a moment, if it could be called that, where everything was in its place, and his safety wasn't a concern.

Scrap could have all the glory he wanted. Josiah just wanted a decent meal and a good night's sleep.

It didn't take long to reach McNelly's tent. They followed the same path Robinson had, and ended up in nearly the same spot, with a crowd gathering around them, anxious to see and hear what had happened since they'd left.

Scrap stayed mounted on Missy for a moment longer than he should have, surveying the men around him, nodding to no one in particular. It looked like he was trolling for applause, aching for a return worthy of a conquering hero — but none was given. There were only coughs and shuffles. No hands against each other. No praise offered to the boy for doing nothing more than he was sent out to do.

Captain McNelly pushed through the flap of his tent, exiting with curiosity. He was followed closely by Lieutenant Clement Robinson.

The flap remained open for a long second, and it looked like they had been planning an attack. There were maps on a table, scattered with papers and brass distance-measuring devices. A full coffeepot simmered on the fire in front of the tent.

Scrap jumped off Missy and hurried back to Garcia. "Get down, greaser." He grabbed the Mexican's arm and pulled at it, but Josiah was there next to him in a flash.

"Let the poor man get down on his own," Josiah commanded.

"He ain't no man. He's a prisoner."

"No sense treating a man like an animal just because you were," Josiah said. He could care less that McNelly stood watching them; he'd had enough of Scrap's mistreatment of the Mexican.

Scrap jerked his head back like he'd been smacked. If they had been anywhere else, in private company instead of standing in the middle of a crowd, Josiah was certain that a fight would have ensued. As it was, Scrap held his tongue and glared in return.

"Let the man get down on his own," Captain McNelly said. Robinson stood over his shoulder, promising a swift response if a scuffle of any kind broke out.

"Yes, sir," Scrap said, standing back. "You heard the captain, greaser, get down here now."

Josiah exhaled loudly and offered Garcia his hand. "Come on. You'll not be hurt here."

"That's right," McNelly said. "Untie the prisoner, Wolfe. Show him we mean what we say."

"Todos ustedes son unos mentirosos," Garcia said, as Josiah loosened the rope that

190

had bound his hands.

"Do not think there are none in this camp who are fluent in your native tongue, sir," Captain McNelly said. "Not all of us are liars, as your statement implies."

Garcia scowled as he pulled his hands free and shook the circulation back into them. "I have no reason to trust any Anglo."

McNelly nodded and watched closely as Josiah helped Garcia off the horse. "Bring him inside the tent, Wolfe."

Josiah touched Garcia's shoulder gently to guide him into the captain's tent. Scrap followed.

"Not you, Elliot. You can wait outside," McNelly said, then turned and made his way inside the tent.

The crowd of men responded with more coughs and discomfort, but none of them said a word, just watched with unblinking eyes. Scrap must have felt like he was a pile of meat, surrounded by a circle of hungry wolves waiting for the first drop of blood to fall to the ground. Scrap was wounded, but McNelly had delivered a blow to the boy's ego and had left his flesh for another enemy. If Josiah was a betting man, he knew the chance to see blood fall was in the offing and would come sooner, rather than later, especially when McNelly found out that the shipment of rustled cattle was expected on the steamer the next day.

Scrap stood wordlessly, obeying the captain's command, the hardness on his face tightening even more as Josiah and Garcia left him behind and joined McNelly and Robinson inside the tent.

The flap snapped closed loudly behind them and sounded just like a slap to the face had been delivered to an unsuspecting scoundrel.

CHAPTER 21

A thin stream of black coal oil smoke rose up to the ceiling of the tent. The vent flap was wide open, and there was a noticeable draft, making it as easy as possible for Captain McNelly to breathe. The heat from the day had yet to fully subside, and the interior remained warm, like an oven that refused to cool.

There were three lamps inside the sparsely furnished tent, all of them burning so brightly Josiah had to squint his eyes and adjust to the light. After riding for so long under the darkness, being in camp and inside the tent was a jolt to his entire system.

It looked like no time had passed at all. But Josiah felt different. Weaker in some ways and stronger in others. He had freed himself of Pearl — for the moment, anyway — but was still haunted by his time with Francesca. He wasn't sure he would ever see her again. He wasn't sure that he wanted to. Leaving again would be difficult. Staying would be impossible.

As he had already assumed, a planning session had been interrupted by their arrival.

A map of the King Ranch lay sprawled out on the table. The ranch had been founded a little more than twenty-five years before by the former river pilot Richard King and a Texas Ranger, Gideon "Legs" Lewis. Their first purchase consisted of more than fifteen thousand acres, and continued to grow to this day. There was not a man in South Texas who did not know the Running W brand and the power and influence behind it. The longhorns with that brand were, of course, favored to be stolen by Juan Cortina.

Beyond the map of the King Ranch lay another one, this one showing all of the coast of the Gulf, with a few X marks in red, where Josiah surmised the captain and Robinson assumed the steamer might be waiting. There were also a few charted red lines that showed the possible trek from Cuba to the coast of Texas. But nothing looked certain, including the frustrated look on the captain's face.

Josiah took a breath. He had been in the tent before, but it had been quick. He did not have a personal relationship with Captain McNelly, even though they had shared some time together, normally only under dire circumstances or Ranger business. Josiah was not Leander McNelly's friend. The closest person to McNelly seemed to be Clement Robinson, and even that relationship seemed born of duty.

And after the incident in Arroyo, Josiah still felt a little nervous being in closed places, even though he was on soil that was securely Anglo.

A cot, covered with a familiar type of second-issue Army blanket, tan with dark brown stripes, was stuffed neatly in the corner of the tent. Other than two chairs, one with a tarred haversack carefully hung over it, the table, and the cot, the room was vacant of anything other than a wood chest that looked like it had seen a lot of miles. Leander McNelly liked to travel light, and the almost bare command tent was proof of that.

McNelly sat down at the head of the map table. Robinson stood at the flap, his holster unsnapped, at the ready.

Robinson was tall and imposing and eyed Garcia with suspicion and distaste, but didn't express himself as freely as Scrap had. Just by the look of the man's clothes, nearly a uniform, even though one wasn't required, and his perfectly trimmed long beard, it was easy to tell he was a man of great ambition. Josiah had no doubt that the man would someday become a captain in the Rangers.

Josiah guided Garcia easily to the captain. They all remained quiet for a moment, sizing one another up.

McNelly finally spoke to Garcia. "Sit down."

"I would rather stand and face my *problemas.*"

"As you wish."

"I wish to be free, *Capitán.*"

"That is not possible. At least at the moment."

Josiah stood stiffly next to Garcia, sure to keep his mouth closed until he was called on to speak.

"I am well aware of your desires, *Capitán.* I am just unsure of the price I will pay if I give you what you want. I have a family that I would like to return to. A job in the boatyard that I have worked at since I was a *niño.* I am not a greaser." The derogatory term hung in the air between Garcia and McNelly. Scrap had used the word freely, as he was apt to do. To Mexicans it was a demoralizing slur, originally used by troops in the

Mexican-American War in the 1840s. The lowest occupation a Mexican held, according to them, was greasing the axles of an ox cart. "I am a fine citizen of my country, and I obey all its laws."

"So you are not a member of Cortina's raiders?"

Garcia's head lowered. "*Sí,* I am."

"So you are not a fine citizen, as you say." McNelly stared at Garcia calmly, but he was not going to remain patient for very long. He tapped his finger on the table like a drummer leading a condemned man to the gallows.

"I am a desperate man. I needed the *dinero,* the money. Not all of us are thieves every day. Cortina has taken our weakness and made it his strength. The times in my country are difficult. I am a poor working man with a lot of mouths to feed. Do you have any *niños, Capitán*? Surely, you understand?"

McNelly flinched, then ignored the reference. He had two children — a boy, Revel, and a girl, Irene. He rarely spoke of either. "Do you know Rafael Salinas?"

"*Sí,* I do. I am under his command," Garcia whispered.

"Then you can speak to him if that is necessary to gain your trust. No harm has

197

come to Salinas, and none will come to you. You have my word."

"I do not trust your word." Garcia lifted his hand up and touched the raspberry bruise under his eye as softly as he could.

"Tell me of how your capture came to be," McNelly demanded. There was a sharp edge of annoyance in his voice.

Garcia looked up to the ceiling of the tent, then returned his hard gaze to McNelly. "There were three of us, riding rear guard, protecting those that had collected the beeves. I got separated, and we had agreed we'd meet up in Arroyo if any of us did not return. But I was not lost, or had not tried to outrun the Rangers. I was trying to go back home. I decided I wanted no part of what was to come. I am no killer, either, and I was afraid for my own life. What happens to my *familia* if I am dead? They will surely starve. Their desperation would be worse, not better. I was a fool, thinking an easy *peso* was the solution.

"So, while my two compatriots waited at the cantina, I was sneaking home. They made a grand mistake by showing their anger and guns to the Ranger here, and his hotheaded *amigo*."

"Is that true, Wolfe?" McNelly asked.

"There *was* a shoot-out in the cantina,

198

sir. I was shot in the shoulder, and these wounds on my face came from a scatter-gun," Josiah answered. "I am lucky to have survived, and if it wasn't for the kindness of strangers in Arroyo, I wouldn't be standing here with you now."

"And Cortina's two men?"

"They are dead. Buried properly in the mission graveyard in Arroyo. They pulled their guns almost as soon as Elliot and I walked in the door. We had no choice but to protect ourselves."

"And this is true?" McNelly asked Garcia.

"I was not there," Garcia said, looking to the floor. "But Ranger Wolfe has been *honesto* with me and treated me like a decent human being."

"And Ranger Elliot?"

"He treated me like a *conejo.*"

"A rabbit?" McNelly said.

"*Sí,* he hunted me down slowly, toying with me like a *zorro,* a fox. I knew he was there long before he attacked, but I could not outrun him. I feel lucky to be alive."

Captain McNelly looked annoyed by the news of Scrap's actions but said nothing to that effect. "You are safe here."

"I have no choice but to believe you."

The captain turned his attention to Josiah. "Your trip was eventful."

"We are both lucky to be here."

"Nothing has shown itself since you left. All of the other scouting teams are either still out or came back empty-handed."

"Garcia has confided in me, Captain," Josiah said. "The steamer is expected in the bay tomorrow."

"Is this true?" McNelly asked the Mexican. His breathing seemed to calm, and his face tightened with happy anticipation.

"*Sí*, it is."

"Then we ride at first light," Captain McNelly said, almost jubilantly.

There was nothing to celebrate as far as Josiah was concerned. The coming dawn meant going into battle once again. And he had stopped looking forward to the opportunity to kill a long, long time ago.

CHAPTER 22

Dismissed, Josiah was the first man to leave the tent. He hesitated for a long second, concerned about Garcia — but quickly decided that if he couldn't trust Leander McNelly and Clement Robinson with the man's care and safety, then he didn't belong in the Ranger camp in the first place.

He took the order that they were riding at first light for what it was. Garcia seemed resigned to his fate, too. If there was more to tell, then it was not for Josiah to hear. The Mexican was a prisoner now — and safe from Scrap's rage.

The scouting assignment had been successfully completed, even though it had come at a higher cost than Josiah would have ever dreamed.

He pushed through the tent flap and found himself the direct focus of almost every man in the company. They had not moved since he and Scrap arrived. Every man in the camp looked anxious to know about the prisoner and what was next for them all. Not a one of them seemed to share Josiah's dread of battle.

The perfectly formed arch around the entrance of the tent was still intact. There were familiar eyes, and some not so familiar, all tinged with a demand for answers.

To Josiah's relief, someone had had the decency to see Clipper to the horse line. The Appaloosa had his head focused on a mound of fresh hay and was tied comfortably in among all of the other Rangers' horses.

Satisfied that his horse was cared for, Josiah scanned the crowd quickly, ignoring the desire of the men in the company to know the outcome of the meeting. It was not Josiah's place to tell them of McNelly's plans. Once he saw that Scrap was nowhere to be seen, he made his way silently through the crowd.

Several men tried to stop Josiah, hoping to know what was afoot. Josiah just dropped his head and made his way up the hill, as far away from the captain's tent as possible, as quickly as he could. Sergeant or no sergeant, he wasn't about to break ranks with McNelly. The captain still had plans and decisions to make.

Josiah returned alone to the fire where he'd taken up residence before leaving for Arroyo. No one had bothered to follow him once they figured out his lips were going to remain shut tight.

The spot looked the same, only it was vacant now since the men who had shared the fire remained waiting in front of McNelly's tent for their orders.

Josiah was relieved, glad for the moment alone. His body ached, his stomach begged for food, and his wounds, still fresh and sore, reminded him how much had changed since he'd left the Ranger camp.

It was obvious that nothing had changed much for the other men who had remained behind in camp. They had been stuck waiting. Waiting for whatever was next. It was a hard fact of life for the soldiering kind. Hurry up and wait. Be ready at a moment's notice to fight to the death. Josiah would have traded places with them if he could have, not gone on the scouting trip at all. Save for the time with Francesca — but now even that encounter was looking to be a mistake. His shoulders had been heavy with regret from the moment he'd left the cantina. Still, he was glad to be back in camp.

"What the hell did you do that for, Wolfe?" Scrap walked out of the shadows from behind a boulder half the size of a house. He still wore his gun belt, the holsters unsnapped, two ivory-handled Peacemakers within reach.

Josiah jumped in his skin but tried not to show Scrap that he'd startled him. "I was just doing my duty."

"Protectin' a greaser?"

"Garcia's a man with a family just like us."

"He's the damn enemy, that's what he is. Woulda slit your throat, too, if he'd had half a chance." Scrap stopped about ten feet from Josiah, his eyes black with anger and his body stiff as a board.

"Really, Elliot, what are you going to do? Shoot me? Or do you want to fight me? Go at me with your fists, like you did with Garcia?" Josiah's tone was easy, without stress or fear. He didn't move from his spot, either. He wore a swivel rig, allowing his own Peacemaker to always be at the ready, but he didn't think of it as a weapon that would be needed for this fight. He wasn't afraid of Scrap Elliot now, and he never had been. *Sometimes,* Josiah thought, *all the boy really needed was a good ass-whippin'.* But it wasn't his place to deliver it, no matter how much he wanted to.

Scrap didn't seem to know how to respond to Josiah's easiness.

"Come on now," Josiah said, "get it over with. There's no one about. I won't pull rank on you, or hold you accountable to the captain." Josiah threw his hands up in the air, in offering. "You think punching at me will solve your problems, you just come right on and have at it."

Scrap squeezed his fists tight.

The fire burned brightly between them. A log had obviously been thrown on it when they arrived in camp, and it allowed Josiah to see Scrap's rage. The boy's face was as red as the embers in the bottom of the pit, and sweat had started to bead on his lip. It wasn't the first time Josiah had seen Scrap mad as a rabid skunk. What concerned him was the fact that Scrap seemed to always be angry, and unpredictable, instead of just every once in a while.

"I ain't gonna shoot you, Wolfe."

"Well, that's good news." A quick burst of pain throbbed in Josiah's shoulder. He was weak but couldn't show it, couldn't respond to the pain. He wasn't sure what Scrap was capable of, at least not at the moment.

"You made me look like a danged fool."

Josiah shrugged. "You didn't need my help with that." He stepped toward Scrap. "Look, why don't you sit down and take a load off.

It's been a long couple of days for us both. I'll rustle us up some beans and coffee. The last thing I want to do is fight with you, or anybody else for that matter. Fighting will come soon enough for us all."

"Tomorrow."

"First light. But you keep that to yourself, at least till McNelly gives his orders and makes his assignments."

"Maybe I won't go."

"That's always your choice."

"I suppose it is." Scrap exhaled and looked up at the sky. "Why is it I never get my chance to be the one that gets noticed for doin' brave things? I can't never win. I'm never gonna be nothin' but what I am."

"You ever think maybe you try just a little too hard?"

Scrap shook his head. "I don't think I try hard enough."

There was a tone in Scrap's voice that almost allowed Josiah to take pity on the boy. Almost. "Maybe you ought to think a little before you act on a thought that passes through that thick head of yours. You might just get yourself, or someone else, hurt one of these days if you don't start doing that pretty soon."

CHAPTER 23

The night passed quicker than Josiah had hoped it would. Racked with pain, along with his growing fear that the infection was returning, he had found sleep difficult to come by. When he did manage to drift off, uncomfortable and uncertain dreams invaded Josiah's mind.

He couldn't quite call the dreams nightmares, because he couldn't remember them clearly. They seemed to be made up of a collection of bad memories, of places he wished he'd never been, and of people he wished he would've never met — or lost. Every waking and sleeping moment felt like it had been touched by regret, and that emotion seemed to be as much an infection as the green pus that had seeped out of his wound in Arroyo. There was no one to tend to him now like there had been when he was shot, no soft comforting hand, or the presence of someone watching over him, making sure he was all right, that he would live to see another day. Juan Carlos and Francesca were gone.

When he had been awake during the night, tossing and turning on the hard ground, his thoughts danced to his living past, and to other nights before battle. They all had been a mix of fear, anxiety, happiness, and joy. Sometimes, it seemed there was no other time Josiah had felt more alive than when he was pulling a Springfield bayonet out of a Yankee's belly, or pulling the trigger of a Henry rifle with certainty and confidence of his aim. He was good at killing, and at surviving. Sometimes too good.

Memories of the war seemed to run all together.

Day after day was a shower in blood. Screams became the music of life. It was never easy killing another man. But it was battle. It was kill or be killed. Just like now. Just like the day that waited for him. He was sure of it, could feel it in his bones and deep in his chest. Just the memory of killing sped up the beat of his heart.

Cortina's men would show no regard for his life, any more than he would for theirs. The attack in Adolfo's cantina was proof of that. Two men had met their end only because they had chosen the wrong allegiance, had decided to die for a cattle thief instead of living by the laws of the great state of Texas. Josiah felt little grief over the death of the two men. They had made their choices, had pulled their guns before any words of peace could be offered.

Still, Josiah wondered if the fighting in his life would ever end. If killing and all of the blood and battles would ever become too much for him. It surprised him that he even thought of quitting, of laying down his guns and walking away from the fight. He wondered if it were even possible.

Until a few days ago, the possibility of leading a normal life in Austin had seemed like a true hope for his future, no matter how distant that future really was. There would come a time when it would be right to leave the Rangers, maybe even remarry and start a new family.

Spending every day with Lyle would be a nice change for him, even though he would have to figure out exactly what it meant to be a full-time father. Ofelia would most likely tire of having him underfoot, but she would adjust. Josiah knew he took the Mexican woman for granted, but how could he not? She loved Lyle like he was her own flesh and blood, and she had been there since the very beginning, when there had been no choice but to cut the boy out of his dead mother's belly — Lily had died from the fevers before she could give birth to the boy.

And then there was Pearl.

Josiah had thought that they could work through their time apart, that his time with the Rangers wouldn't conflict with their courting. Maybe things would have been different if he would have stayed in Austin and found another way to make a living. But being one of Sheriff Rory Farnsworth's deputies held little attraction to him. There was little else, outside of being a lawman of one kind or another, that Josiah felt qualified for.

Working as a deputy in the sheriff's department was far more political than being a Ranger, considering it was an elected office and constantly in turmoil, and far more than he ever wanted to deal with. He had been an appointed marshal once, briefly in his earlier life, and that was enough for him. It seemed like he was always beholden to someone on the town board, or some businessman, for one thing or another. He couldn't imagine the politics of a big city like Austin, especially considering all that had happened recently — the sheriff's banker father having recently been accused of murder.

He could follow Pearl's example, if it came to that. Her life had changed dramatically. Once, she was the belle of the ball, a debutante — until her father was killed and her mother went crazy, mad as a stepped-on rattlesnake, and lost the family home. Pearl, with the help of Juan Carlos, had picked herself up and gotten back on her feet. She said she never again wanted to be dependent on anyone else in her life.

Josiah respected her grit, her ambition, but he saw very little opportunity for himself other than riding with the Rangers. He was too old to go to some school to become something he didn't know anything about.

Starting over held little appeal to him. The move to Austin from Seerville had been enough of a change, one he wasn't sure he was quite used to just yet the way it was. He still missed the comfort and familiarity of the piney woods of East Texas and preferred them over the bustling and constantly changing city.

The thought of Juan Carlos had cost him even more sleep.

Josiah feared that he had lost the man as his friend, because the Mexican knew nothing of Pearl's letter. He hoped he would have a chance to explain himself to Juan Carlos at some point soon, but there was no guarantee that Josiah would ever see the man again. Especially if their friendship *had* ended.

Regret was most definitely dangerous. A poison that would not go away, no matter how much Josiah tossed and turned.

Finally, just before dawn, before the first light broke over the horizon, Josiah pulled himself up off the ground and put a fresh pot of Arbuckle's on the fire.

The other boys around the fire were still sleeping, mostly buried under their blankets. A cloudless sky had allowed the air to turn cool even though it was early summer. It was like that sometimes, so cold at night that a man thought it could turn up and snow. That surely would have been a sight and most certainly would have started the day on a much different foot than anyone expected.

The weather, though, was of little concern. It would most likely be a clear, hot day — adding sweat and discomfort to the blood and violence that was almost a given.

Josiah squatted before the fire, his eyes focused on the coffeepot, the blue glaze mostly blackened from years of daily use. He knew better than to try and hang on to the dreams and nightmares, if that's what they were. Wrestling with his past, angels and demons, offered little aid or comfort for the coming battle.

All he could hope for was to survive to fight another day, and return home as soon as he could . . . all in one piece.

CHAPTER 24

Something had changed in Captain McNelly's demeanor. He sat on his horse stiffer, and his hard blue eyes were eagle-like, boring through the distance, searching for anything that moved. He had spoken very little since he'd exited the sanctuary of his tent, other than to organize the boys into two twenty-man units. One long line of men stood at the ready behind Clement Robinson, and the other line behind McNelly himself. Not a man said a word. The morning was quiet, solemn, even though there wasn't a cloud in the sky.

It was common knowledge by now, with the capture of Rafael Salinas and Garcia, that the number of Cortina's men was small. Sixteen in all, according to both men. That was very few men to rustle three hundred cattle and see them safely to a waiting steamer.

As far as Josiah was concerned, it seemed

highly possible that there were more men, perhaps that neither captive was aware of — or that neither was speaking of. Their stories were remarkably similar, which made them seem suspect, or like the truth — one or the other. It was hard to trust prisoners. But as far as Josiah knew, their stories had not strayed.

Surely, Cortina didn't think that the Kings, and other ranchers in South Texas, would not call on the governor, or General Steele, to supply a company of Rangers to patrol the area and put a stop to the thievery that was robbing them of their profits and filling Mexican coffers. Cortina had to know he was in Coke's crosshairs, a thorn in the governor's side.

Josiah was sure Cortina wanted a fight and that there was a trap laid somewhere close — most likely inside their own camp if Josiah was a betting man, which he mostly wasn't.

With the horses lined up nose to tail, Josiah was two men back from McNelly. The men ahead of him were longtime riders with the captain, familiar to all of the boys who rode in the company.

Joe Startman was a lanky cowboy-turned-Ranger who said little but was always the first man to step into a boxing match if one sprung up. He had a long reach and was a powerful inside fighter for a tall man. Josiah respected the man's talents and dared not challenge him in any way.

There had never been any official indication that Startman held any rank, but he was always close by the captain, always in the know, or consulted, about any plans, so that was all that needed to be said — he was afforded the same courtesies and respect that were expected regarding Lieutenant Robinson. As far as Josiah knew, Joe Startman had only lost one fight in the time he'd been riding with the Rangers, and that was because he'd been drunk the night before.

Pip Howerson was settled in right behind Joe Startman, on a chestnut mare with legs made of lightning. The high-strung horse was a sure bet when the races were on.

McNelly was tolerant of both horse racing and boxing matches only because they served as distractions. One of the worst things about Rangering was the time a man had to himself. It seemed like the company was always waiting on something. More information. Mail. Supplies. Word from Austin about where to go next. Something. It was always something coming or going. Rarely was the camp set up in, or near, a

216

town. Trouble was easy enough to find without asking for it. Betting games seemed the lesser of any other evils encountered on the trail.

Pip's horse was a dandy. She was fast off the start and only got faster once Pip would give her her head and let the horse run full out. Somebody had told Josiah that she had a real wild streak in her, and that was easy to see. Josiah had never seen a horse that liked to run as much as Pip's horse.

To be fair, Scrap's blue roan mare was a good runner, too. And Scrap was a fine horseman, but he was outmatched every time Pip Howerson edged his mare up to the starting line. Scrap hadn't won one race against Pip and wasn't likely to anytime soon. Needless to say, Scrap wasn't too fond of Pip Howerson, a short man with a rodent-like face, but he was smart enough to be real careful of his mouth and opinions when he was around Joe Startman.

Scrap was right behind Josiah, three men back from McNelly, up a good ways in the line.

There wasn't a Ranger in camp who didn't know, or probably think to himself, that Scrap was where he was so Josiah could keep an eye on him, keep him in tow if things got ugly. Scrap's position in the line wasn't due to any promotion in rank, though it might have been a reward from the captain to Scrap for bringing Garcia in alive and in one piece.

"Wolfe," McNelly called out, waving his arm forward, motioning for Josiah to join him.

Hearing his name didn't register at first to Josiah. He was staring off over the horizon, trying to numb his mind to the coming day.

After a long second, Scrap directed Missy to nudge Clipper. The Appaloosa stepped to the side, annoyed with a snort. "Wolfe," Scrap demanded through clenched teeth. "The captain wants ya. Best get a move on."

The horizon was void of any clouds, and a thin pink line was fading away as the morning sun, already red and shimmering with heat, ascended into the sky. A steady breeze pushed out of the south, bringing with it the taste of salt and the realization that the ocean was near. Gulls and terns kited in the air in the distance, their black silhouettes indistinguishable but certain, like flies starting to swarm over a dead body.

Josiah snapped out of his daze and answered, "Yes, sir?"

"Come here," McNelly bellowed. It was his turn to be annoyed.

Josiah eased Clipper up alongside the captain and his horse, a tall black gelding with an old jagged scar shooting down its glossy neck. "What can I do for you, sir?"

McNelly side-stepped his horse next to Josiah so they were almost touching, knee-to-knee. "Garcia was an advance man. They're driving the beeves to the river and then down to the Gulf. There's another motte closer to the river, a good place to hole up and hide from the drovers. I've got scouts at every point to locate them. I think they'll be in the Laguna Madre if we have no word of them as of yet. Do you know of it?"

Josiah shook his head no.

McNelly sighed. "The lagoon extends inward from the Gulf. It's a swampy prairie of short grasses, mesquite trees, and prickly pear. It's a good place to graze the beeves before loading them on the steamer. There's not many places to hide, and an open herd will be easy to spot. I don't think Cortina will leave them there long, but it will do him no good to deliver a bunch of hungry cows to Cuba."

"You think Cortina has more men than we think?"

"I am almost certain of it. Once we get to the motte, I want you to break off and head south toward the lagoon. Scout it out, see if

I am right."

"Alone, sir?" Josiah asked.

"You're sure you're up to it?"

"There's no worry. My wound has yet to seep, and the pain is tolerable. I don't need a nursemaid, or an extra hand that could get in the way."

McNelly nodded and pushed off, moving away from Josiah, heading out with a single order, the sun glimmering on his back.

Saddles squeaked and adjusted. The noise of movement met Josiah's ears like a slow beat to the start of a hymn he'd heard more than once in the war. The procession started without any urgency, but a fine cloud of dust rose into the air as the Rangers headed out to find Cortina, leaving the safety and comfort of camp behind them.

Josiah waited for his spot in the line, slid in behind Pip without any acknowledgment to Scrap, and joined the rest of the company as they moved toward the certainty of battle.

CHAPTER 25

The motte was like most others that Josiah had seen or spent time in. It was a grove of tall trees, pecan and oak, in the midst of a stand of grasses, offering shade and protection to any creature who claimed it as its own. Mostly there were squirrels and snakes, all scattered and hiding, roused by the heavy tramp of horse hooves on the ground. Sometimes, this far south, a motte could give den to a wildcat or a jaguar, depending on the structure of the rocks inside the oasis, but there was no sign of any predator, furry or otherwise.

Even with nearly forty men under the canopy, the motte seemed huge, ten times larger than it needed to be for them all to be comfortable. It would have made a good base to fight from.

Some of the boys set out to explore as soon as they jumped off their mounts, to see what kind of critters they could kick up for an easy meal. Most likely it would be rabbit stew for dinner, if the company stayed at the motte that long. Josiah had no idea the depths or details of McNelly's plans.

It was nearing two in the afternoon.

Shade from the blazing sun was a welcome relief, and good water was easy to find. Any true rest would be short-lived. Josiah had his orders, and he planned on moving along quickly — as soon as Clipper was tended to and ready to hit the trail again. Long rides were easy for the Appaloosa. Easier for the horse than for Josiah at the moment. He felt tired and weak, like he needed a hearty dinner and a long sleep. But there was no bed in the offing.

A slow-moving creek wound through the motte. The water was brown and brackish, but Clipper didn't seem to mind. The ride to the motte had been hard and hot.

Scrap let Missy drink right next to Clipper. The two horses didn't mind each other's company, since they'd spent plenty of time around each other. But there was no affection there, either. Clipper got giddy around Pip Howerson's speedy mare, but Pip was nowhere close. He was up next to the captain, talking in hushed tones with Robinson and Joe Startman.

"You look like the ride's beat the hell out of you, Wolfe," Scrap said.

"It's this wound." Josiah tapped his shoulder gently. "Took more out of me than I thought."

"Your face is healin' up fine. Gonna have a scar like a cat got a good scratch at ya."

"Been a better tale if that was the case, I 'spect."

Josiah fidgeted with Clipper's reins, flipping them back and forth, glancing at Scrap, but keeping his attention focused on the captain as much as he could. Scrap noticed.

"What're you all nervous about, Wolfe?"

"Nothing. It doesn't matter."

Before Scrap could say anything else, Pip Howerson broke away from the captain, mounted his horse, and headed straight for Josiah.

Clipper noticed and gave up the drink with a snort and a paw at the muddy bank of the stream.

"Easy, there boy," Josiah said. Clipper pulled to the right, opposite of Josiah, wanting to turn to the mare. Luckily, Josiah still held the reins securely in his hand. He pulled tight, flipped them a bit, and with a loud click of his tongue, got the horse's attention. "Whoa, now, Clipper."

"Get you mount under control, Wolfe,"

Pip Howerson ordered.

Josiah cast the man a hateful glance. "Your mare coming into season, Pip?"

The man shrugged. "Ain't my fault you ain't made a geldin' out of that spotted boy if she is."

"Yeah, Wolfe," Scrap interjected, "why ain't you never had 'im cut?"

"I guess I just never got around to it."

"Seems to me like you best think about it," Pip said.

"When the time's right."

Pip Howerson nodded. "Captain changed his mind. He wants me to ride with you."

Scrap flinched and shot Josiah a curious glance, tinged with anger. "What's he talkin' about?"

"Captain wants me to do another round of scouting."

"Last time didn't turn out so well for you," Scrap said.

"That's why the captain wants me to ride along," Pip said.

"Me and Wolfe ride together," Scrap replied.

"You want to tell the captain that, Elliot?"

Josiah wrestled Clipper back under control, pulling him away from Pip's mare as far as he could. Pain pulsed through Josiah's right side, and he tried not to show any weakness. The last thing he wanted was the captain to think he couldn't handle his duty, that he'd be an ill weight in the coming fight. Josiah wanted nothing more than to be ready to face Cortina, or Cortina's men, however it came, with one hundred percent of his being, physically and emotionally.

The injury threatened his very existence and those that rode alongside him. He was certain he could fight the good fight. There was no other alternative. Go to battle or ride back to Austin and face his life alone. He found it curious that his mind did not wander back to Arroyo, to Francesca, but it didn't.

"No," Scrap said. "I ain't tellin' Captain McNelly nothin'." He looked up at Josiah. "You be careful out there."

Josiah steadied himself, then climbed onto Clipper's saddle. He had his back to Scrap, so he couldn't see the boy's face, but he could tell from the tone of his voice that he meant what he said. "Nothing's going to happen to us," he said. "Pip's a good shot and a good rider."

Josiah could tell that words bubbled on Scrap's tongue, but he held them back, kicked the ground, turned, and walked away without saying anything else.

Josiah watched Scrap stalk off and heard

Pip chuckle at the same time.

"That boy sure is a firecracker," Pip said.

"He's my friend." Josiah spun Clipper around so he was facing the same direction as Pip's mare. The Appaloosa groaned as Josiah fought to stop him from getting too close. Clipper's nostrils were flared, and every muscle in the horse's body was hard and tense.

"Never said he wasn't," Pip said. He looked at Clipper, annoyed and disturbed, but said nothing else. Like Scrap, he just moved forward, out of the motte and into the bright, hot sun.

Josiah had no choice but to follow him.

CHAPTER 26

The land was flat, a clear, uncompromised vista for as far as the eye could see. The sea shimmered on the horizon, but if a man didn't know it was there, he'd just think he was staring at more flat land; a distant oasis lacking trees or promise.

The area surrounding the Laguna Madre offered no shadows, shade, or protection from the blazing sun overhead. A smattering of mesquite trees that had somehow managed to survive the unrelenting sun and chaotic weather normal to seasides and floodplains were all stubby and short. Any green leaves within reach of a mule deer's pull had been stripped away as soon as they'd appeared, leaving the gangly trees mostly barren. Sometimes, in the night, the trees looked like skeletons, standing sentinel over a land roamed by hungry and aimless creatures just trying to survive.

Adding to the flatness of the floodplain

was the offering of tall grasses. The long, sharp blades were already starting to brown from the summer heat and the surprising lack of rain in the spring. There were still streaks of green at the base of the grass, trailing to the root. Sustenance could still be found by a knowledgeable creature with a strong enough cud and the will to search it out. But beyond the grass, and on the well-worn trail, the ground was crusted white with salt and brine. Clouds of flies rose into the air at each step the horses took. The horses swished their tails furiously, but to no avail. The flies were as hungry and as relentless as the scorching sun.

Josiah had his collar turned up, his long sleeves pulled to his wrists, and his bandana up to his nose, covering his mouth and half of his face like an outlaw. He could have been shrouded in rain gear, too, and that wouldn't have stopped the flies and no-see-ums from penetrating his clothes. Some of them bit, and thanks to the intensity of the heat, he itched from the inside out. It did no good to swat away the insects. That just seemed to encourage them to band together and attack even more furiously.

Five feet separated Josiah from Pip. It was the most comfortable distance for Josiah to control Clipper around Pip's mare. He didn't know the horse's name. Pip had never called it anything other than "girl" or "horse," with some affection but never with definition. It was entirely possible that the horse didn't have a name. Some fellas were like that — refused to name their mounts. They were neither pets nor friends to them. Pip Howerson struck Josiah as one of those fellas. He kept mostly to himself — except, of course, when it was time to run a race and fill his pockets with money.

"Seems like an odd place to bring three hundred head of cattle," Josiah said. He didn't whisper, but he was aware that his voice would carry farther and faster in the open.

"Why's that?" Pip's mouse-like nose twitched. The only thing missing from the man's rodent-like face was a pair of whiskers and teeth sharp enough to chew through wood, Josiah thought, but didn't say.

"No place to hide them."

"Plenty of grass for 'em to feed on."

"True enough."

"You ever punch a drive?" Pip asked.

They walked the horses at an easy gait, not in a hurry, and not too concerned about being spotted. No one would know they were Rangers from a distance — or up close for that matter. They'd most likely be mistaken for a pair of bank robbers instead of lawmen. One of the advantages of not having to wear a uniform or badge was the withholding of any identification at all.

"Not for a living," Josiah said. "Not now, not ever I hope."

"What's that supposed to mean?"

Josiah drew a deep breath and eyed the horizon. He thought he saw an odd movement in the grass about fifty yards ahead of them. Reeds crossing over the opposite direction against the breeze. "I tagged along on one for a few days some time ago, rode drag. Turns out Clipper wasn't much of a cut horse, and I wasn't much of a cowboy."

"Well, hell, that horse ain't built for chasin' after stray cows. I ain't bein' mean or nothing, just telling you what I see."

"I know. It takes a horse accustomed to the demand. He's a good one for distance, just not at the run." Josiah gently tapped Clipper's neck with his open hand. The flies took offense to the motion, or were drawn to it, one or the other. They swarmed at Josiah's hand, convincing him to dig into his pack for a pair of gloves.

"Those Appaloosas are some fine, healthy horses on a drive. This little girl was a green-broke horse booted off a drive for too much spirit. I happened onto her for a few dollars. Damn fools didn't know a treasure when they saw it. I wrangled a remuda for a while myself, but that life wasn't for me."

"We had a cow when I was a kid, but I don't know anything about herds of cattle."

"Why was you taggin' along?"

"Just trying to blend in."

"Oh, that's right. You was doin' some spy work for the captain. Lord come Nelly, I sure hope like hell he don't tap me for that kind of thing. I can scout with the best of 'em, but actin' like I'm supposed to be somebody else, oh no, that's not for me."

"It's not my favorite duty, either. But duty it was, so I went along with it."

After Josiah had killed Captain Feders in self-defense some months back, he was sent to Corpus Christi as a spy to gather information about Cortina's rustling operation. Unbeknownst to Josiah, Cortina had plans to invade and take Corpus Christi as his own. It wasn't the first time in the Mexican's history that he had tried such a thing. After the initial battle, Josiah had found himself in a situation where he needed cover to meet up with Captain Leander McNelly and his company of Rangers coming to Corpus to root out Cortina. The cattle drive was a perfect place to blend in — until a stampede was started with intention, and Josiah was sent after the instigator.

"There's some fellas who say you're lucky to be alive, Wolfe," Pip said.

Josiah ignored the comment and slowed Clipper to a stop. He thought he saw the grass in the distance move again.

He knew it could be anything. A big cat, a coyote, or a fox, hunting its way along some invisible trail. Or it could be a scout for Cortina, on the lookout for Rangers.

"What is it?" Pip asked.

"Not sure," Josiah answered, easing his Peacemaker out of the holster.

A quick glance around told him that they were more out in the open than he'd real-ized, and their only cover was the knee-high grass itself. There were no trees worthy of hiding behind, or rocks, or boulders of any size within sight that could offer them pro-tection.

The bad part of this kind of country was that they were exposed to all of the ele-ments, with no place to run if it came to that. The good part was hard to find.

Heat rose up from the ground, offering a putrid, rotting smell, not welcoming at all; the stench got worse the farther into the plain they traveled, not better. And the flies remained unbearable, as much for the men as the horses. Josiah was glad he was outfitted to endure the insects.

He felt tension rising up the back of his neck, an instinct, honed in war and in the years riding on the right side of the law, that something was amiss. They were vulnerable. Too vulnerable.

Josiah slid off the saddle and chambered a cartridge in his Peacemaker.

Pip remained on his horse, stopped next to Clipper, and had opened his mouth to say something when the first gunshot echoed from the horizon.

But even closer, right behind him, Josiah heard a *thump, thump* — two bullets striking flesh. He knew the sound just as well as he knew his own voice. Horrified, he turned and saw what had been the unseen shooter's target.

Pip Howerson's chestnut mare whinnied and screamed, then stumbled sideways. Blood exploded out of the mare's muscular neck, just below the reins. Pip tried to wrestle the horse away, but she was staggering in the opposite direction. Without any choice, Pip jumped from the saddle just as the horse collapsed to the ground with a gasp, moan, and relaxation of its anal muscles. The bullets had only missed Pip by inches.

Josiah slapped Clipper as hard as he could on the rump and yelled, "Run!" then dove to the hard ground, disappearing into a black cloud of flies, his nose instantly buried in the smell of death.

CHAPTER 27

Another round of gunfire crackled in the distance — soft thunder that barely had any energy at all. Josiah was certain the gunfire was from a pistol, not a rifle.

It was hard to tell if they'd stumbled on another scout, or if they'd managed to ride straight into Cortina's men, set on delivering the herd of cattle. If so, it was sixteen against two. Not good odds in any circumstance. Even worse when a horse had been lost. There would be no quick escape, no fast run back to the camp. Returning alive would be difficult at best, and impossible if they were as outnumbered as Josiah thought they were. Cortina would not take kindly to prisoners, if it came to that, like Captain McNelly had.

Pip crawled to his mare and hugged her bloody neck.

A murky, forked river of blood oozed out from the horse's body. The flies celebrated their remarkable stroke of luck, of being in the right place at the right time, and made their way to the red feast in swarms. The mare's smooth chestnut hair looked black, black as the horse's terrified eyes as she struggled with all of her might to stand and flee. Her heart would not allow such a thing; weakness had set in — death was near, but not near enough. The shots would have been more humane if they had struck the horse in the heart and killed her outright. As it was, she foamed at the mouth, gasped for air, all the while fighting to run one last time.

Shock had worn off of Pip's mousy face. His cheeks were twisted in fear and anguish. His eyes were as dark as the horse's, and his entire face was as white as the salty ground they lay on.

The grass gave them cover, but the shooter knew where they had fallen and was methodically firing into it. A gunshot exploded about every ten seconds. Bullets ripped across the top of the grass, thumping into the ground five or six feet away from where the horse struggled to live, as Josiah and Pip watched in horror.

Their own luck wouldn't last long, Josiah was certain of it. He had no idea if Clipper had made his way to safety, or if the Appa-

loosa lay dying, like the mare, close by —
only alone.

The ambush had come amazingly quick,
and though they shouldn't have been surprised by it, it was obvious that they had
been. One minute all was right with the
world, they were riding along talking, and
the next they were lying in a growing pool
of blood, trapped with no way out.

Pip stared at Josiah, then rolled to his side
and looked up to the sky, then back to the
dying horse just as quickly. He had pulled
his gun from the holster, a long-barreled
Colt Dragoon and, without hesitation,
settled the cold metal barrel behind the
mare's ear and pulled the trigger.

For a moment, all Josiah could see was
the bright orange flash. He was immediately
deafened by the shot. Blood splattered
across his face; a warm, unwelcome salve
on the scabs left behind by Francesca's scattergun.

The putrid, rotting smell of the ground
mixed with the metallic blood and the
gunpowder. If Josiah closed his eyes and
blinked, the smell reminded him of Chickamauga, one of the bloodiest battles he'd
fought in. Josiah knew full well that he had
been lucky to survive that day, and he'd be
even luckier, it seemed, if he lived through

this one. It was a different war, but the stakes were the same at the end of the day. Victors walked away with their lives and memories. The defeated were left behind to rot and feed the ground and the flies.

The mare quivered and shook, then exhaled one last time. Her suffering was over, her fear removed, given way to darkness and, hopefully, peace of some kind. If an animal could know such a thing.

Pip's face was covered with blood and sweat. Streaks of moisture trailed down from his sad eyes, like rivers cutting a canyon through the mud. It was hard to say if what Josiah saw was tears or not. It could have been. Regardless, Pip had done the right thing and ended the mare's life as quickly and as painlessly as he could.

Another bullet whizzed overhead just as all of Josiah's senses started to return. He knew he had to do something. They were nothing more than sitting ducks if they stayed where they were. "We have to move," he whispered with as much force and authority as he could muster.

Pip Howerson glared at Josiah. It took him almost a full minute to respond. "Where to?"

"I don't know. Away. You go to the right. I'll go to the left. Looks like the shooter is about fifty yards north of us. Retreat back as far as you can. Stay off the trail. We'll meet back up. I'm hoping my horse is still alive and can see us back to camp."

"We need to find Cortina."

"I think they may have just found us. You let me worry about McNelly if it comes to that. Two dead men won't have much to say otherwise."

Pip said nothing. He was lying prone on the ground, propped up on his elbows, his chin resting just above the mare's forehead. "Fastest damn horse I ever rode, Wolfe. If she had wings, we coulda flied around the world. I knew she was special the first time I spied her."

"I know, I'm sorry. We'll come back for her."

Pip took a deep breath, nuzzled his forehead against the horse's head, and then crawled around to the saddlebag and scabbard. He loaded up with as much ammunition as he could carry, grabbed his Spencer rifle, and made his way through the grass as gently, and as quietly, as he could without looking back.

Josiah watched Pip disappear, pulled his hat off, and peered up over the grass as cautiously as possible.

The sun was bright, and the heat of the

day had continued to intensify. He could see clearly for a good ways. There was nothing to see — just a sea of grass, standing erect, not moving at all. What breeze there'd been had died. It was like the whole world had stopped just to see what was going to happen next.

If there was a herd of cattle in the distance, then they were well hid in some unseen and unknown valley. There wasn't the slightest hint, sound, or smell that suggested they'd run up on the rustled herd or Cortina's army of bandits. Just the opposite. It looked to Josiah that they'd stumbled onto another scout, one man, not an army.

Just as he was about to slide back down to the ground, the shooter popped up and fired off another shot.

He was too far away to make out any features, whether the man was Mexican or Anglo, friend or foe. There was no use trying to negotiate with a man who'd already opened fire on them. Josiah had two choices: he could ignore the shot or return fire, exposing his own position, letting the shooter know with more certainty that he had not moved.

He chose to return fire. Only he didn't restrain himself. His Winchester rifle was still on Clipper's back, so the only other weapon he had left besides his Peacemaker was an eight-inch Bowie knife attached to his fully complimented gun belt. He'd need that if he came face-to-face with the man.

The gun smoke hung over him like a heavy gray cloud in the unmoving, thick air.

Josiah dropped back to the ground and crawled away from the dead horse as quickly as he could, trying his best not to rattle the grasses, showing his path. But that was impossible, and he knew it.

CHAPTER 28

Josiah was surrounded by tall grass and silence. For a brief moment, he had no idea what direction he was heading, or which way he ought to go.

Meeting up with Pip, at some point, was the ultimate goal, but the thought of running away from the shooter, hoping to survive by hugging the ground and hiding, rubbed Josiah the wrong way.

Running or hiding had never won him a fight, and this fight wasn't one he could afford to lose. He was weak enough the way it was, hobbled to a degree by the wound he'd taken in Arroyo. The cauterization had surely stopped the spread of infection, but it had slowed him down. Good thing for Josiah that he'd been in prime health beforehand. He'd still have been bedridden otherwise.

He pushed away the thought of Francesca as soon as it showed itself. She was the last thing he needed to be thinking about at the moment. But the thought had stopped him long enough for him to notice a game trail heading in the direction of the shooter. It was thin, but well-worn. There were fresh weasel tracks in the salt. He hoped he could ease along the trail without disturbing the grass too much, without alerting the shooter to his exact location.

With a deep breath, and his Peacemaker in hand, Josiah started to crawl slowly through the grass on his elbows, weaving around thick stands of the sharp blades when he could. Ignoring the flies was difficult, but he had gotten used to them. He'd wiped as much of the horse's blood off his exposed skin as possible, but the flies still favored him. Mosquitoes, too, had joined in the attack. Ignoring the bites was difficult, but he had no choice but to endure the hungry insects and move on.

The sun continued to beam brightly overhead, but down inside the grass was still full of shadows and unknown holes. His sense of direction was strong, but for all he knew, without anything to pinpoint his ultimate destination, Josiah could have been crawling in circles, making a fool of himself, or heading straight for unseen trouble.

He was alone, that was all that he was certain of, lost in the grasses, trailing, he hoped, in the opposite direction from Pip.

It felt like he was the only man alive in the world. He was the army of good against the unknown evil that searched for him as eagerly as he searched for it. He knew he was out-manned, could feel it deep in his bones. Killing a Ranger would only buoy the shooter's spirits, make him a hero in Cortina's camp. Especially once Josiah's identity was made known.

It wasn't the first time Josiah had felt that way, alone in the world, alone in battle, left to fight for all he owned and believed in. But somehow, this felt different, like it was really the truth, like he really had been left to his own devices. McNelly and the boys were miles away, and he had never fought with Pip at his side, didn't know if the man was a good shot, full of courage or fear, or what. Especially now that his horse was downed.

Oddly, Josiah felt himself missing Scrap.

At the very least, Elliot had his back, most of the time, when he wasn't half-cocked and bent on a rage about something or another. Still, Josiah wished the boy was alongside him. The shooter surely wouldn't have had a chance then.

He stopped about ten yards into his trek.

The world had remained silent. Disturbingly so. There wasn't an insect, outside of the local flies and mosquitoes, or a bird within a mile, at least not one that was willing to offer a chirp or a peep of happiness or need. Josiah could hear his own breathing and his heart beating and nothing more.

He peered slowly up over the top of the grasses and saw nothing either way.

All that remained of the incident behind him was an indentation in the grass where the chestnut mare lay, waiting for whatever scavenger would come along and devour it.

A pair of vultures appeared in the sky overhead, circling silently, watching and waiting for the right opportunity to glide down from their heavenly perch and partake in the sustenance left to them by one of Cortina's men — at least, Josiah assumed it was one of the rustlers that had fired the deadly shot. It could have been anybody with a grudge, uncertain of their cause. Still, it made sense to him that it was one of Cortina's men. Who else would shoot first without any other provocation? Who else, indeed?

Just as Josiah dropped down to the ground, another gunshot crackled in the distance. Only this time, it wasn't so distant. Maybe fifteen yards north of him.

Another gunshot answered the first one. Most likely Pip returning fire from behind him. To his credit, Pip didn't stop with just one shot. He emptied his chamber, fired off all six rounds, in rapid succession, just like Josiah had. Both men wanted to avenge the horse's death.

All Josiah could do, at that moment, was lie on the ground and hope like hell one of the bullets didn't find him.

It would've been a shame to die from a bullet fired by a friend and compatriot after all of these years, after all of the battles he'd fought in. Bad luck would surely have a last laugh. Fate would howl with glee at the irony of it all. Truth be told, Josiah should have been a dead man a long time ago, and he knew it. He knew his luck was running thin.

But none of the bullets found Josiah. And the thunder and crack of the Colt Dragoon that belonged to Pip died away.

Silence quickly returned to the open grass plain, but at least this time around Josiah had lost the feeling of being alone. Pip was still in the fight, shooting from behind him. It gave him a bit of confidence that he'd been lacking.

With that new fuel and comfort, Josiah set out again, crawling slowly in the direction of the shooter.

It only took a journey of about five yards before he heard a rustling in the grass ahead of him. Josiah stopped and froze. There was nowhere to hide, nowhere to run to, as far as he knew.

He had a cartridge chambered in the Peacemaker, the hammer pulled back. Sweat dripped down his forehead, running into his eyes, stinging them, blurring his vision. But Josiah didn't feel any fear. He didn't feel anything. He was just focused on the movement ahead of him.

Whoever, or whatever, it was, it was coming closer.

Surely, if it was a man standing up walking, then Pip would have had a clear shot and taken him down. Save Josiah the trouble. But as it was, Pip seemed to have vanished.

A shadow dropped over Josiah, and for the first time, he could see boots pushing through the grass toward him. The man was bent down in a crouch, keeping as close to the top of the grass as possible.

It only took Josiah a second to see that he didn't recognize the man, and another second to pull the trigger of his gun.

CHAPTER 29

The bullet caught the Mexican in the right shoulder, propelling him backward with a surprised scream.

The shot had unsettled the man, but he hung on to his six-shooter as he tumbled to the ground. As soon as he hit the ground, the Mexican rolled on his side and started shooting. Luckily for Josiah, the man was just as disoriented as he had been deep in the grass, and his shots were off about five feet. It only took a heartbeat for all six cartridges to be spent, and none them had found their target.

Josiah lunged up onto his feet in a crouch, shooting, using his last bullet. For a moment he was lost — until the man jumped him and wrestled him back to the ground.

The smell of hate, fear, and blood overwhelmed Josiah, and his breath got caught in his throat. The wind had been fully knocked out of him when he'd hit the ground.

Josiah didn't panic. He fought back. Without any hesitation or thought, he pushed up and swung at the Mexican, whose brown eyes were wild and bulging with anger. Drool ran out of the corner of the attacker's mouth, mixed with blood and hate. He must have bit his tongue.

The punch missed, caught nothing but air. The man had anticipated Josiah's reaction and cocked his head out of the way just in time.

It was then that Josiah saw the knife in the man's hand. It careened downward toward his throat with all of the Mexican's might behind it.

Josiah rolled out of the way, and the knife blade, glimmering and at least ten inches long, stabbed into the ground less than an inch away from his skin. He felt the wind of metal and was almost blinded by its silvery reflection.

The Mexican let go of the knife and jumped onto Josiah, straddling him, pinning his feet to the ground with all of his weight. He reared back then and punched Josiah in the cheek as hard as he could with a balled fist.

Josiah's teeth rattled, and his brain felt

like a cantaloupe in a bucket that had just been dropped to the ground. The hit dazed him, and the Mexican knew it — he followed up with his other fist on the opposite side of Josiah's face.

Josiah wasn't sure if he yelled out. He thought he did, thought he heard himself scream, then groan with pain, but he didn't lose control of all his senses. Pain ricocheted through his body, but he didn't lose consciousness. The pain just made him angry, more determined to fight back. There was no question that the Mexican had the advantage at the moment, but Josiah was going to do everything he could to change that.

With as much force as he could muster, Josiah jammed his knee upward, catching the Mexican directly in the crotch, sending him spiraling backward in immediate agony. His thrust had been on target, creating an opening the Mexican hadn't considered and hadn't protected himself from.

Josiah twisted to the side and grabbed the man's knife. He pulled it out of the ground and jumped up, searching for where the Mexican had come to rest.

All of Josiah's primordial instincts had taken over now. This was war. Hand-to-hand fighting. Death was close. He could taste it, smell it, feel it. Every vein was wide open inside his body. His blood was pumping at full capacity, orchestrating as much opportunity and physical edge as possible. Adrenaline drugged him into believing he was invincible, that he couldn't be hurt, that he wasn't going to die. Not today. He had too much to live for, too much life in him to surrender to one of Cortina's thugs for nothing more than a few stolen cattle.

His life didn't pass before him. Unresolved memories and heartaches had no place in this fight. All that mattered to Josiah was his immediate and ultimate survival — and the only way he could be certain there would be another tomorrow for him was to kill the Mexican, before the Mexican killed him.

Even the flies and mosquitoes had found the sense to flee the melee. If silence had been the norm in the grass plain before the fight started, it had been elevated to dead silence now. There was only the fight — the heavy breathing, the groans and moans of life and death, of two men determined to kill each other — and nothing more.

There was no sign of Pip.

The Mexican was up on his knees now, scrambling forward, pushing off the ground with the all the energy he had, looking over his shoulder, trying to escape.

Josiah dove forward, the long knife firmly in his grip. His vision and accuracy were clouded by the shadows on the ground and the hurriedness of his jump. He missed the Mexican's leg by an inch. But that didn't stop him. He yanked the knife from the ground and pushed forward with as much rage as he could channel.

He could hear the Mexican struggling to breathe. He hadn't realized how big a man the attacker was. There wasn't time to size him up, to judge his opponent's skills. There was only the attack. Now it looked as if the man's size and lack of physical prowess were proving to be the Mexican's downfall. He had a thick belly the size of a beer barrel and stubby legs that had never had any hope of speed or coordination. He was a work-horse, if that, not a beautiful runner — like the one he had killed.

They were both scrambling. The advantage had turned in Josiah's favor, but that didn't promise to hold.

The Mexican was fumbling with his gun, a short-barreled Colt, trying to load one cartridge while attempting to gain his footing and run off.

Josiah leaped forward and brought the knife down into the back of the Mexican's thigh with as much force as he could push into it. He felt the blade tear into flesh and careen off bone. There was a slicing, sucking sound that met with a loud exclamation of pain and surprise from the Mexican. Josiah twisted the knife out of the man's leg, causing as much damage and pain as possible.

The attacker hadn't stopped scrambling or given up because of the pain. He tried even harder to escape, to get out of Josiah's reach.

The knife was covered in blood, the glimmer and perfection of the honed steel gone, as if it had never existed. Josiah thrust the knife down again, penetrating the back of the man's calf. The meat of his calf was more compact, harder than the thigh, and required more pressure to push through. Somehow with the force of the stab, the blade escaped out the other side of the Mexican's leg.

There had been very few times in Josiah's life that he'd heard a scream so loud and full of pain. The only way the wound could contribute to the man's death was if he bled to death, if the sharp knife had sliced a big vein of some sort. But Josiah had seen more than one man left to die on the battlefield from wounds less than the one he'd just delivered to the Mexican.

He pulled the knife out again, with another twist. The Mexican collapsed face-forward to the ground, continuing to yell and scream — all in Spanish, words that Josiah didn't understand, but he knew they were words of rage and anger, not retreat and surrender.

Josiah stopped for a second, regained his breath.

The Mexican started to crawl away. It was a slow escape, like he had a ton of bricks piled on his back. The leg was useless, limp and favored, blood pumping out of it in quick spurts. The faster the man's heart pumped, the more the ground turned red.

Flies and insects couldn't resist any longer and attacked almost in swarms. The air was suddenly filled with focused buzzing, and overhead, more vultures had joined the original two. Shadows danced from the sky as the long-winged black birds passed in front of the sun.

Anyone within a mile could have heard the screaming and shouting.

Josiah wondered about Pip, and then Clipper's fate, but pushed away any concern as he watched the Mexican gain strength, or at least effort, as he climbed to his knees.

Josiah jumped up as well and dove again at the man. The knife led into the calculated fall, zeroing in and coming to rest just where Josiah aimed: the nape of the man's neck.

The knife went all the way through the neck, cutting the spine, the tip popping out just underneath the Mexican's Adam's apple. Guttural sounds and blood exploded everywhere, covering Josiah with warmth and stickiness.

He jumped back with the knife, letting the Mexican fall forward. The man twitched and hit the ground in a hard, final thump. Death was instant. If not humane, at least it was over. The fight ended, and somehow, with his own wounds, pain, and disabilities, Josiah had survived.

Nothing else around him mattered. The world had stopped turning. His heart beat rapidly, and he could taste the Mexican's blood on his tongue, feel it trying to invade his skin, covering his face and hands.

This was not the first victory for him. Hardly. But it was the most recent. He'd been a young man the first time he'd had to fight a man to the death. He had vomited then, felt a hole tear in his soul, felt regret, fear, and revulsion. Now he was only glad to be alive.

He had no pity for the Mexican. He'd engaged Josiah from the start, known what the risk was, what was at stake — he'd taken his life into his own hands and lost. That's all there was to it.

Josiah drew in a deep breath, sighed, wiped his face with the back of his sleeve, and stood up.

He hadn't been paying any attention, had lost himself in the fight and forgotten where he was.

A gunshot in the distance greeted him. It didn't come from the direction Pip had fled, but from the direction where the Mexican had first attacked.

Just like flies, where there was one Mexican fighter, there were more. Josiah had only fought a battle in a war that promised not to relent. And he stood in an open field, unsure of where his gun was, where his horse was, alone and spent, certain that if he was faced with another fight like the one he'd just fought, he would surely lose, surely die a miserable death, like the Mexican who lay before him.

Chapter 30

Another gunshot quickly followed the first, urging Josiah to drop to the ground for cover. But he didn't move, he stood gazing into the distance, trying to comprehend what he was looking at.

He'd found himself on a slight rise, allowing him to look down into a dip in the earth, a slight roll just as the land reached out and met the calm ocean. The sun glared off the water like a mirror, hurting his eyes, causing him to look away.

The ground rumbled under his feet, and then another familiar sound met his ears: screaming cattle, scared out of their heads, pushing and bucking to get away from something. Josiah knew what a stampede sounded, and looked, like. He'd been in the midst of one earlier in the year, just outside of Corpus Christi. That stampede had been started with intention, and he wasn't so sure that this one wasn't started the same way.

Each gunshot spooked the cows more, causing them to run up along the coast, some staying huddled together, like a swarm of birds trying to outmaneuver a diving hawk, while others strayed off, running on their own, taking their chances in the grass plains that skirted the sandy beaches.

All of the cattle were running in the opposite direction from Josiah. The gunshots were not for him but for something else. That, at least, was a mild relief. He wasn't sure if he could stand for another fight on his own.

Cortina had employed some *vaqueros* to herd the cows, all longhorns, to the steamer, but they were not doing the shooting, either. They were riding hard, too, trying to outrun a company of oncoming Texas Rangers.

McNelly was easy to identify, leading a hard line of the boys from camp, obviously having found the herd without Josiah's and Pip's help. The captain was doing his best to rescue the cows, to fulfill his duty.

Some of the *vaqueros* were on foot, running full out, trying to escape the onslaught of Rangers. Even with the rumble of the ground and the fearful cries of the longhorns, Josiah flinched as the sound of crackling gunshot met his ears. Small puffs of gray smoke erupted in the air above the rushing horses. A man-made storm that promised both death and destruction. If nature had no conscience, then she was surely outmatched by man's taste for war and battle. The worst tornado or hurricane was no peer to the human desire to conquer and kill.

The man Josiah had killed must have been riding the perimeter, scouting a broad circle around the herd. There were so few men in Cortina's band of rustlers, he must have been the only one to the north of the herd. It was a matter of luck for Josiah. Two men would have been impossible to fight. He would have been a dead man, instead of a man still alive, trying to regain his strength and reestablish his bearings.

He had no choice but to join the company of men now, even though there was more of a fight coming than he was up to, all covered in blood, the taste of death still rattling around in his mouth. Avoiding the battle was out of the question. The company needed him . . . and he knew he needed them. Being out in the open, remaining alone, was dangerous and stupid, and he knew it.

Josiah turned then, any thought of acknowledging the physical pain he felt pushed quickly out of his mind. He needed to find his gun and his horse. And there was the question of Pip's safety. He hoped that the man hadn't met a fate similar to the Mexican's, that he hadn't come across another scout who'd fought him hand-to-hand to the death, too. It was entirely possible that his fellow Ranger had met his maker, that the smell of death that inhabited the inside of Josiah's nose was not only the dead Mexican and the roan mare, but Pip, the hard-riding stranger who never seemed to lose a race.

He turned his back on the Mexican, who was obviously dead, though still bleeding heavily. The man lay in a red pool of his own blood, the invisible and small predators of the insect world already celebrating their luck and bounty. His face was twisted in pain, reflecting the intensity of his last living moment.

Josiah quickly searched the ground for his Peacemaker. He tracked back through the trampled-down grass to where it had flown out of his hand. It was pretty easy to find with the sun beaming down from the sky so brightly. The barrel gleamed on the ground, even in the shadows of the grasses. He rushed to the gun, glad for its presence and the safety it offered him. At least now he could defend himself if the need arose.

The Peacemaker felt good in his hand. He opened the cylinder and reloaded the trusted gun. Then he checked the barrel to make sure it wasn't blocked with dirt or silt. Holstering the gun was not an option, not with a battle breaking less than two hundred yards from him.

Unfortunately, Clipper wasn't the kind of horse that came running to a whistle or call. Josiah had just never trained the Appaloosa to be much like a dog.

Before moving on, Josiah stripped the Mexican of his guns and knife. He threw the cartridge-laden belt over his shoulder, carrying the holstered gun, another Colt .45, under his arm.

He took a deep breath and looked in the opposite direction of the stampede and saw nothing but open land. The way from which he'd come seemed to offer peace and sanctuary — but Josiah knew it would be a mistake to assume anything at the moment. Calling out to Pip didn't make much sense, either. He didn't want to give himself away or bring any undue attention to himself. He wanted to join the fight when he was ready, not bring it to him any sooner than necessary.

Each moment brought Josiah more

strength.

He wasn't going to be at full fighting strength anytime soon. There was no question about that, not with the wounds he had suffered in Arroyo, and now in the fight with the Mexican scout — but he still had value, something to offer the company. He could still sit on his horse and shoot, could run down any of the *vaqueros* on foot. He just needed his horse.

Crouching as best he could, he made his way through the knee-high grass back to where the chestnut mare lay dead. It was easy to divine Clipper's path through the grass.

The horse had bolted to the east, almost straight back to where they had come from.

Josiah wondered if Clipper had tried to go back to the camp, to someplace safe. It would have made sense, but the company of Rangers were a good distance away, not in a destination Josiah could arrive at quickly on foot.

Clipper had always been an easy horse to ride in battle, had never been afraid or skittish of loud noises or gunshots, so it made little sense that the Appaloosa had bolted or gone very far. Still, there was no sign of the horse, and that concerned Josiah more than the growing battle behind him.

He ignored the mare and pushed through
the grass, staying as close to Clipper's trail
as he could.

CHAPTER 31

Josiah was not surprised when he found Pip facedown in the grass, a single bullet hole in the back of his skull.

The blood had already started to congeal, goo up, but there was no saving the man. He was as dead as the Mexican. Both of them had been on the run, trying to escape, didn't see death coming, though the Mexican surely had to have known as much as Josiah had that every breath taken bordered on being his last. It was hard to say what Pip had thought. Maybe he saw refuge and safety over the rise, hoping like hell that the Mexican was a bad shot when he heard the report of the Colt from behind him. If there was any comfort to be taken, both men had died quickly, each in a fight he'd believed in.

Josiah knew little of Pip — if he had kin who would care about his passing, where he hailed from, or what his hopes for the future were. It was that way with most of the boys in McNelly's company of Rangers. You'd find out more about them after they died than you had when they lived.

It seemed easier for most of the Rangers not to talk about their lives back home. Including Josiah. Talking about his son, Lyle, only made him homesick and regretful. He knew he was missing a good chunk of the boy's life, knew the time away could never be replaced, so focusing on his absence was dangerous. Especially in a moment like the present, when life and death hung in the balance, were nothing more than a lucky shot — or an unlucky one, depending on where you stood.

The thunder and explosion of the battle behind Josiah faded away for just a second. All that remained was an echo and the smell of gunpowder on the breeze.

He leaned down and put his finger on Pip's neck to make sure the man was truly dead. Pip's skin was warm and sweaty, but there was no pulse, no sign of life. Just to make sure, Josiah put his ear to the man's back to see if he could hear a heartbeat. Nothing. Nothing but more smells of death and the wind rolling gently through the grass.

Josiah's senses were nearly numb now.

Some smells become solid, unnoticeable, even comfortable, after enough time. But the smell of war never became that way for him. He could taste the gunpowder, the metallic tang of blood. It was an unnatural aroma and taste, foreign, forbidden, but all too familiar.

With a deep sigh, Josiah reached around and gently closed Pip's eyes. If it were possible, he'd try to bury Pip with his horse when everything was said and done. That seemed fitting.

For a second, Josiah thought about loading up with Pip's weapons, too, like he had with the Mexican's. But he didn't want to weigh himself down so severely that he couldn't move easily — or run if he needed to.

When he looked up, a wave of relief flowed through him. He saw Clipper standing about fifteen yards ahead of him. The Appaloosa seemed to glow in the bright sunlight, his white even whiter, and his black even blacker. The contrast of colors was striking, as the horse stood stoically, almost like a statue, staring at Josiah.

The only shadows that reached down from the sky came from the vultures, who were circling higher and higher, floating off to the north, over land instead of the ocean, trying, it looked like, to escape the madness of the men below them. They wouldn't go far, just out of shooting range, but they would rush back in to survey the carnage first thing, just after the dust and smoke settled to the ground.

A slight smile crossed Josiah's face. Seeing the horse was like seeing home after a long journey. There was little comfort and pleasure to be had in what lay ahead for them. Knowing that he would be in his own saddle, on his own horse, buoyed Josiah. If the horse had been dead, had been shot like Pip's, it would have only added to his weakness and his rage. Other than Scrap, Clipper was the closest thing to a friend Josiah had on, or off, the trail, and riding into battle with a trusted steed would give him some much needed strength after what he had just been through.

Josiah walked easily up to Clipper, straining to hear all of the noises that surrounded him, on the ready for any attack, seen or unseen. The horse didn't spook, didn't seem nervous at all. He swished his tail and raised his head up and down as Josiah touched his neck. A quick glance told Josiah that the horse bore no visible wounds. All was well — for the moment.

After unloading the Mexican's gun belt,

Josiah climbed up easily into the saddle and settled in. He felt bad about leaving Pip to the insects, vultures, and whatever else wandered by, but he had no choice. Joining the rest of the company mattered the most at the moment.

From the rise, Josiah could see several miles to the west. The vista was broad and wide as the land, mostly free of trees of any kind, flattened out to infinity, barely differentiating itself from the sea. The only way to tell the land and water apart was the thin strip of brown sandy beach that separated the two. The grasses covered the land, waving in the breeze, making it look like waves flowing up from the sea, jumping the beach, then continuing on for as far as the eye could see.

The sky was cloudless. Perfect summer blue. The color of cornflowers and calmness. Saltiness and moisture tinged the air with noticeable effect. It was a smell and taste that Josiah had come to enjoy — but not now. The residue of battle had pushed away any memories of pleasurable times on the coast.

A steamer sat a good twenty yards off the coast. Smoke streamed up from the dual stacks slowly. The big wheel on the back sat stationary, and there were no deckhands visible. A captain's tower jutted upward, and where the cabins of a passenger steamer would have normally been, there was only an open space, fenced off like a floating corral. It was still empty. Somehow, the captain had found the herd just in time, stopping Cortina's plan, or putting a dent in it, at the moment.

The frightened cattle were scattered up and down the coastline, for almost as far as Josiah could see. They stuck mostly to the beach, but a good portion of them were rushing through the grass, unconcerned that it was chest-high. From what he knew, the longhorns preferred open spaces. Fear had set them on a course of escape no matter what the resistance.

A few *vaquer*os tried to wrangle the longhorns back into a herd, but Cortina's men were at the leading end of the frantic stampede. Josiah feared there was another battalion of Mexicans hidden in the distance, waiting for a raid like the one McNelly was conducting. It made sense to Josiah that there would be a backup plan in place. This was a valuable shipment for Cortina. Too valuable not to protect with more than sixteen men. Fewer than that now.

McNelly and the boys were still trailing

the rear of the herd of longhorns, the sound of battle overcoming the screaming and mooing cows.

Some of the Mexicans were on foot, and a few of the Rangers had jumped to the ground to join the fight, hand-to-hand.

Josiah sucked in a deep breath and urged Clipper forward, joining the fight without reluctance.

He spied McNelly first and headed straight for the captain, unconcerned now about whether he could be seen or be a target. There was no turning back.

He had his own Peacemaker in his left hand, and the Mexican's gun in his un-bound holster, loaded and ready for when the cartridges of his own gun had been used up. Whether he was physically up to the fight was not a question, or a choice to be made. He had no choice. But he hoped to stay on horseback and avoid another ground fight, if that was possible.

He pushed Clipper to a full run. The jostling caused him some pain, but he pushed it away, allowed the call of battle and the adrenaline that came with it to cure his ills — as much as that was possible.

Killing the Mexican had come easy as he looked back on it, using the incident to whet his appetite for what was about to come.

Regrets might come later, in the middle of the night, deep in a sleep, if he was lucky enough to survive and come out of the fight whole. It was an assumption that he hoped held true. He couldn't go into a fight thinking he was going to die.

Lieutenant Robinson rode close behind McNelly, his sword drawn, as he bore down on a Mexican who was on the run.

The Mexican was screaming in Spanish, fumbling with a gun, loading up another round of cartridges. Robinson didn't relent, didn't slow down. The man was too close to McNelly. With a hard and calculated thrust, Robinson plunged the blade of the sword forward, catching the man in the kidney. Robinson twisted his wrist fluidly and continued to ride forward, pulling the sword out of the man's side with ease. It was a skilled maneuver, one that Robinson had obviously used before. He had the makings of a captain.

The Mexican screamed out in agony and collapsed to the ground, rolling, still clutching his gun, still screaming words that Josiah didn't understand but knew the meaning of somehow. Dying in battle in any language needed no translation for him.

Josiah's view was suddenly obscured, covered in gun smoke, a black powder fog that pushed any pleasantries of the seaside away. The smoke rose quickly in the air, pushing northeast on the wind rolling in off the waves. For a long moment, it felt precarious to aim at the enemy.

In another second, Josiah heard a familiar yell rise up from behind the Mexican, and watched as Scrap appeared not far behind Robinson, pushing forward as hard as he could, riding his blue roan mare, Missy.

Scrap aimed his rifle, a Spencer repeater, at the Mexican, and happily pulled the trigger. The shot was sure, and caught the man right behind the ear, finishing him off. Scrap yipped and yeehawed, celebrating his shot, making sure the Mexican was dead, and unable to cause the captain, or any of the other Rangers, any harm.

Josiah was glad to see Scrap, and even happier still to know that there were men in the fight who had each other's back. He yelled himself, and then, having caught Scrap's attention, he loosened the reins in his hand, gave Clipper his head, and joined the fight.

CHAPTER 32

The horn from the steamer blasted loudly, rising above all the sounds of the battle like an alarm, or a call to duty. It was like the world took a breath, took notice that there were actually human beings inside the boat. Until the moment when the horn blasted, the steamer could have been a ghost ship, just sitting in the water waiting to transport its cargo, not a threat to anyone.

The gunfire stopped so suddenly, the echoes seemed never to have existed at all. Screams and yells settled down, but the thunder of the running cattle *did not* cease — it only grew dimmer, farther away, heading up the coast and into the interior of the arroyo.

Josiah swerved as he rushed ahead, pulling up on the reins, allowing Clipper to jump over the dead Mexican that Robinson had stabbed and Scrap had shot. He turned then and headed straight for the beach.

There was nowhere to run, to hide, and he knew immediately that if there were men on the steamer, and they were going to take up their arms, they had to be stopped. They would be Cortina's supporters, the beef more valuable to them than gold, to feed the hungry population in Cuba.

Josiah bit the reins between his teeth, switched the Peacemaker to his other hand, then pulled his fully loaded Winchester rifle from the scabbard. An orange blast exploded from around the base of the smokestack, on the starboard side of the steamer, just as Josiah settled his finger around the trigger and rested the butt of the gun against his injured shoulder. The kick was minimal, and he wasn't concerned about the pain it caused him. The shooter on the boat was his only concern.

The man by the smokestack fired again, this time taking direct aim at Josiah.

Josiah was just on the edge of the grass and could see the man's shadow on the deck. With as much accuracy as possible, he unloaded all six shots of his Peacemaker, holstered it quickly, then fired five more shots from the rifle in rapid succession. Clipper galloped confidently toward the ocean, unfazed by the noise and warfare around him.

Like Josiah, the rest of the Rangers had reengaged in the fight with Cortina's men after the momentary lapse. The sound of gunfire rose up behind him like a storm drawing energy from its lull, only louder, more violent, and determined to destroy whatever lay in its path.

Smoke, and the taste of gunpowder, overwhelmed Josiah's senses. His eyes burned. His vision was blurry. He was numb, beyond feeling. He knew each breath he drew in could be his last, as out in the open as he was.

A gun exploded to Josiah's immediate right, and a quick glance told him that Scrap had joined his side.

Josiah nodded, then turned his attention back to the boat. Scrap followed suit, both of them firing directly at the captain's tower and at the man next to the smokestack.

Wood chips exploded off the front of the steamer as each bullet found its mark. It looked like it was raining around the front of the boat as the residue hit the water.

It took less than a minute for the first shooter to collapse. It was hard to tell who had hit the man, and it didn't matter to Josiah whether it was him or Scrap who'd delivered the deadly shot. It was one less gun pointed in their direction.

But that didn't stop the rest from shooting. Another gun had appeared, pointed out of the tower's well. Obviously, the captain was defending his ship, was going to fight for control of it to the death. Surrendering was his only other choice, and that didn't seem likely.

As Josiah reloaded, Scrap fired from both his Spencer rifle and his own Colt. Then when it was Scrap's turn to reload, Josiah took his turn and traded fire with the captain. The tandem of responsibility was unspoken between them. They had been in enough battles together to know how to survive without speaking.

A five-minute gunfight can seem like an eternity, especially when you're as exposed as Josiah and Scrap were. Anyone could have shot them from the front or the back — but they'd trusted Robinson and Captain McNelly to cover them.

Both of the officers had seen Josiah's intent when he'd rushed the steamer, and they'd taken up a position not twenty yards from him, firing in the opposite direction, covering the assault.

There were very few of Cortina's men left on horseback. Any thought of rescuing the mission was lost. The *vaqueros* were now nothing but bandits on the run. Most of them were on foot, easy to run down.

The shots coming from the steamer stopped. There was no way to tell if the man in the captain's tower was dead, if one of their shots had found its target. All Josiah could do was assume that a bullet had ended the exchange. As far as he was concerned, Scrap Elliot had the eyes of an eagle and could shoot the spot off an ant's butt at a hundred yards.

"Let's head back up and help the captain," Josiah yelled out.

Their horses were standing nose to nose, and Scrap was settled stiffly in his saddle, reloading his Spencer. The carbine held seven shots and was tube-fed in the butt of the stock. Josiah had no idea how Scrap had come to possess the Spencer, since it was a weapon of the War Between the States and had some age on it, but the boy seemed comfortable with it. A skilled shooter could shoot off about twenty cartridges in a minute with that gun. Scrap had those skills, times ten.

Scrap slapped the tube in, closed the slide, pumped a round into the chamber, then cocked the rifle, ready to shoot. "Let me pound a few more rounds thataway. My gut tells me the bastard's a-hidin' in the bowels of that boat."

Josiah didn't object, just dropped his chin. "I haven't seen any movement for a long minute."

"What the hell happened anyway, Wolfe?" Scrap eyed the steamer, then pulled the Spencer's trigger, not giving Josiah a chance to answer. He fired off all his rounds without stopping.

The smoke was thick, catching in the wind off the water, pushing away quickly. Gunfire still popped behind them, but it was more infrequent. So were the screams from the men. There was hardly any noise from the longhorns. Distant moos. Nothing close, like the sounds of an imminent stampede, to be concerned about.

Josiah waited for the smoke to clear before saying anything, watching the boat as closely as Scrap. He saw nothing. "We came up on a scout. He shot Pip's horse."

Scrap's eyes widened. "The chestnut mare?"

Josiah nodded. "Killed it outright."

"Damn. That was a fine horse." Scrap unconsciously patted Missy's neck.

"I went after the scout, and Pip went in the opposite direction, but he must not've kept low enough. The scout shot him, too."

"Kill him?"

"I'm afraid so."

"That's a damn shame, too. Pip was a good fella. I liked him good enough — except when he took my coin."

"Which was frequently."

"Ain't gonna wish a man dead over a bad bet."

"I'd hope not."

"There'll be more dead before this day's over with," Josiah said, casting a glance at the sky, eyeing a vulture in the distance.

"Let's hope there's more Mexican blood spilt than Anglo. I bet that coward Cortina ain't nowheres near here. Probably sent all his lowlifes to do his biddin'. I can't abide a man like that. I surely can't."

Neither of them spoke after that — they let the air settle around them. Nothing else needed saying. There was a toll to be paid in a battle such as this, and they both knew they were lucky to be alive.

Scrap reloaded again, and Josiah turned his attention away from the steamer. He heard horses approaching. He expected to see the captain coming his way, and he was right. The captain was riding toward him, the ridge and area behind them all secured by Rangers taking stations at strategic points. But Josiah was surprised to see another rider with the captain other than Robinson, who was at McNelly's side as well.

The other rider was Juan Carlos, come to join the fight.

CHAPTER 33

"I'm pretty certain I kilt them fellas out-right on that boat, Captain," Scrap said to McNelly. He didn't make eye contact with Juan Carlos, didn't even acknowledge his presence.

All five men were huddled in a circle, on their horses, about twenty-five yards from the shore, just inside the grass line. Robinson held his rifle, ready to pop it up and shoot at a second's notice.

"Pretty certain could get us all killed, Elliot," McNelly said. "Dead certain is more the course of action that interests me at the moment."

Scrap lowered his eyes to the ground. "Yes, sir, I just ain't seen no movement for a good while, and I unloaded a belt full of cartridges on that floater. Wolfe, too. We got one man for sure. It don't look like there can be more than that, and the captain, on-board."

McNelly looked at Scrap warily. "You'd serve yourself to not think, Ranger Elliot. I admire your shooting skills, but Cortina's as smart as a hungry coyote and sly as an old fox. Just because you see something doesn't make it true. Especially in the heat of battle. But you're too young to understand that."

Scrap bit the corner of his lip, visibly fighting to keep any words swirling around in his head from jumping off his tongue. Every man in the Ranger camp knew that McNelly didn't suffer fools gladly, and that sentiment must have surely been ramped up since they were in the midst of battle, a battle they'd all known was coming for days on end.

Josiah was impressed by Scrap's restraint.

Juan Carlos hadn't spoken a word since coming to a stop, and he didn't look interested in being thrust into the middle of any confrontation between Scrap and Captain McNelly. He sat stoically, and uncomfortably, on a gelding paint that looked as old and haggard as Juan Carlos himself.

The man looked to have aged ten years since Josiah had seen him last — uneasily in the shadows from Arroyo. All of the lines in the old Mexican's face looked deeper, his face sunken like he hadn't had a decent meal in weeks. His clothes, hardly anything more than rags, orange, brown, and dirty, hung off his skinny body like a blanket thrown over a rotted scarecrow's frame. Raggedy and dirty was not an unusual look for Juan Carlos, but something seemed different. He looked to be at death's door.

It hadn't been that long ago that the Mexican had nearly died, had been shot precariously close to the gut, and Josiah wondered if the injury had come back to haunt Juan Carlos. He surely understood the effect that a recent injury could have on a man's constitution.

Of course, they were all ragged and skinny — being on the trail and in the midst of battle had its price for every man.

Captain McNelly eyed the horizon, then turned his attention to Josiah. "I want you to sweep around behind us and make sure there aren't any strays, Wolfe. The steamer doesn't pose any threat that I can see. The delivery has been averted, and I'd dare say that the scoundrel Cortina has a backup plan. I would if I were him." He hesitated for a second, casting a glance to Scrap. "Take both Elliot and Juan Carlos with you."

"Yes, sir."

"Be wary, Wolfe. This battle is far from

over. Nothing will end until Cortina is dead and buried, his ambitions put to a final end. This is a war to him. There's more at stake than just rustling these cows out of Texas. Do I make myself clear?"

Josiah nodded. "Yes, sir," he said again. His voice was unwavering. He was glad to have the company of Scrap and Juan Carlos — but the old Mexican's presence made him uncomfortable. There was some unfinished business to tend to, at least as far as Josiah was concerned. He was certain that Juan Carlos had seen him in an embrace with Francesca. Luckily, Josiah still had Pearl's letter inside his coat pocket. He hadn't thought to discard it, not that he would have, but leaving it behind with the rest of his belongings might have been preferable. A constant reminder of the rejection was the last thing he needed on his mind as he ventured into battle.

"Very well then." McNelly readjusted himself in his saddle. Gun smoke still clouded the air, and the pops and pings of gunshots rang in the air, although more infrequently now than when the battle first began.

Josiah could hear the rattle in McNelly's chest and see the strain on his face.

"Onward, Robinson," the captain commanded, punching his horse urgently with both ankles.

Dust, and a cloud of flies, kicked up as McNelly and Robinson sped away. Josiah watched them carefully for a long moment, his hand on the trigger of his Winchester just in case an unseen shooter popped up somewhere and they needed covered. "Let's get out of range of the steamer," Josiah said.

"I kilt every living being on that boat, Wolfe."

"I hope you're right, Scrap. I damn sure hope you're right."

Josiah had al lowed Scrap to take the lead. They crested the rise and circled around Pip and his dead horse. Both were hard to miss, but Josiah didn't linger, didn't replay any of the prior events that had brought on both deaths. And Scrap was happy, for once, to keep his mouth shut.

There had been several dead Mexicans littered about on the way up the rise, but Josiah didn't stop to count them, though the thought of it occurred to him. If Garcia and Rafael had been telling the truth about the number of men assigned to the rustling operation, then it would've given him a better idea how many men were left living.

Fighting in the distance faded, and for all

intents and purposes, the battle was over. Still, Josiah understood McNelly's concern. One man could return to Cortina's camp and tell him of the outcome, could cause the bandit to re-outfit and send another wave of fighters — if he actually did have a backup plan.

"I am glad to see you, Juan Carlos," Josiah said.

"Is that so?"

"Yes, of course it's so." The discomfort that Josiah had detected upon first seeing Juan Carlos remained. The Mexican looked like he could hardly contain his anger. "There's something we need to speak of."

"This may not be the time, or the place, señor."

"It may be the only place and time." Josiah looked away from Juan Carlos's penetrating eyes, making sure that Scrap was far enough out of earshot and focused on the trail, and sweep, like he was supposed to be.

"If you insist," Juan Carlos said.

"It is about Pearl."

"My concern for her exceeds that of my own life."

"I understand that. And your friendship is important to me. I owe you my life."

"And I am indebted to you for mine more

than once. But there are limits to a man's gratitude."

Josiah tapped his chest. "I received a letter before Scrap and I left for Arroyo. A letter from Pearl. She has decided that she doesn't want to live the life of her mother, always waiting on bad news from the trail or wondering of my safety. She wishes to get on with her life without me in it."

"And from that news, you rush into the arms of another woman, señor? I thought you were a different kind of man than that."

"I am simply a man," Josiah said, almost whispering. "I have the letter if you would like to see it."

Juan Carlos shook his head no. "I believe you. Pearl has always been very *inquieto,* um, restless. The shadows of both her mama and her papa haunt her. She wishes to stand on her own two feet. I am happy for that. I just wish she could have been patient. You, too."

"I will seek her out once I return to Austin."

"Remember you are a fighting man."

"What's that mean?"

"You are alone in the world. Moments of weakness or desire rise infrequently. Pearl's father was a *guerrero,* a warrior, too, just like you. She knew the consequences of her choice when she gave herself to you." Juan Carlos looked away for a brief moment. "If our friendship has survived to this day, then a beautiful woman will not sever it. You have not betrayed me."

Josiah sighed, relieved, and nodded.

Ahead, Scrap stopped, wrapped the reins loosely around the horn of his saddle, and drew his Spencer out of the scabbard. "Wolfe, you best come have a look at this," he said, easing his finger onto the trigger.

CHAPTER 34

The afternoon sky had burned white. It was like the ocean had sucked all of the blue out of it. The only sound reaching the trio was the waves, crashing into the land, the tide rising, pushing the steamer precariously close to the shore.

It was not the sight of the boat coming to shore that had caused them to turn back; what happened to the vessel was of little concern to them. If it crashed on the rocks and broke apart, it would be viewed as a good thing, voiding the opportunity for the boat to be used again by Cortina, or his men, to transport anything for their cause. What did concern them, though, was the bloodied man standing at the bow of the steamer, waving a white flag, obviously unable to flee, to right the ship and save it, or himself.

Scrap had stopped Missy on the ridge, looking down to the ocean. Josiah knew what the boy was thinking, could see his trigger finger twitching — Scrap wanted to ignore the white flag and shoot the man outright.

"I'd take a deep breath if I were you, Elliot." Josiah eased Clipper alongside Scrap. Juan Carlos gave way to Josiah and held back. He bore no expression on his face, and kept his attention focused on the man on the boat.

"One shot, Wolfe. It'd be over quick," Scrap said.

"You going to explain that to the captain?"

Scrap glared at Josiah out of the corner of his eye. "Who says I'd have to?"

"The man is surrendering."

"Tell me the truth. You ain't never kilt a man who was offering himself up as a prisoner?"

Josiah looked away. "It was different in the war."

"This is a war, too," Scrap said with clenched teeth. "Ain't no damn different. If that man there had the opportunity to kill me right now, he would, and you know it. Fact is, he don't have that opportunity. Should've thought of that when he hooked himself up with the likes of Cortina."

"You're just angry because you made a stand to McNelly, proclaiming all of the men on that boat were dead, victims of your excellent shooting skills. And it's not true. Kind of makes you look bad, if you ask me."

"Nobody asked you." The veins in Scrap's neck and forehead pulsed as his face turned red. "You ain't gonna let me shoot him, are you, *Sergeant* Wolfe?"

The emphasis Scrap put on the word "Sergeant" made him sound like a little boy about to throw a fit because he didn't get what he wanted. Josiah was very familiar with the attitude since he had a toddler son, but he didn't flinch. "You shoot if you have to. Not until."

"Yes, sir."

Juan Carlos eased up alongside Josiah. "Here, señor, this may help." He handed Josiah a brass telescope much like an officer would have used in the War Between the States.

Josiah gladly accepted the telescope and looked through it with one eye cocked and closed.

The man on the boat was still swinging a white rag. There was blood on his shirt, and no sign of any weapons. He was dark-skinned and could have been a Mexican or Cuban, it was hard to tell.

Josiah was concerned the surrender was a ploy, a trick. He'd seen it happen more than once when he was fighting the Yankees. The enemy would lure their opponents to them under the guise of injury, or willingness to give up the fight, only to open fire from which there was no escape. It was an age-old trick, but still effective to the man who led with his emotions instead of his brain.

From what Josiah could see, there was no other movement on the steamer. He held the telescope as steady as he could. The rising tide was pushing the boat toward land quickly, on high, aggressive, waves. It would only be a matter of minutes before it washed ashore.

Josiah pulled his sight back from the man and the deck of the boat and slowly scanned the grasses for any kind of movement or shadows of men hiding. He saw nothing. Just the wind dancing across the top of the grass like before, dancing naturally from gusts off the water.

Satisfied, he pulled the telescope from his eye. "Looks clear, but that doesn't mean it is. However we proceed, we need to be cautious. We're right in the middle of a desperate hour for Cortina's men."

The shooting in the distance had died down; it was infrequent now. There was no sign of the herd of longhorns or the *vaqueros* charged to get them on board the steamer. If there was any kind of battle, or hand fighting, going on, it was out of sight, and out of earshot.

It was almost like the three of them had been abandoned. And with the exception of the dead Mexicans littered on the beach, there was no sign or indication that any kind of fight had ever taken place at all.

"The captain ordered us to circle around and sweep for strays or snipers," Josiah said. "We need to take this man in alive, if we can. He sees us, knows we're here. Fire a warning shot, Elliot. Crack the wood just at his feet to show him we're serious."

"Just the wood?"

"Don't miss. That's an order."

Scrap sighed, settled the butt of his Spencer rifle to his shoulder, and pulled the trigger, hitting exactly where Josiah had told him to.

The man on board the steamer jumped and started yelling louder. He danced wildly, waving the white rag even more frantically than before. He was barely able to hang on as the boat pitched and yawed heavily to the starboard side. A paddle on the rear wheel snapped off and crashed into another one, causing the entire mechanism to shatter. The steamer groaned and ground ashore, coming to a stop — luckily, all in

293

one piece, causing the man to stop, hang on, and not tumble over the railing.

Josiah didn't move, just watched the crash with interest. "Scrap, you stay up here and cover us."

"You think that's necessary?"

"Might not be, but I'd sure hate to regret not giving that order."

"Suit yourself." Scrap lowered his Spencer from his shoulder and pointed it to the ground, allowing the weapon to be raised and fired on short notice.

CHAPTER 35

"Ease on down here. Once you get on the ground, put your hands behind your head, and you won't get hurt," Josiah said, with the man on the boat's head squarely within his aim.

Juan Carlos fought to hold his old horse steady a few feet from the water. The waves seemed to make it nervous. He held a Colt Open Top as best he could. The Open Top was a predecessor to the Colt Single-Action Army, the Peacemaker. It fired .44 rimfire cartridges, and from what Josiah had seen in the past, Juan Carlos was a decent shot. The outdated weapon was nothing to be concerned about. But the advantage always fell to the newer model Colts, like the Peacemaker Josiah carried, and to the man with a steady horse and a steady hand. The hair on the back of Josiah's neck was on end, and he was alert to every sound and movement around him.

The man on the boat nodded, then started to climb over the rail.

"Slow now," Josiah commanded. "I'm in no mood for any tricks." He tilted his head back to the ridge without taking his eyes off the man. "And that fella up there? He's got a real itchy finger. He's done killed a few of your men today, and my guess is, he isn't ready to quit anytime soon. *Comprende?*"

Josiah wasn't sure if the man spoke, or understood, English. He assumed he didn't. Speaking Mexican was uncommon for Josiah, and it felt odd rolling off his tongue. He hoped the man didn't think he was fluent in the language, but if that were the case, Juan Carlos could step in. That was one of the reasons Josiah had the Mexican come along with him instead of ordering him to stay with Scrap.

"*Sí,* I understand," the man said. He climbed down from the bow of the steamer gingerly, since the hull was still rocking, still being pushed forward by the unrelenting force of the waves. As soon as his boots hit the ground, the man pasted his hands to the back of his head. "Please don't shoot, I am only a lowly deckhand. I am no thief or outlaw. I know nothing of these troubles I have found myself in. I just signed up for the journey to serve on the boat."

Josiah was relieved the man spoke the Anglo tongue as well as he did.

"No se acueste," Juan Carlos said to the man. His voice and eyes were steel-hard and direct as an executioner's.

Josiah had no clue what Juan Carlos said, but he offered the same attitude, the same glare. The man was a fool not to take either of them seriously.

"Do not lie," Juan Carlos interpreted, glancing quickly at Josiah with a nod. "You are a dead man if you do. *No habrá redención.*"

Not knowing the language was a weakness for Josiah. Especially when he was home, in the midst of Lyle and Ofelia.

Ofelia was teaching Lyle the language, and at the age of four, the boy could hold a conversation in Mexican in a way Josiah could not. There was no use protesting the idea. Josiah saw the advantages that Lyle would have over him as an adult. The world was changing. Honest contact with Mexicans, regardless of the current situation, was becoming more frequent. Prejudice still existed. Josiah imagined it always would, even as far as he was concerned to a degree, but life would be a lot different in the future for his son than it was for him. He pushed away the thought of Lyle as quickly as it came into his mind. There was no place for regret on the battlefield.

The deckhand glared at Juan Carlos. "Lying would be a foolish thing to do with so many guns pointed at me, wouldn't it, *amigo*? And my redemption is none of your concern. Just because you have a gun on me does not mean you own me, or my soul. Our Father blesses me."

"As you wish, *mi amigo*," Juan Carlos said.

Josiah shifted his weight in the saddle a little nervously. "Friends don't normally point guns at each other."

Juan Carlos backed his horse away from the crashing waves so there was no water touching its hooves, and it settled down immediately, allowing him to steady the Open Top Colt. "Are you the last man on board?"

"*Sí,* the captain is dead. Killed in the volley of gunshots. We were a short crew. There were to be *vaqueros* along for the return once the *vacas* were loaded and we were on the way back to Cuba."

A smile winced across Josiah's face and disappeared as suddenly as it appeared. "That'll make Scrap happy."

"How do I know that you are telling me the truth?" Juan Carlos asked. "How do I know that there are not more men hiding in the captain's quarters?"

"You don't. You must trust what I say, or you can kill me, it is up to you. I prefer to live, as I am sure you do, too."

"I do not wish to see another dead man on this day," Juan Carlos said. "Enough men have lost their lives for Cortina and his simple *codicia.*"

The deckhand held a steady gaze, glaring at Juan Carlos. "There is more than greed to every war. There is power and influence. Cortina wishes to create a legend for his own reflection to live in. Every general is the same, no matter the country."

Juan Carlos nodded, the look in his eyes stern. Every wrinkle on his face seemed to be as creased as a starched shirtsleeve. "I'm in no need of your wisdom or opinions."

"Then you will have to trust me," the deckhand said. "Allow me to live. I mean no one any harm. I just wish to return home to my *mujer* and my *niños.*"

Juan Carlos exhaled deeply. "I cannot promise you that will happen anytime soon. Your fate will be in Captain McNelly's hands. You are his prisoner now. Not ours."

"A prisoner of *Tejas*?"

"*Sí,* a prisoner of the Texas Rangers."

"Then I am a dead man." The deckhand genuflected, made a cross on his chest, from his head to his sternum with blazing speed.

"Not if you do as you are told," Juan Carlos said.

Satisfied, Josiah loosened the reins in his hand and backed Clipper up about five feet so that he and Juan Carlos's horse were nose to nose. "Come on then. We best get started. It's a long walk to the camp."

Juan Carlos put his hand out to the right, stopping Josiah. He shook his head. "I do not trust this *hombre.*"

It was nearly a whisper, but serious enough for Josiah to abide by the implication. He lowered his hand and looked quickly over his shoulder to make sure that Scrap was still in place, still had the deckhand in his sights. The boy hadn't moved. Scrap looked like a statue standing on the hill, the sun shining on him like he was in the middle of a spotlight. The only shadows on the ground came from the returning vultures, floating over the bodies left from the fight, with the smell of death and opportunity surely swirling in their nostrils like intoxicating nectar.

Before Josiah could issue an order, Juan Carlos slipped off his horse. "You make one false move, *amigo,* and I will blow your head off." He had the Open Top pointed directly at the deckhand's forehead.

The man did not react. Just stood solemnly with his hands to his sides.

Josiah had the man squarely in the sight of his Winchester, too. The only sounds he could hear above his beating heart were the crashing of the waves and the agitation and crunch of the sand against the bottom of Juan Carlos's shoes as he walked slowly to the man.

The old Mexican's intent was to search the deckhand's body for a hidden weapon of any kind.

There was hardly ever a need to command a man like Juan Carlos. His instincts were as sharp and alert as any solider's Josiah had ever known, no matter his age or implication of physical weakness.

Juan Carlos had ridden with the Rangers as long as any man Josiah knew of, in all of their various forms through their history, never serving in an open or equal capacity, but serving nonetheless. It was when his half brother, Captain Hiram Fikes, was still alive that Juan Carlos rode even more clearly next to the men who served the state of Texas in one capacity or another.

To say Juan Carlos was well trained is an understatement. He was a natural fighter, a ghostlike spy, a man comfortable with the knowledge that war never ends; it is ongoing no matter what it is called, from one battle to the next, raging through some years stronger than others, for the cause of new borders, liberty, freedom . . . or simple greed.

Juan Carlos stopped directly in front of the deckhand.

A sudden series of gunshots erupted in the distance. *Ping, ping, ping.* Not thunder. Not lightning. Just three shots, come and gone. Loud enough, close enough, though out of sight, to distract Juan Carlos for more than a long second.

But the long second of distraction was all the deckhand needed.

In one swift motion, he pulled out a hidden Bowie knife from inside the waist of his trousers and thrust it with lightning speed directly into Juan Carlos's chest.

CHAPTER 36

Juan Carlos grimaced, pushing away a look of surprise as the deckhand yanked the knife out of his chest.

Josiah's eyes blurred. The world went quiet for a breath. His finger trembled against the warm metal trigger, but compression came naturally, a reflex out of shock and other emotions that would not be revealed until later — if ever. He was reacting now without concern for what was right or wrong. Survival mattered, nothing else. If there were any implications to his actions, or mistakes to grieve over, then that would have to come later. All that mattered now was pulling the trigger — and making sure the deckhand was deader than dead, unable to hurt anyone ever again.

A crack came from behind Josiah. An expected snap of thunder, followed by another gunshot, and then another and another.

As Juan Carlos fell to the ground, knees

first, the first bullet tore into the deckhand's face. It was hard to tell which reached him first, Josiah's or Scrap's shot. It didn't matter. The right half of the man's face exploded instantly. There was no reading his expression, no need to. Surely, he had expected to meet his death. Escaping was out of the question, out of the realm of possibility. Whether he was surprised or not would never be known. It was a desperate move, stabbing Juan Carlos. There was no way out, no way to survive. That wasn't the plan. It couldn't have been.

Josiah couldn't resist his rage as he saw Juan Carlos fall facedown into the sand — he fanned the Peacemaker, cocking it with his palm as quick as he could pull the trigger, never missing his target, never looking away from the pain and destruction he was inflicting. It was an action he rarely allowed himself to perform. Fanning was showy, immature, not worthy of a Ranger or a man of shooting stature. But righteousness and maturity were lost in the moment. He could not comprehend what he was seeing. Juan Carlos had been shot before and survived, but it had weakened him, hobbled him in a noticeable way. Being stabbed with such precision would, most likely, be fatal.

Scrap kept shooting, too, emptying every

cartridge the Spencer could hold, blasting away at the deckhand. His head first. Then his chest. Then his gut. There wasn't a bit of exposed skin left on the man that wasn't covered in blood. His clothes, too, were soaked red. He looked like a papist cardinal, minus the grace, following an avenue into heaven — if such a place existed.

The spray of blood looked like someone was throwing paint into the ocean. The constant shots were raining sinew, muscle, and shattered bone directly into the water.

A school of starving bait fish relished their good fortune and exposed themselves, some of them squiggling along the shore, driving themselves into a frenzy, nearly pushing out of the water, to gobble at the bounty as it fell from the sky.

The deckhand collapsed in a bloody mess about five feet back from Juan Carlos. The knife slid out of his hand and lodged directly into the ground, the hilt sticking up like Excalibur, waiting to be discovered by its true owner. He was dead before he hit the ground, before he knew what hit him or had the chance to recant, change his mind, and give himself over as a prisoner to the Texas Rangers.

The air smelled of revenge and decay, riled by a rising wind, and an out-of-control steamer that was being pushed and pulled by the current.

Smoke vanished, and the reports of the Rangers' gunshots echoed away, riding the wind like a bad omen that had come true.

The boat groaned and creaked, offering notice to Josiah that it still existed, that there very well might be more armed men stowed away, waiting for a moment of surprise of their own, attempting to save themselves and redeem anything they could out of the mission set on them by Juan Cortina.

Josiah blinked and saw that Juan Carlos was not moving. There was no desperate heave of his chest, no sound of life or motion at all. He lay on the beach, facedown in the sand, blood draining out of him, surrounding him in a pool, leaving his body limp, like a sinking island in an unknown sea.

A rushing noise caused Josiah to look away, to glance over his shoulder and see that Scrap was heading in his direction, leaving his post on the ridge. The boy still held the Spencer, ready to shoot at anything that moved.

Scrap's presence gave Josiah a moment of confidence, a moment of clarity. He was no doctor, but he had battlefield skills. If Juan Carlos could be saved, if he was not dead already, then it would come from Josiah's hands — but first, he had to make sure that he himself would survive the moment to help.

To save Juan Carlos, he had to save himself.

Josiah jumped down off Clipper and scanned the ground quickly. It didn't take long for him to find what he was looking for: several small, fist-sized rocks. He grabbed up a couple, realizing that every second counted, his attention flitting to the deck of the steamer every few seconds, looking for any sign of movement or unnatural shadow.

Scrap and Missy approached quickly.

The boy stopped a few yards from Josiah, jumped off his horse, and ran straight for Juan Carlos. "Wolfe, what the hell are you doing?" he shouted, as he leaned down to the Mexican, checking for a pulse.

Josiah ignored Scrap. He hurried back to Clipper and tore open his saddlebag. The horse stood still, ignoring the steamer and anything that was going on around it.

It only took a second for Josiah to find what he was looking for. A small bottle with coal oil in it and several matches bound together with a small bit of twine.

"He's still alive, Wolfe," Scrap yelled out.

"Try and stop the bleeding," Josiah answered back.

"Don't know if I can. What the hell are you *doing*?"

"Never you mind. Just tend to Juan Carlos the best you can and keep an eye on that steamer. I don't believe a word that man said. Could be more men on it, just waiting their turn at us."

Scrap nodded, and Josiah turned back to the task at hand.

What he had planned was a long shot, but it was all he could think to do, other than sending Scrap alone onto the steamer to face whatever might wait there. He wasn't doing that. He'd already lost Juan Carlos, seen him injured at the very least, killed at the very worst, with the decisions he'd already made.

Seconds seemed like hours as Josiah rummaged through his saddlebag. Finally, he found what he was looking for — three soiled bandanas. He quickly wrapped one around a rock, knotted it, doused it with coal oil, lit it on fire, and flung it as hard as he could onto the deck of the steamer.

He did the same thing with the other two rags, only he was more cautious with his toss. The first one shattered through what remained of the glass in the captain's tower, and the other landed next to the starboard-side smokestack.

The air smelled of coal oil and smoke, and all Josiah could do was hope that the fire would catch, ending any speculation at all whether there were still any men left on board the boat.

CHAPTER 37

Scrap had rolled Juan Carlos onto his back and was putting pressure on the knife wound. The flow of blood looked to have slowed, but there was a healthy red puddle growing underneath the old Mexican. Scrap's hands were soaked with blood, but he didn't seem to notice or care. The look on his face was grim, ashen. He seemed genuinely concerned about Juan Carlos even though they'd had their fair share of differences in the past, and Scrap wasn't too fond of any Mexican — especially, at times, Juan Carlos.

Juan Carlos was staring straight up at the cloudless sky. He turned and focused his eyes on Josiah as he leaned down next to him. "I was foolish, señor. I could feel it in my bones not to trust him, that he was a threat to our safety. Now I have paid the price of my arrogance and ignorance. I thought we had won the day."

"Let me have a look," Josiah said. He made eye contact with Scrap. The boy's face remained expressionless as he tried to shake his head no as subtly as he could.

"No, there will be no need," Juan Carlos choked to say. "The wound is deep, and I have not fully recovered from the gunshot I took on our adventure to Durango. We tried to stop Cortina then as now. The results are the same. I have learned my lesson."

"We have to get some help for you," Josiah demanded. "I'm not going to just stand here and do nothing."

"There is no time, señor." The words were almost a whisper and came with a gasp at the end. "Moving me would be too painful. I can feel the weakness rising up from deep inside. If I move, I will only bleed more. You have seen this before, in the time of the war. You know what I say is the truth."

"You will die here." Josiah sighed, resigned to the surety of what his eyes saw. Battlefield memories flittered in the periphery of his mind like bats swarming in the graying of night.

"*Sí,* death is just waiting its turn at victory. I do not fear it. I have tricked it many times, but just as I felt the man's lie, I feel the truth of my impending death now. It will wait for me no longer. I am out of luck and favor."

Josiah exhaled deeply and lowered his head. "I'm sorry."

"There is nothing to be sorry about. I have had a long, happy life. What more can a man ask?"

"You do not deserve this. I could have prevented this."

"I believe in very few things, señor, but I believe in fate. I have never been one to acknowledge a God or the presence of another life after this one. The mission bells did not draw me in but sent me running from their condemnation and judgment. Perhaps, I should have listened to the *padres* when I was young, but I was stubborn as a *buey*. Like you, unmoving like an ox. But it would have made this time easier, I think, believing in something other than the darkness that surely awaits me."

Josiah looked away. "I have no words of comfort for you."

Scrap cleared his throat but offered nothing.

"I know," Juan Carlos said.

"You deserve better." Josiah couldn't let go of the idea that the entire incident was his fault.

"Deserve? How many men have lived the life I have and how many have lived only half the time? I am *mucha suerte*. Very lucky, Señor Josiah, to have lived the life I have lived." Juan Carlos coughed painfully and turned his head so that he was looking away from Josiah, down the beach, into the distance. "When I was young, all I wanted to be was a fisherman. A simple fisherman like my *tío,* my uncle. He wasn't really my uncle, just a man that my mother kept in her house. He was a good man. I called him Luca, and longed for him to be my real *papá,* but he was not, could not be. My father was Anglo, and it was difficult for him to see me, so he did not ever come around. I only knew his eyes. The ones that looked back at me in the mirror, and my mother's that bore nothing but bitterness at her choice whenever she looked at me on sad days. It was Luca who taught me how to catch my bait with a net, like I showed you. He taught me the most important things that I would ever need to know. Like when to run, when to stand your ground, and when the end is the end — like now."

"I remember fishing with you," Josiah said. He tried to push away all of the rising emotion he could and looked up at the steamer.

One of the flaming rocks had taken seed. Fire was starting to climb up the outside of the smokestack. He could smell the smoke, and it made him happy. Revenge always tasted like acid in reality. Sweetness was just a child's game.

The memory of standing in the ocean, fishing with Juan Carlos, was sharp as the knife that had been thrust into the old man's chest. It was a good memory, a fine, perfect day, when all Josiah had hoped for was going home to Austin with Juan Carlos's blessing and permission to court Pearl. Now all that he had gained that day was nearly gone, nothing more than a dream that had slipped woefully into a nightmare.

"It is fitting," Juan Carlos said, "that I die on the edge of the sea. Luca would see the irony in it. I feel the comfort of it."

Josiah was still staring at the growing fire. Black smoke was spiraling out of the captain's tower, too. It wouldn't be long before the entire steamer was ablaze. "Keep an eye out," he said to Scrap. "If there are any men left on the boat, the fire will flush them like the rats they are."

"Dead rats," Scrap said. His Spencer rifle was only a few inches from his reach. He still had his hand on Juan Carlos's chest, putting pressure on the wound, but there was no mistaking his readiness. "They ain't gonna be nothin' but dead rats."

"Those were fine days," Juan Carlos said. "But my best days were spent on a horse, riding next to my *hermano.*"

Josiah knew *hermano* meant brother. Juan Carlos had used the word several times in the past when he spoke of the dead captain. "Yes, those were good days, all of us together with Captain Fikes. I still have a hard time believing that he will not ride up and save the day one last time. I look for him out of the corner of my eye when we are riding, but all I see are shadows."

"Those days are gone, lost in the river of time," Juan Carlos said.

Josiah nodded. The battle in the distance had fallen silent. There had not been a gunshot in several minutes, not since before the deckhand stabbed Juan Carlos. He wondered if the fighting was over. "At least we have stopped Cortina."

"Only on this day. He will scurry into the light again. Now he hides like the *cucaracha* that he really is." Juan Carlos licked his lips and drew in a deep breath. His chest rattled louder than McNelly's.

"I will hunt Cortina down if it is the last thing I do, and make him pay for what he has done."

"Be careful of such oaths made in anger, señor. Cortina is more powerful than you

315

think. He has many arms and many eyes. You are already his enemy. Your rage makes you weak, not strong. Look at me, lying here in my blood, twice wounded by my desire to stop him."

"You have served proudly."

"Not as proudly as you think."

The words drifted off on the wind and mixed with the smoke. A flame jumped the length of the smokestack, flaring bright orange as the flames spread across the roof of the tower. It was like the sun had crashed to earth.

A wave of heat rushed over Josiah and Juan Carlos, gobbling at all the oxygen it could consume. An eruption of showering sparks followed. One hit Josiah's neck, and it was like being stung by a giant, angry wasp. He slapped it away, knowing there would be more.

"We need to move you," Josiah said.

Juan Carlos shook his head no, then stared at Josiah, his chest heavy, clanging with death, and filling with fluid. "I will ride at the side of *el capitán* once again. Tell Pearl not to be *triste.*"

Josiah didn't know what the word meant, but he could feel its intent: pure, unadulterated sadness. Air caught in his own throat as he fought to breathe. His effort to push away any emotion was failing. His heart was racing. His mind screamed from deep inside him that there was something he should be doing to try and save his friend. But there was nothing he could do, and he knew it. A tear welled up in his eye, then slipped from the rim and trailed down his cheek. He sobbed then, like a boy. A flood of rage, uncertainty, and grief released like a pent-up dam, disabled with fissures and scars of time, finally weak enough to just . . . give.

The world had vanished. Every image was blurred. Every memory of death and loss, close to the surface. Lily slipping away in his arms, broken, but still harboring life in her swollen belly. Lowering his father's coffin into the grave. The aftermath of Chickamauga. Smoke rising. The air filled with the smell of blood and defeat. The ground hallowed, to be forever haunted by innocent men, just following orders to serve a cause. Just like Juan Carlos.

When Josiah could finally get ahold of himself, he cleared his tears away and watched as the old Mexican arched his back, smiled, and took his last breath with as much confidence and bravery as he could muster.

Chapter 38

Captain McNelly and the rest of the company appeared on the horizon, rushing toward them with dedication, speed, and ferocity. They were little more than silhouettes, but hard to mistake. Josiah could identify McNelly, and his horse, a mile away.

The steamer was fully ablaze, from bow to stern, billowing black, angry smoke into the perfect cloudless sky. No other men had jumped to safety; no rats fled the heat and destruction like Josiah had thought might happen. It looked like the deckhand had been telling the truth. This battle was over. He had been the last man standing — and he'd made the most of it by killing Juan Carlos.

Josiah and Scrap had moved Juan Carlos's body up into the grass and covered him from head to toe with a blanket. They were far enough away from the burning steamer but could still feel the heat from the fire, have their noses filled with flying ash, and be assaulted by the occasional, wayward spark. But they weren't leaving. Not yet.

They had left the deckhand where he lay; at the border of the sand and water. If his clothes were not wet and blood-soaked, Josiah was certain that the sparks would have already found a home in them and caught fire. It would have been a fitting end for the man. As it was, Josiah was considering the possibility of tossing the man's body onto the blazing steamer. But exerting any undue effort to bury the man, or do away with his body, churned his stomach.

A few seagulls landed downwind of the steamer, on the open beach. Three of them eyed the dead man's body, bobbing their heads, looking for a way to get close enough for a peck of fresh flesh. Other seabirds circled overhead, looking for the same thing. Unfortunately, the fire was too hot and too close to the deckhand's body for any of them to get to it.

After noticing the hungry birds, Josiah reconsidered the thought about leaving the deckhand where he lay. It might be more suitable to let the scavengers have at him, tear him apart bit by bloody bit. That thought made him feel better. He left it at that, though, and looked away from the boat and the man.

Josiah stared to the ground and tried to moderate his breathing. His face was covered with blood, sweat, dirt, and tearstains. Wiping away the consequences of the battle hadn't occurred to him. Nor did he care if the company of Rangers saw the remnants of emotion on his skin. He didn't care about much of anything at the moment. He was numb.

Scrap shuffled his feet, nervously waiting for McNelly to arrive. He stirred up a tiny cloud of flies.

They swarmed to Josiah's face, and he batted them away, glaring at Scrap. "Can't you stand still for a single minute?"

"I itch now that I stopped movin'. You think this is over?"

Josiah nodded. "McNelly wouldn't be leading the company back if it weren't." His head throbbed, and just the sound of Scrap's voice irritated him. He wanted nothing more than to just leave, to walk away — alone. But he knew he had to wait on the captain to come to collect them . . . and Juan Carlos.

There had been no consideration, or discussion, about what to do with Juan Carlos's body. Leaving it to the birds was out of the question. Burning it right away wasn't an option. Juan Carlos deserved more. There'd be a proper burial, in one place or another, when the time came. But that decision — when, where, and how — would be left to Captain McNelly. Josiah was sure of that.

"I wonder if they herded the beeves? Might be steak for dinner. You know one or two of them got shot during this here fight. I sure could go for some good meat instead of beans, couldn't you, Wolfe? I mean, I ain't complainin', but I'm hungry now that this is over with. I could eat a whole cow on my own. Don't you get hungry after a fight, Wolfe?"

The thought of food, of eating, of a return to normal life, seemed disrespectful to Josiah. He turned to Scrap, prepared to tell him to shut up. *Just please shut up.* But the words wouldn't come out. His mouth went dry, and for some reason, all of the pain that had been restricted because of the attention and adrenaline of the battle, washed over him in a wave. Not only was he numb, but now he felt weak. His knees trembled, and for a brief second, he thought he was going to fall face-first to the ground.

"You all right, Wolfe? You look pale as a ghost," Scrap said. He stopped talking, stopped fidgeting for a brief second, releasing his own nervousness from the battle, for a moment.

"I'm fine."

"You oughta sit down."

"I'm fine."

"Have it your way then."

"I'm just trying to steady myself." Josiah watched McNelly and the company ride toward them. They were about thirty yards down the beach. It was the whole lot of them. From what he could tell, it didn't look like they'd lost a single man.

Robinson was in place as second in command, and all the familiar faces, Tom Darkson and the other fellas, all looked to be right where they were supposed to be. Of course, Josiah wasn't about to go on counting. Some men had surely been left behind to tend to the herd of cattle, and some of the men in the line were most likely prisoners, certain to join the others that had been captured on the scouting trips.

It would be fine news to hear, or see, that Cortina had been shackled, captured alive and put on the path to justice. It would have been even better news if the man were dead, his dying moment slow and painful. Josiah would hope for that. The dangle of a slack rope. He hoped the man suffered just like

Juan Carlos had, knowing full well that he was going to die.

He didn't see a heavy guard on any of the Mexicans as the company drew closer, so that thought was most likely a false hope. But Cortina's death was still a hope. The only thing better would be if he was the one to deliver the blow to Cortina. At the moment, he wanted nothing more than to be the one to kill Juan Cortina and end his reign of terror and thievery.

"You sure you're all right, Wolfe?" Scrap asked. "I ain't never seen you like this."

Josiah glared at him, then looked up as McNelly approached, ten yards away. They made eye contact, and Josiah looked away. "I'm fine."

"Sure you are."

"Leave it alone, Scrap."

Scrap exhaled, pushed all of the air out of his chest, then bit his lip. "You know," he said, "none of this would be happening if you would have let me shoot that there man when I wanted to."

"What'd you say?"

"I'm just sayin' Juan Carlos would still be alive if you woulda let me do what I saw fit to, when we had the time."

Scrap acted like he was going to continue on, his nervousness and arrogance controlling his tongue, but he was stopped flat by Josiah.

The rage and pain Josiah felt could no longer be contained. It exploded up from the tips of his toes and careened completely out of control, bypassing his brain and launching his hardened fist fully from his heart. He reared back and punched Scrap in the jaw as hard as he could, sending the surprised boy spiraling backward, tripping and falling to the ground with a painful scream.

Chapter 39

Scrap bounded up from the ground just as McNelly brought the company to a halt. Scrap's eyes were wild with rage; he looked like a rangy dog snarling after being kicked by its owner. Blood ran out of the corner of his mouth. His lip was busted, and the possibility that he had bit his tongue was almost certain. He was tense as a rope stretched tight between two trees, and his fists were balled tightly, ready for retribution. Seething with anger, he was nearly unleashed.

Thunder from the company and the roar of the consuming fire on the steamer were all Josiah could hear outside of his heartbeat. He couldn't think at the moment. All he wanted to do was keep hitting Scrap, keep hitting him until he shut up, until he stopped his condemnation and pontificating on things he didn't have a right to. But something deep inside Josiah pulled him back, made him stop and try to regain his senses.

He knew if he stepped one foot forward, if he actually had a go at Scrap again, he'd most likely kill the boy. Kill him right there and then, right in front of McNelly and the other Rangers.

It wasn't the consequences of his own actions that concerned Josiah, that had stopped him. It was the right and wrong of killing. The day had been full of it. Enough was enough. Scrap didn't deserve to die. He just needed to learn a lesson. Killing for spite was not something Josiah wanted to live with. He was no outlaw and didn't intend to be anytime soon.

"What the hell are you doin', Wolfe?" Scrap scrambled toward Josiah, not paying any attention to the fire or the location of the captain and the company.

Josiah focused all his energy on breathing deep breaths, on stepping back. He didn't want to hurt Scrap any more than he already had, but he would defend himself if he had to.

Guilt and regret would possibly come later for punching the boy, but now all Josiah was concerned about was restraint.

He knew himself well enough to know what he was capable of, how far to go, when he was about to snap and not care about right or wrong. The punch was as close as he'd come to that line in a long time. The best thing to do was let go of it, realize that Scrap hadn't meant what he said. Emotions were raw and tender after everything that had happened.

Josiah couldn't even look at the lump in the grass covered by the blanket. He couldn't stomach the thought that Juan Carlos was really dead.

"That will be enough, Elliot!" It was McNelly's voice, booming over the ruckus and fire. He rode straight between Josiah and Scrap and came to a sudden, authoritative stop. "We do not fight with each other. We save that for the enemy!"

Scrap stopped his rush and stared at McNelly like he was God come down from the heavens, issuing a commandment. "He started it," Scrap said, pointing at Josiah with a trembling finger.

Josiah lowered his head and didn't offer to defend himself.

McNelly climbed down off his horse and came to a stop face-to-face with Josiah.

The captain had taken a nick over his eye. The blood had already congealed, and a dried crimson rivulet cut through the grime of battle. "You need to tell me what's going on here, Wolfe. What has happened that has caused you and Ranger Elliot to come to fisticuffs?"

Josiah sucked in a breath of ashy air and said nothing. He couldn't bring himself to speak of Juan Carlos's death.

"Well, come on, man," McNelly demanded. "Cat got your tongue, or is it shame that's stuck in your throat?"

"Neither, sir," Josiah finally said.

The company circled around Josiah, McNelly, and Scrap, with the exception of Robinson. He rode past them all, splashed along the edge of the water, and circled around the dead deckhand. He said nothing, just looked up at the burning steamer and rode back into the company, dodging a spray of sparks as a large wave rocked the boat, tilting it toward the beach. Robinson stopped and took the reins of McNelly's horse into his thick hands. He looked bloodied and battle-weary, too.

"I'm in no mood for shenanigans, Sergeant Wolfe. The day has been long, and Cortina still eludes us," McNelly said.

The emphasis of his rank caused a shiver to run up and down Josiah's spine. With the lack of uniforms and precise military demands, it was easy to forget that he had duties to fulfill. Restraint was even more important to him in that moment. "You have captured the herd, though, stopped this operation?"

"That was not the prize."

"I'm sorry, sir." Josiah broke eye contact with the captain and watched Robinson in the periphery as he dismounted his horse, handing off the reins to Tom Darkson, then circled Juan Carlos's body. "Juan Carlos was killed. We lost Pip Howerson, too. I think the battle set me and Elliot on edge. Nothing was meant by it. Just nerves that got the best of us."

"Doesn't look that way to me," McNelly said, perusing Scrap from head to toe. He exhaled deeply. "I'll want a full account of this incident once we're back at camp. I'm very disturbed by your actions, Wolfe."

"I understand, sir."

"There are no others left to fight then? All of the men on the boat are dead?" McNelly asked with a cock of his head toward the steamer.

"There's been no jumpers since I started the fire. The deckhand seems to have been the last man standing."

"Well, at least the boat is destroyed. That doesn't make up for a life, but it makes up for something." McNelly turned, grabbed his horse's reins from Darkson, who was standing stoically, and started to hoist his boot into the stirrup, but stopped and returned his attention to Josiah. "Bring the bodies back to camp with you. We'll need to see to a proper burial before the critters come along and think they've stumbled upon a feast."

"Yes, sir." There was no enthusiasm in Josiah's voice, and it was noted by the sharp look that crossed McNelly's face.

The captain climbed up on his horse and looked down at Scrap. "You're riding with us, Elliot. I suggest you find your mount and join us. Doesn't look like being left behind is in your best interest."

Scrap didn't object, just tossed a hateful glare at Josiah, rubbed his check, then stalked off, looking for Missy.

CHAPTER 40

The steamer broke in two unceremoniously, weakened by the fire that had completely consumed it as it was tossed to and fro on the rocks just beyond the shore. There was a great cracking sound, like an egg dropped to the ground, that echoed across the beach then vanished out to sea, like chunks of the boat itself. The sky was filled with black smoke, and now that the company had moved on, the only sounds surrounding Josiah, beyond the crackling of the remaining fire, were the calls of seabirds scouring the ground for any opportunity that showed itself.

Juan Carlos's tired old horse had made its way off into the grass, grazing alongside Clipper like it didn't have a care in the world, like it had found a new friend, instead of losing a master. Expecting realization of another's death from a horse was silly, but oddly, Josiah *did* expect some kind of show of sorrow from the horse. He felt it himself.

It was hard telling how long Juan Carlos had been in ownership of the shaggy horse. Josiah had never seen it before. The old Mexican had showed no loyalty to any animal for as long as Josiah had known him. Juan Carlos was not a mean horse owner, he didn't flog his ride like Josiah had seen a lot of men do, but he wasn't a soft or caring owner, either. So it may have been for a very good reason that the horse showed no emotion. That or it was plain-out impossible for a horse to realize that its owner had been killed.

Feeling a little safer now that he knew the company was returning to camp, Josiah allowed himself to relax just a little bit. He was still alert, his hands ready to pull his gun if the need arose, but now only a little more than he normally was when he was out alone. McNelly would have a ring of men at watch, too, all on edge, expecting retaliation from Cortina and his men. The battle was over, but not the war — not if Cortina lived on. And he did, according to the captain. So the end to this fight was not imminent. South Texas would still have to live with the real threat of violence and theft. Even more so now. Cortina wouldn't just whimper away, lick his wounds, and change his ways. The loss to McNelly would only fuel Cortina's rage, Josiah was certain of that.

The first thing Josiah did was make his way to Clipper. He dug out the canteen from his saddlebag and gulped down a solid drink of water. Then he poured some of the warm water into his hand and wiped it across his face, being gentle on the scatter-shot wounds. The water spread the dirt, blood, and his sweat, and it stung under the scabs of the wound, but Josiah persisted. He feared more infection, especially in his face, now that he had time to think of such a thing. Surviving the battle was never certain, especially in his condition.

His face was as clean as it could be for the moment. Josiah gathered up Clipper and the black horse and made his way to the blanket that covered Juan Carlos's body. He ignored the gunshot in his shoulder. He could feel that it was wet, was seeping, that it had most likely been torn apart. Oddly, it didn't hurt. Just felt tender and raw. Once he was back in camp, he'd have it looked at. One of the boys they rode with, Verlyn Tinker, the one they all called Doc, had a way of healing things even though he wasn't a schooled doctor.

Josiah stood over Juan Carlos's covered body for a long time, minutes that seemed to stop, and reflected back on his time with the man. He felt an overwhelming sorrow growing inside of him. He didn't need Scrap to blame him for Juan Carlos's death. He was already blaming himself. And something told him that he always would, that he would forever remember the deckhand driving the knife into Juan Carlos's chest, and the surprised look on the old Mexican's face. It was a dark memory that would rest alongside others that ended in death. This one, the most recent, seemed to hurt more than others had, even Lily's, and he wasn't entirely sure why.

He had properly met Juan Carlos in San Antonio on his first mission with the Frontier Battalion when Captain Fikes, Juan Carlos's half brother, was still alive and had called on him to help bring Charlie Langdon, an outlaw that Josiah had a history with, to justice. Charlie was in a jail in San Antonio, and his gang was desperate to break him out. One of the outlaws tracked Josiah down to the Menger Hotel, and it was his good fortune that Captain Fikes had put Juan Carlos in the hotel to watch out for such an attack.

Juan Carlos saved Josiah's life, and from

that moment on, the two had shared a bond that seemed unbreakable. But there were limits to their friendship. Partly because Juan Carlos was seen entirely as a Mexican, not half-Anglo like Josiah knew him to be, and partly because of Josiah's lack of understanding of the Spanish language and Mexican customs.

It hadn't been that long ago, after Juan Carlos was wounded and sought refuge in the fishing village, that their relationship had thoroughly been tested.

Josiah had made a mistake that ended up costing the life of the woman Juan Carlos had long loved, Maria Villareal. The episode still haunted Josiah, and now it felt like it had happened again, that he had caused the loss of another life by a choice he had made — or not made.

Josiah knew Juan Carlos would argue with him, that what had happened was just how their lives had turned out. Fate had interceded. But there was no way he could not feel responsible, like a failure, like an unreliable sergeant with too little knowledge to lead — making him dangerous, not only to himself but to the men he was responsible for.

Blood had soaked through the blanket that covered Juan Carlos, making the death even more real, more certain.

Josiah hesitated before he pulled the blanket off, then took a deep breath and went ahead with the task. He knew he had to follow McNelly's orders and return Juan Carlos's body to the camp, but he was in no hurry. It seemed more like a punishment than a duty.

Juan Carlos lay on his back, faceup, his eyes closed like he was sleeping. There was no pain on his face. He looked serenely peaceful. The only evidence of trauma was the wound in his chest. The blood had started to dry. Other than that, and the grime of the battle, Juan Carlos hardly looked any different than he ever did.

It was, however, the touch to Juan Carlos's skin that confirmed to Josiah that death had really came and taken his friend. He was cold and starting to get stiff.

Josiah rolled Juan Carlos in the blanket, fighting off a regiment of sand flies the whole time. In return, they attacked any visible skin on Josiah they could. He felt nothing. Their bites were common now. Common, and he was numb. He didn't go to combat with them. He knew he would lose.

With as much ease as he could, Josiah lifted Juan Carlos's lifeless body with the intent of securing it over the back of the shaggy black horse.

The horse grunted and groaned, seemed immediately uncomfortable, and tried to skitter away. It was a reaction that Josiah hadn't counted on, but had hoped for from the beginning, some sign of recognition — and he nearly dropped the body before finally getting it settled in place.

Maybe the horse knew something was wrong after all. Maybe there was a smell to death that humans couldn't detect — or a lack of smell, vanished with the last breath of the man. Or maybe the horse just knew what death was, after all.

Clipper eased up alongside the horse and nudged it with his nose. It was as much a show of emotion as any man could expect from two beasts void of voices or sense.

Josiah gently and respectfully tied Juan Carlos's body down over the saddle, then tied the reins of the horse to his own saddle.

He stared out to the sea for a long moment afterward and watched the waves wash in and out. He wished he had a way to take the body out into the water and dump it there for burial. Juan Carlos would have liked that. He loved the ocean. But that was not to be. There was no boat to afford such a journey. The only one in sight was now in two pieces, burning from end to end. The flames had started to die as the fire ran out of fresh, dry wood, and it wouldn't be long before there was nothing left but a broken skeleton, lying wrecked on the beach for wanderers-by, who would speculate what had happened and why.

If there had been any men onboard the steamer after the deckhand showed himself, they were definitely dead. There was no way any man could have survived the fire.

As for the deckhand, Josiah decided to just leave him where he was, riddled with bullets, the waves washing his blood out to sea. Josiah hoped the birds would come along and peck his eyes out. The only thing that would have been better was if the deckhand had still been alive and could feel the pain and terror of the attack. But there was no hoping for that. The deckhand was as dead as Juan Carlos.

Then, for a brief moment, Josiah wished he was a religious man, a believer in God and all things from that realm. That way he could wish the deckhand a quick journey to hell. But that moment passed just as quickly as it came. Josiah had lost any faith he might have ever had on the battlefield, seeing the brutality of man and no intervention from an unseen force to stop it. And at the bedside of his dying daughters and his dying wife. If there was a God, that would have been the time for Him to show Himself. That hadn't happened, and as Josiah led the shaggy black horse away from the beach, he was certain nothing like it ever would.

The only fires of hell were the ones he was walking away from. The thought, and something else, stopped Josiah; a slight movement out of the corner of his eye caused him to bring Juan Carlos's horse to a sudden halt.

A lone rider sat up on the farthest hill, looking down at Josiah. Any man that was a decent shot could have taken him down in two breaths. Josiah reached for his own gun and eased behind the shaggy horse, set on using it for cover.

The rider could've been Juan Cortina, come to survey what was left of his plan, or a scout, sent to report back on the defeat. It could've even been another Ranger, left behind to cover Josiah's return to camp, but he doubted it. McNelly hadn't said a word of such a thing. The battle was over, at least for the Rangers. That had been certain when the captain headed back to the camp.

Josiah settled himself behind the horse and brought the unknown rider into his sights. He felt no fear, just the long-held desire that the rider be Cortina. He wanted to face the man and put an end the Mexican's raids and tyranny. A bad taste washed through his mouth; the mystery of the man's identity enraged him. He blinked, trying to get a better look, but when he cleared his vision, the rider was gone. He blinked again, making sure he was right, and he was. There was no sign of the rider at all — but that didn't mean the danger of another man's gun, or Juan Cortina, was gone, or satisfied with defeat. It meant the war continued.

CHAPTER 41

Before returning to camp, Josiah stopped and retrieved Pip Howerson's body, bundling and tying it in a blanket like he had Juan Carlos's, then loading it over Clipper's saddle. There was no other choice. He was going to have to walk back to camp.

It had been his hope to bury Pip along with his horse, and that still might be a possibility, but something told Josiah that it wouldn't happen. McNelly wouldn't want to waste the manpower, or energy, to dig a hole big enough and deep enough for both of them to fit in.

The mare was a damn good horse, and she deserved better than to be left behind. But that was the way it was after a battle. A month from now there would only be a skeleton left behind, and rumors on the wind that something bad had happened on the surrounding grounds. So maybe it was best to leave the horse behind and let nature be nature — but still, Josiah hesitated. It felt like he was committing a crime of some sort, leaving the horse to the vultures and other meat eaters. *Maybe,* he thought, *Pip would be offended.* But Pip was dead. Deader than dead. Just like Juan Carlos. It didn't matter what happened to the horse. But that didn't make it right — or make it feel right, just leaving it all behind, but he had to, and he knew it.

The heat of the day had not subsided, nor had the feeling that he was alone. A big orange dinner plate radiated in the sky and had started to slope down from its apex, easing slowly toward late afternoon. Dusk wasn't that far off, and darkness would follow then, washing the day behind it, too. Time would march on. As it was, the sun beamed brightly, and there continued to be no clouds to be seen. Only the wind off the ocean made walking back to camp tolerable, and it was tainted with the smell of smoke and destruction. Escaping this battle was going to be difficult.

Each step Josiah took was like walking in mud, even though the ground was dry. He was tired, sore, and sad from the turn of events of the day. It had been like that before for him after a long fight, sadness welling up under his skin — but somehow, this felt different. Like it was the end of something bigger.

But it wasn't the end of the fight; the sighting of the lone rider had reaffirmed that notion. Cortina was still alive, most likely planning another raid, or hatching another scheme to rustle and sell longhorns to the Cubans.

What Josiah was feeling wasn't about Cortina. It was about *his* life, about what was next. He wasn't sure he would fully recover from what he'd just experienced, not like he had in the past.

Josiah missed Lyle, missed the normalcy of everyday life — even in Austin, a city that still felt foreign to him. Still, even though it didn't feel like home to him, he would have given anything to crest the rise he was trudging up and see Austin spread out before him, instead of the Ranger camp.

He hungered for Ofelia's *menudo,* and as odd as it was, he longed for the smell of Pearl's toilet water . . . and her touch, even if she no longer desired his touch — or presence in her life.

The fight had taken a lot out of him. Losing Juan Carlos would be hard to swallow, but he knew he would have to deal with it somehow, put the man's death in perspective and accept blame or find redemption from the cause, one or the other. But what he was feeling was as much about the living as the dead.

Regret and guilt, the rawest of uncontrolled human emotions, always sneaked in after battle, after killing a man. Some men fought it off with heavy doses of whiskey, or in the arms of a welcoming whore. Neither appealed to Josiah. Like always, he would think his way through it, occupy himself with a puzzling exercise or some other task to take his mind off the immediate past. That was what had worked for him before.

He knew he shouldn't have lost his temper with Scrap, punched him as hard as he had — but the fact was he had, and he couldn't take it back. Whether Scrap would see that it was nothing more than a reaction to the day, to the fight, to the loss, was yet to be seen. It was hard to say if there was any forgiveness left in the boy's heart — or the desire in Josiah's to seek it. From what Josiah had seen, from what he knew about Scrap, he was left with his doubts. The boy's heart could be cold as a winter day in the Dakotas. Seeing your parents killed senselessly by the Comanche would do that to any man. It had angered Scrap, hurt him in a way that very few people would, or could, ever understand. That event stunted him, too. He'd stopped maturing, stopped feeling compassion for other folks. Josiah knew what he was dealing with. He and Scrap shared more in common than either one of them was willing to admit.

After a long, winding walk that seemed to pass more quickly than he had expected it to, Josiah led the two horses into camp solemnly, not having to say a word to the men on watch. They had obviously been told to expect him.

Josiah was happy to see the camp throbbing with life. It was a distraction from his troubled mind.

There was smoke in the air from freshly built fires, overwhelmed by the smell of cooking beef — Scrap's wish for a killed cow had come true. Someone was playing a fiddle at a fast, happy pace, and it echoed off the rocks that surrounded the camp, making it seem louder than it really was. Tents were aglow, and every face he saw had a smile on it — at least until they made eye contact with him and realized what cargo the two horses carried. It wasn't only the Mexicans who had paid a price that day. So had the Rangers. Most everyone scurried by Josiah, busy and eager to be as far away from the cost of war as possible.

Josiah kept his head down, his shame and

regret impermeable. The horses followed close behind, the reins lose in his hand.

He made his way slowly to Verlyn Tinker's tent, not in any hurry to part with the bodies.

Tinker was as close to a doctor as the camp had. There was no saving Pip or Juan Carlos, but Tinker also had the unfortunate job of preparing the dead for burial if such an event occurred, as well as looking after cuts and scrapes and such. Josiah wanted his shoulder looked at as well. He'd felt a tear in it earlier.

The flap to Tinker's tent was pegged open, and the inside was fully lit with several coal lamps burning brightly. Josiah tied the horses to a sprawling live oak just to the north of the tent's entrance.

Josiah made his way to the tent, his head down, each step still difficult. He stopped before entering, clearing his throat to garner Tinker's attention.

Verlyn Tinker was probably ten years older than Josiah, maybe fifteen, making him nearly fifty years old. He was a tall man with stooped shoulders and a narrow face. Put a beard and stovepipe on the man and he would have looked a lot like Abe Lincoln. He was dressed simply in black trousers and a white linen shirt that was dotted with blotches of blood — just like his hands.

Tinker stood over a shirtless young Ranger that on second look turned out to be Tom Darkson, blotting a wound just above his ribs dry.

"Ouch, Doc, damn it, that's stingin' the beejesus out of me," Darkson said. It looked like he'd gotten grazed by a bullet. The wound was long and shallow. Darkson was little more than a boy, his face fresh, his upper lip dotted with peach fuzz. He was younger than Scrap, and Josiah was almost certain that the battle with the rustlers had been one of his first engagements.

Tinker noticed Josiah and cocked his head, inviting him into the tent. "Don't be a girl, Tom. You're lucky you're not hurt more than you are. Feels like you have a cracked rib or two as well." He had a Yankee accent. Not a Massachusetts one, but from somewhere east. It was hard to tell from where, exactly — but easy to tell that the man wasn't Texan, born and bred.

"Ain't gonna hurt when I ride, is it?" Darkson asked. "That shot knocked me clean off my mount. I need to get back up on it, you know."

"Have a seat, Wolfe," Tinker said, pointing to the chair by the door. "I'll be with you in a minute."

Josiah nodded, but stayed standing. The tent was warm, and a slight breeze snaked in through the open flap and out the back, where another flap was untied, loosely, waving about softly. The tap of the canvas sounded like a distant drumbeat.

The inside of the tent was tidy and well organized. Along with the two chairs, there was a table that Josiah supposed was for surgery, and a cupboard full of medicines and salves. Several unlit hurricane lamps sat at the base of the table, offering the opportunity for more light if the need called for it. A private quarters was draped off with a green army blanket, pocked with moth holes, that hid Tinker's cot and personal belongings. All of the equipment had been transported by a buckboard.

The camp had been outfitted for the long haul and was more a base than just a camp, since they were so far from everything they might need. The investment to put an end to Juan Cortina was a huge one.

Josiah could smell the whiskey that Tinker was using to clean Tom Darkson's wound, and there were other smells inside the tent, too. Mostly unpleasant, sterile, or like something had crawled into the corner and died. Luckily the breeze kept fresh air circulating.

Tinker turned his attention back to his

patient. "I think it'll hurt you to piss for the next month or so. Riding a horse will not be pleasurable."

"Damn it."

"It could be worse," Tinker said. "The fall most likely busted a rib or two. I'll wrap you up. That'll help a little bit."

"Will whiskey take away the pain?"

"Depends on how much you drink."

Josiah stood stiffly, staying out of the conversation. He had his own pain and wounds to consider. He'd busted a rib before, too, so he knew Tom Darkson was in for more than Tinker was telling him.

"As much as I can, Doc, as much as I can," Darkson said, wincing as Tinker wrapped a strip of cloth around his torso.

Tinker smiled a warm smile and focused on the task at hand. He had a gentle, fatherly way about him that immediately put most people at ease. There wasn't a man in camp that would say a bad thing against the man. Not that Josiah had ever heard. And he had no reason to say anything bad, either. He hardly knew Tinker, hadn't had need for his services on this trip — until now.

Darkson grimaced and complained again as Tinker continued wrapping his ribs tighter and tighter.

Josiah felt uncomfortable, didn't want to see another man's pain. "I'm going to step outside," he said.

Tinker looked up. "Suit yourself. But don't go far. I got a message from Captain McNelly for you."

CHAPTER 42

The shade from the live oak that stood over the tent made it look like evening instead of late afternoon. Light dappled the ground through the thick, broad leaves, dotting everything in sight with shadows and grayness. Wood smoke filled the air, overtaking the smell of meat cooking over the flames; campfires were being started for the coming night, warming up a few of the tubs that had been brought along for baths.

Fiddle music floated in the air, and someone up to the north of where Josiah stood, near where he and Scrap had camped, laughed heartily. Another hoot and holler followed and echoed through the shallow canyon the camp had been set in, but Josiah ignored it. He wondered why McNelly would leave a message for him with Doc Tinker. The substance of the message mildly concerned him, but instead of celebrating his own safe return, or worrying about his fate with McNelly, all Josiah could think of was burying Juan Carlos.

It would be an odd world without the Mexican. Juan Carlos was like the shadows that danced across the top of Josiah's boots. One minute he was there, and the next, he was gone, only to appear months later, unexpected, but just at the right time, when Josiah needed him the most. He never knew why that was.

Even now, Josiah expected to see Juan Carlos ease up the trail, his death only a ruse, not really true, but some greater strategy to get closer to Cortina. But Josiah knew he was deluding himself. Juan Carlos was dead. He would never show up again, not when Josiah was safe in Ranger camp, and not down the road, when circumstances were the most dire.

Tom Darkson walked out of the tent stiffly, unpegging the open flap, his ribs bound tight, forcing him to stand straight and walk as easily as possible. The flap of the tent snapped back quickly into place, the breeze catching it just right. "You're next," Darkson said.

"Thanks."

"Doc says I ain't gonna be up to snuff for a few days, but I think he's wrong about that. He don't know nothin' about me. I heal like a lizard. Momma said I'd grow a finger back if ever one got cut off by mistake."

Josiah just shook his head. It sounded like something Scrap would say. Must be the folly of youth, believing that they would heal overnight. Maybe he had been that way himself. He didn't remember it. Didn't care to. His first battle had been bigger and bloodier than the one they'd all experienced today. Still, there was no comparing the times. They were different. So was the war.

"You'd do yourself a favor to pay heed to what Doc said to you. He's been through this a time or two. I've seen men stronger than you fall over and die from injuries that seemed far less than you've suffered, I'm sure," Josiah said.

Darkson stopped just past Josiah and ran his hand through his hair, like he was confused. His hair was a wiry black rat's nest, and his hat was nowhere to be seen. Probably left out on the battlefield.

Darkson's eyes were wide, and his face still dirty from the fight. "I was born too late to fight in the War Between the States, Sergeant Wolfe. I always feel like there's a story I'm missin' when I'm standin' in the room with two men or more that served. I'm not in the know. But after today, I feel like I understand a little more. I saw things today that I never thought I would. Blood and death ain't as easy to swallow when it's a man, even a Mexican, compared to a squirrel or another piece of meat. I can't tell you how many times I slit the throat of a deer, bled him out. But what I saw done today, well, I don't think Momma would be too proud."

Josiah wanted to tell the boy that there was no way he would ever understand what a survivor of the War Between the States had gone through, and that he should be glad of it, but he said nothing. He just stared at Tom Darkson and wondered if he'd killed his first man today, since he didn't come right out and say so. If that was why he was jittery.

The guilt and depression would come later. In the middle of the night, when the boy was alone. Or maybe in his sleep, when the dead man proceeded to turn a comforting dream into a nightmare — one that would never go away. Josiah still walked with the dead in his sleep, visited the bloody battlefields of his past. But they were dimmer, farther away, not so urgent and real.

Still, the nightmares were enough to wake him and make him feel like he was still there. His stomach always burned with regret for days after, and nothing would calm him. Some called the affliction Soldier's Heart, but Josiah never liked to put a name to such things. He just considered it a bad memory that came from a boy serving in a war that, in the end, had nothing to do with him.

"Did you see Elliot return to camp?" Josiah finally asked.

Darkson looked at him oddly, like he'd been expecting him to say something entirely different than he did. "Yeah, I saw him. He rode in with the captain. Why?"

"Just wanting to know he was here somewhere."

"Last I saw him, he was sportin' a good shiner and tippin' back a bottle of whiskey."

"Good to know, thanks." Josiah turned away and walked back inside the tent, leaving Tom Darkson to go wherever he was going next.

Verlyn Tinker opened up the cupboard, exposing a row of bottles and crockery that was previously hidden from sight. He grabbed a fresh bottle of whiskey and closed the cupboard. When he turned back to face Josiah, there was a tiredness in Tinker's eyes that had not been there before — or had not been seen.

"So who'd you fight with?" Josiah asked.

"I wasn't out there today." Tinker sat the whiskey bottle on the table next to the chair Josiah was in. "Take your shirt off."

Josiah started to undo the buttons on his sleeves. "I mean in the war."

"Oh. Pennsylvania, the Second Regiment, Company K to start. I was raised up near Wellsville in York County."

Josiah nodded as he slipped his shirt over his head. Pennsylvania explained the man's undefined Yankee accent.

"Wasn't in the regiment long, though," Tinker continued, "I found my way to the Ambulance Corps pretty quickly. I had the stomach for blood, the knack for healing when I could, and a soft touch with a saw. Antietam was really the first battle I served in as litter-bearer, but I went on from there to other things medical. Never had time for school. Everything I learned, I learned on the battlefield."

Tinker poured a dab of whiskey on a cloth and started to reach toward the cauterized wound on Josiah's shoulder — but Josiah drew back instinctively. "Antietam?" he asked. There was a coldness in his voice that was unmistakable. All of the years that had passed since the war vanished, and the old priorities and hatreds entered the tent as if on command. It was like the air just stopped moving and winter invaded the room. Josiah shivered.

"You were there," Tinker said. It wasn't a question, but a statement. The range of emotion in Tinker's voice stayed steady, didn't change from his normal warm tone to cold like Josiah's had. "The war's over, Wolfe. That was thirteen years ago. A lifetime ago."

"We didn't have an Ambulance Corps."

"It was a bloody day."

"The bloodiest." Josiah eyed Tinker differently, with apprehension as the doc stood frozen, holding the cloth, waiting, it seemed, for permission to carry on with what he had started — caring for Josiah's wound.

Josiah drew in a deep breath and closed his eyes briefly, doing his best to push away images from that day. It was almost impossible as they mixed with the fighting of the current day. When he opened his eyes, Tinker was staring at him compassionately, just waiting.

"I mean you no harm," Tinker said gently. "What I learned in those days only aids in my efforts today. We all carry our scars from the war, Wolfe, but our motivations and loyalties are the same now. I laid down my sword a long time ago. Most of the men here have done the same, at least as much as possible. I'd assumed you had, too."

Josiah nodded. "You're right. It's just . . . I lost a lot of good friends that day."

"There's no need to explain. Words like 'Antietam' are powerful. You look of age, and I should have been more careful in what I spoke of. I think little of the past these days. That fight has been replaced with another enemy, and the battles continue." Tinker motioned with the cloth. "Do you mind? Your wound needs to be cleaned and sewed up."

Josiah glanced at the wound. Tinker was right. He needed tending to, even if it was by a Yankee. He nodded, and soon felt the cool touch of the wet cloth. "Why'd you come to Texas and ride with the Rangers?"

Tinker shrugged. "One thing led to another. Home was different when I returned. I wasn't comfortable there. I needed a new start, so I headed west. A lot of us did that."

"With bushwhackers and the like?"

"Hardly." Tinker pulled back and poured more whiskey onto the cloth. "I ended up here because of matters of the heart." A slight smile passed across Tinker's face, then he went back to work, wiping away the dirt on Josiah's skin. "But I'm restless, have been since the war, I suppose, and that relationship didn't work out. I'd had enough of winters, and the weather suited me here — still does as far as that goes, so I stayed. The cause of the Rangers suits me, too. I guess my home is on the battlefield sewing up fellas like you, making them feel better, if I can. Just because you're born in a place doesn't mean you belong there for all of your life."

All of the hesitation Josiah felt about Tinker faded away as the man talked on and worked at fixing up his wound.

Letting go of his own anger over the war had happened a long time ago, or at least he'd thought it had. Josiah had ridden with Yankees before, worked with them, one way or another, to set things right, like in Austin, when it came to freeing Scrap from the jail. The two men who had helped him the most were from Massachusetts.

"You might want to take a swig of this," Tinker said, offering the bottle of whiskey to Josiah. "It's going to hurt a bit when I sew you up. Your muscles are tender, and the skin's raw around the wound."

"I'm fine."

"Have it your way. I do have to say, though, that whoever set things right with this wound did a fine job. You'd most likely be dead now if it hadn't been cauterized."

"Juan Carlos," Josiah whispered.

"I'm sorry?"

"Juan Carlos. He saved my life one last time. I couldn't save his life though. I failed him."

Recognition crossed Tinker's face as he sat the whiskey on the table and picked up a needle and thread. "One of the men who was killed in the battle?"

"Yes, a good friend." Josiah paused as Tinker came at him with the needle. "You said you had a message for me from Mc-Nelly. What is it?"

Tinker sighed and froze his hand in mid-air again. "You're to leave the bodies with me. I'm supposed to prepare them for transport, and you're to see Captain McNelly first thing in the morning."

"Transport?"

"I don't know the details, I'm just the messenger. The captain looked pretty tuckered out, so I think he was heading to his tent for some rest. I did what I could for him, but that was little, in his condition. He didn't want to be bothered for the rest of the day. You sure you don't want some of this whiskey?"

Josiah stared at the bottle, reconsidered, and nodded yes. "It might smooth things out. Might just take the edge off how I'm feeling."

"Yes," Tinker said. "It might just do that."

CHAPTER 43

By the time Verlyn Tinker finished his doctoring duties with Josiah, it was early evening. Josiah stood outside the tent, his stomach grumbling with hunger, and his veins and throat still a little numb from swigs of whiskey he'd taken to get through being sewed up.

Tinker followed Josiah outside the tent and lit a torch that stood just to the side of the entrance. The tall, rangy man stood back then and dug a little bag of tobacco out of his vest pocket. He proceeded to roll himself a cigarette with quick skill, producing a perfectly round, tight smoke that suggested he'd been exercising his fingers in such a manner for a number of years. Scrap's quirlies always looked sloppy and burned quickly.

"I'll get one of the boys to help me move the bodies," Tinker said. "But you might take care with the possessions, saddlebags and the like. I don't want to be responsible," Tinker said.

Josiah took the man's words to be an order, though they weren't delivered with a demand, just quiet authority. "Howerson had little on him. His personal possessions must be in his tent. Juan Carlos had a saddlebag on his horse, but I don't know what else. I don't even know where he slept."

Tinker shrugged. "Can't possess something if it's not there, now, can you?"

"I guess not. What are you going to do?" Josiah asked, staring in the declining light toward the two horses. They stood still as statues, unconcerned with anything that was going on around them.

"I told you, prepare them for transport. Like we did in the war. Nothing's changed since then except what I use to finish off the chore. Used to be a simple soldier would just be buried in a mass grave, or in the hole where he dropped."

Josiah nodded. "I dug my fair share of graves."

"We all did." There was a nod of acknowledgment, of the shared experience that neither of them seemed to be able to escape.

"Just for soldiers."

"Well then, you know the well-to-do soldier, or an officer, would be sent home for burial. We used creosote, arsenic, mercury, turpentine, all combined with whatever alcohol was handy to preserve the bodies. But since the war, formaldehyde simplifies the task. Of all the things I learned during the war, the skills I gained from spending time with an embalming surgeon were the least favorite. I've got a good dose of formaldehyde in the crockery in the tent; though my practice is rusty, I figure I can serve the dead adequately, but I'm no undertaker mind you. Two different things anyhow, an embalmer and an undertaker. There's no coin in this task for me. I expect the chemicals were brought along in case McNelly or Robinson took a fall and died. I'm mildly surprised that the captain is willing to use the formaldehyde for someone other than them, but those were the orders I was given, so I'm just following them and not asking any questions."

Josiah looked away from the dead bodies, bent motionless over the horses' backs, and dropped his gaze to the ground. "You didn't ride with Captain Fikes, did you?"

Tinker shook his head no. "The Frontier Battalion? No. I've ridden with Captain McNelly from the start of this new incarnation of the Ranger organization. I knew little of

Fikes. Only what I heard of him when he was killed, and then I didn't know what to believe was true or a legend birthing itself. You know how things get started."

"I do."

"So what's all of this have to do with Captain Fikes? He died a year ago, or longer, if I remember right."

"One of the men killed today was his half brother."

"Howerson?"

"No, Juan Carlos Montegné."

"The Mexican?"

Josiah nodded yes.

Tinker stuck the cigarette in his mouth, fished a match out of his pocket, and lit it with a deep, thoughtful draw. "Well, I'll be," he said, exhaling a cloud of thin blue smoke after a long second.

"Not a lot of people were aware of the connection," Josiah said. "It was a secret that was uncomfortable even for Juan Carlos. I always got the impression that he wasn't much welcome in Mexican circles, as much as he wasn't welcome in the Anglo world. I saw him act as a servant in his own brother's house on one occasion, and there was no acknowledgment from anyone in the house that he was anything but just that, a servant. I think he was treated poorly in that house after his brother was killed, at least by everyone but his niece, Pearl, the captain's daughter."

The air seemed to disappear inside Josiah's chest as he spoke Pearl's name. He had not considered, until that very moment, how she would react to the news of Juan Carlos's death. He had tried as hard as he could to put her out of his mind.

Obviously, Captain McNelly intended to have Juan Carlos's body returned to Austin. The thought of it, all that such a journey entailed, left Josiah's throat dry, all things considered. He hoped McNelly had other plans. Plans that did not include him, for one thing. Even though leaving Juan Carlos with a stranger at this point didn't seem right.

Tinker drew in on the cigarette, causing the tip to glow brightly. The glow met with the torches that had fully taken hold, causing Josiah to look away.

The torches flickered casually, reacting to the breeze that came and went, offering more light around the tent, as if to announce that the doc was still open for business.

"I don't imagine it was an easy life," Tinker said. "I know little of Juan Carlos. He was like a shadow, always lurking about, gone before you could have a decent conversation with him. He was a spy for McNelly and the whole of the Rangers, I know that much, but little else. His legend will mesh with Captain Fikes's now."

"If the world is to know they were brothers."

"Sad that it might not."

"Juan Carlos had been a spy long before the Frontier Battalion came into existence. He was pretty much Captain Fikes's shadow, even back to the State Police days. He was good at blending in, not being seen. I always wished I had his talent and instinct, but I didn't get to know him until I started riding with the Rangers. Now I think he was one of the closest friends I've come to have," Josiah said.

"That would explain Captain McNelly's decision then." Tinker puffed on the cigarette one last time, then tamped it out on the bottom of his boot. "I better get started if I'm going to see the sack before midnight."

"You sure you don't want my help?"

"No, you've done enough on this day. The lifting will do you no good, only harm. The sight of embalming is not pleasant. I know you've seen worse things, but this is your friend. You don't need that memory."

Josiah started to insist, but let his words fall back down his throat. Tinker was right. "All right. I'll take care with the saddlebag and the horses, then."

"Good. Wait here. I'll be back with help in two shakes."

Josiah watched as Tinker lumbered off in the direction of a small collection of dog tents. In the grayness of the light, Tinker looked old and haggard, like a man who had slaved about all his life in one job or another. Which was odd, because just a few minutes before, he'd seemed lively and warm, full of compassion. Maybe it was the healer in him — or maybe it was what Josiah needed to see, or feel. Either way, he liked the man, and was glad for his skills and presence. His shoulder felt better than it had in days. All he needed now was a good bath and a warm plate of food. But they would have to wait.

CHAPTER 44

The shaggy black horse didn't flinch when Josiah walked up alongside it. Clipper, on the other hand, snorted and shook his head. For some reason the Appaloosa was annoyed, or seemed to be. He was probably hungry and tired, too, Josiah decided, as he made his way to the saddlebag on the other horse.

Once Tinker returned, he'd get the horses settled for the night, then get on with his own quest to put the battle behind him. Clipper was usually pretty easygoing, but it had been an unusual day — battle had its price on a beast, too.

With light bright enough from the torches to see clearly, Josiah made his way to Juan Carlos's saddlebag. He approached the man's horse as gently as possible, touching it with his fingertips, never breaking eye contact with it. "Easy there, fella. Easy," he whispered.

It was all he could to do since there was very little he knew about the horse's temperament. The last thing he needed was to get kicked. Of course, the horse looked like it barely had enough energy to stand up, much less kick, but Josiah wasn't taking any chances.

Someone laughed in the distance, reminding Josiah that the camp was probably going to get even more lively as darkness came on. The fiddle music played on, and luckily, it looked like the night would be clear of weather. There was little to stand in the way of a calm evening, outside of the possibility of retaliation from Cortina. That was always a possibility, but unlikely.

McNelly had chosen the spot for the camp carefully, making sure it was naturally fortified by the cut of the land. Watch had most likely been doubled with the expectation that something might suddenly happen, as opposed to nothing — which is what Josiah was hoping for.

Certain now that the horse was calm, he unbuckled the saddlebag and opened it slowly, like it was a forbidden act or like he was opening a tomb of some sort.

Josiah had ignored the wrapped body tied over the saddle, tried not to consider that it was Juan Carlos wrapped inside the blanket. But he could not ignore the feeling that he was invading a man's privacy as he glanced over the contents of the saddlebag. He had yet to come face-to-face with his regret for his part in Juan Carlos's death, but that moment was coming.

The inside of the saddlebag looked to hold all of Juan Carlos's earthly belongings. There was a change of clothes, some extra ammunition, a packet of Arbuckle's coffee, and a satchel that looked to hold some papers and coins.

Josiah hesitated and looked around to make sure he was still alone, before he dove deeper into the satchel. There was no one to be seen, but he expected Tinker back at any moment.

The contents of the satchel were enough to make an honest man consider the prospect that he was the only person in the world who knew they were there. Josiah was no thief. He instantly knew that the money, and the full contents of the satchel, were not his property, but Pearl's — unless there were instructions, somewhere, that directed him otherwise.

After Captain Fikes had been killed, running the estate and managing all of his holdings fell to Pearl's mother, who was incapable in the ways of money management.

And of timing. The financial markets had collapsed in 1873 because of a high degree of speculation in the railroad business and beyond. Pearl and her mother had previously lived a life of privilege, occupying a social status that brought the governor to their home, on more than one occasion, for dinner. Pearl herself was a debutante, raised with all of the fineries a young woman of wealth could expect in Austin.

As far as Josiah knew, Pearl was the only kin that Juan Carlos had. If the old Mexican had children, they were unknown. But then, Juan Carlos was a private man. It wasn't that long ago that Josiah had learned about Maria Villareal, the woman Juan Carlos loved.

There were bank notes in the satchel. Papers that had more zeros on them than Josiah could put together and come up with a sum — even though he was a good one with math and ciphers.

He heard footsteps coming up behind him, and hurriedly stuffed the papers back in the satchel, then closed it up, followed quickly by the saddlebag, which he pulled off the back of the shaggy black horse.

He wasn't sure if he understood what he had read, what he had seen, but if his hunch was true, Juan Carlos had been a very wealthy man. Wealthy enough to restore Pearl Fikes to her previous station in society, if she really was the sole beneficiary of the saddlebag.

CHAPTER 45

Verlyn Tinker stood back and supervised as two young Rangers pulled Pip Howerson's body off Clipper's back.

Neither of Tinker's helpers made eye contact with or said a word to Josiah. They ignored him, acted like he didn't exist. One of the boys, Ned Johannsen, a tall, blond-haired, blue-eyed fella, had raced against Pip many times — and lost, like everyone else. But Josiah had had little association with him, or the other Ranger, an older man, DuLane Smith, who helped around the chuck wagon and could stir up a decent batch of gravy if he was called on to do so.

Josiah watched them alongside Tinker, holding Juan Carlos's saddlebag securely in his hand. He hadn't said anything to Tinker about the contents and doubted that he would.

At the moment, the amount of money in the satchel was his secret to carry, a burden that he was glad to keep. What Juan Carlos would want done with the money was certain in Josiah's mind, if there were no further instructions to be found.

"Once we get the bodies inside, the boys can take the horses down to the corral and have them cared for, if that's all right with you?" Tinker said.

Josiah glanced at Clipper. There was nothing in his own saddlebag that warranted as watchful an eye as Juan Carlos's, so he nodded, giving silent permission. "I don't know what'll become of that old horse. I've never seen it before."

"Up to the captain, I suppose." Tinker stood stiffly as Smith and Johannsen eased their way past, carrying Pip's body to the tent. The wrapping had held tight, but there was no mistaking that they were carrying a body. "He might just let it wander off instead of taking on the expense of feeding it. Doesn't look like it'd be much use, other than flavoring a stew."

Josiah twitched and cast a punitive glance at Tinker, but held his tongue. Whatever became of the horse had been of little concern to him up until that moment. He decided right then that it would be treated as property, just like the satchel. "I'll speak to the captain about it," he said.

"That Juan Carlos's saddlebag?"

"Yes, I think I best hang on to it, too. I know his niece and aim to see to it that she gets it once I return to Austin. I figure it might be proper for her to decide the fate of that horse, too."

"I suppose you're the best person for that."

"I'm not so sure of that, but I think I might be the only man in camp to take on the task."

Tinker shrugged. "Makes no difference to me."

Silence fell between the two men then. The noise of the camp was hardly deafening, but it had a pulse, between the rhythm of fiddle music and men coming and going from the tent that had been set up with the washtubs.

The flames at the entrance of Tinker's tent flickered and burned consistently, matching with other torches and campfires that had been set in preparation for the coming of night.

Josiah hesitated as he tried to control his breathing. Leaving Juan Carlos behind was going to be much more difficult than he had thought.

Tinker must have been able to read the hesitation on Josiah's face. He put a hand gently on his shoulder and said, "There's nothing else you can do."

"I know, it's just that . . ."

"Blame is a horrible thing to experience, Wolfe. I'm sure you did the best you could for your friend. No matter what you believe, whether there's an afterlife, or a greater beyond, the man's suffering is over. I will treat his remains like he was a member of my own family. It's the least I can do."

"Thank you," Josiah said. He tightened his grip on the saddlebag, squared his shoulders, then reached out and touched the blanket that held Juan Carlos's body and said his silent good-byes.

The return of Johannsen and Smith encouraged Josiah to turn and leave. Tinker was right; there was nothing left for him to do here.

"It wasn't your fault," Tinker said, as Josiah walked away from Juan Carlos.

"Easy for you to say," Josiah answered over his shoulder. "Easy for you to say what was my fault and what wasn't."

Tinker said nothing in return, but Du-Lane Smith coughed loudly as he made his way to Juan Carlos.

Josiah tried to ignore the cough, hoping that it was nothing more than it seemed, and not a note of doubt. If it was truly doubt, then that attitude would spread through the Ranger camp like a sickness, tainting everything he said or did. His rank of sergeant would be in title only, any respect withheld and lost, because Juan Carlos died as a result of the decisions he had made.

The campfire was raging, with flames almost two feet above the ground, reaching into the sky hungrily. A grate and an empty coffeepot sat off to the right of the fire, waiting for the flames to die out and the coals to burn orange as a cooking source. There were a few bedrolls scattered about, but there was no sign of any man in the spot Josiah had previously staked out as his own.

There had been five or six of them that had chosen to sleep out in the open, instead of pitching tents. Including Scrap, whose gear and bedroll were nowhere to be seen. It was like he had vanished, disappeared in the outer realm of the living, just like Juan Carlos had. But Josiah knew better. Scrap was avoiding him, was still angry. And Josiah couldn't blame him. He was still angry at himself for losing control.

He sat the saddlebag down and took a deep breath. All of the energy drained out of him then. The day took its toll, and he nearly collapsed to the ground. He sat as easily as he could, landing on his open bedroll.

He still held the saddlebag tightly, but he let it go, let it slide out of his grasp, then folded his knees up to his chest and rested his head face down on them.

He wasn't sure how much time had passed. Clearing his mind, restraining his emotion, and tolerating the natural pain from the battle were his only goals. It must have been a while later when the shuffle of movement got his attention.

The fire had died down, and the grayness of the evening sky had turned to black. Orange coals pulsed, and the fiddle music had stopped completely. Enthusiasm from the day's events had settled down. Most likely, the baths and the meals had been completed, and the company was settling down to rest.

When Josiah looked up, the sight of Scrap Elliot standing before him, his arms folded and a cross look on his face, was the last thing he expected to see.

Chapter 46

The black eye Scrap was sporting could not be missed, not even in the declining light. Nor could the anger that had settled on his hard-set jaw.

Once Josiah got his breath back, he decided to stay sitting. Putting himself face-to-face with Scrap, on even footing, didn't seem right. Besides, he just didn't have it in him to stand up for another fight. Enough was enough. "I didn't figure on seeing you too soon," he said. There was a hint of exasperation in his voice, but he let that pass, too.

Scrap, on the other hand, had his fists balled, and he looked tight as a guitar string about to be strummed. "You figured wrong one more time, Wolfe. We got business to settle."

There was no use putting off the inevitable. Josiah knew apologizing was the right thing to do — and obviously, the sooner the better for them both. "I'm sorry, Elliot," he said, looking up, "I lost control of myself. The pain of my injuries and the exhaustion from the day just got the best of me. But I don't regret not letting you shoot that man. He was surrendering. I had to believe him. But I shouldn't have hit you, simple as that."

"You don't give a damn that he killed the Mexican? I thought he was your friend."

"I do care. But this isn't about Juan Carlos."

"The hell it ain't. He's dead 'cause of you and your thick head."

"I'm sorry, Scrap. That's all I can say to you. I was wrong in what I did, and I regret it. What else can I say?"

"Sometimes sorry ain't enough." Scrap rubbed his cheek gingerly under the bruise. It looked like he'd stuck his eye in black axle grease.

"I suppose you're right. But fighting with me isn't going to change things. Like you said, Juan Carlos is dead. Doc Tinker is seeing to it that his body is taken care of. And that shiner is going to work itself out on its own. I don't have any hope that you'll just up and forgive me. I've known you too long not to know that you won't do that, but I can't offer you anything else but a promise that it will never happen again. You should be able to judge from my actions in the past that I aim to honor my word. Your anger can't take that away if you're being honest."

"That's it then? You ain't gonna stand up and see this through? Fight me man-to-man? Let me have my chance at you?"

"See what through?"

"I deserve my chance to coldcock you. An eye for an eye. This here is biblical as far as I'm concerned. You owe me a grudge match."

"Is that what you think will make you feel better about all of this? Fighting with me? Giving me a good solid punch at the end of a fighting day?"

"Fair is fair, Wolfe. I thought you was my friend. I mean we've been cross with each other before, but this was somethin' else. Somethin' else entirely. You stepped over a line. We was on duty, fightin' against the same enemy. I'm not the enemy, damn it! The Mexicans are, and here I am the one's that beat up."

Josiah exhaled and stood up weakly. "You *are* my friend, Scrap. What happened out there wasn't about whether that's true or not. I wasn't myself, and neither were you. I've seen it before, felt it before, a long time ago when I fought in the War Between the States. More times than I like to remember.

I thought those days were over, but I guess they're not. Never will be as long as there's somebody shooting at us and there's a battle of some kind raging about."

"It's never happened to me before," Scrap said, frowning.

"I know. Look," Josiah said, extending his hand in an offer of friendship, "I'll say it again, I'm sorry. If you want to take a swing at me, then go ahead. Now's the time. I won't fight back." He relaxed his hand and opened up both arms, giving Scrap a clear and easy path to swing through. It was as close to begging for forgiveness as Josiah was going to get.

"You ain't gonna fight back? You're just gonna stand there and take it?"

Josiah said nothing, just nodded yes.

There were no sounds around them, at least that Josiah could hear. The fire was silent other than an occasional crackle, waiting for another log, and the camping spot was vacant of other Rangers — they were alone, so no one could intervene. The rest of the boys were probably gathered around a larger fire, close to the chuck wagon, finishing up supper. But it was more than that. It was like the rest of the world had vanished. All that was important was standing right in front of Josiah. He meant to put an end to this scuffle with Scrap — properly, if that was possible.

Scrap reared back and clamped his teeth hard together like he was going to put all the power and force he could muster into the punch. But he stopped at the last second, didn't follow through. His eyes grew glassy, and a set of angry tears welled up, threatening to break out and stream down his cheek. He turned away then, not letting Josiah see that happen. "Damn it, Wolfe" was all he said.

Josiah dropped his head and allowed his arms to fold slowly to his sides. "Not everything that happens in a battle makes sense, Scrap. You pick up the pieces and put them back together the best you can. But there's no doubt that things are different. What happened today will change the lives of more than just us."

He was still uncertain if Scrap had given up the desire to fight with him. He might have just been gathering himself and could charge like a territorial bull at any second. Either way, it didn't matter. Josiah had decided he'd take whatever came, though he would have preferred to have Scrap's friendship over his rage.

Scrap sighed, and his shoulders dropped. He stood facing the fire, his back to Josiah.

"All I ever wanted was to fight in a battle. Earn my salt as a Ranger, you know? I figured I would have tall tales to tell in my old age, like them fellas that came back from facing the Northern aggressors, like you. I was too young for that fight. This is all I have, and it's not so pretty as I thought it'd be. That Mexican was kind to me in his own way, and now I guess I was pretty mean to him. I wish I could take back how I acted toward him."

"Juan Carlos never took what you said to him to heart," Josiah said. "He saw you as a spirited colt, and figured one of these days you'd tame down and end up leading us all through the days of blood and fighting. But I understand your regret. I made my own mistakes in that regard."

Scrap turned around and faced Josiah with tears streaming down his face. "You never told me it would be this hard."

"Some things you have to learn on your own. Don't you worry, you'll have your stories to tell. I'm certain of that."

"Yeah, sure, I will." Scrap drew up a deep breath and wiped his face on his shirtsleeve. "Blubberin' about like a baby. I sure won't tell anybody about that."

"Maybe you should," Josiah said.

Scrap glare at him, but it only lasted a second.

Only a few feet separated Josiah and Scrap, and it was easy to see in the glow from the embers of the fire just how young Scrap really was. Sometimes he forgot that Scrap was really just out of boyhood, and it had been a difficult, lonely journey for him.

"I'm sorry," Josiah said, offering a handshake again.

Scrap took it this time, shook it firmly, then let go. "I'm pretty hungry. And you smell like a wallerin' pig. I say we get ourselves cleaned up and find some of that beef I'm smellin'."

"Sounds good," Josiah said, walking past Scrap, picking up the saddlebag. "But we need to keep an eye on this."

CHAPTER 47

The night passed quietly, without episode. Morning came along sooner than Josiah wanted it to, and truth be told, he could have exercised a certain amount of laziness and slept until noon. But he had orders from Doc Tinker to report to Captain McNelly first thing in the morning, so he couldn't afford the extra sleep if he wanted to stay in good graces.

He arose from the bedroll stiffly, stretched and surveyed his surroundings. Five other Rangers lay sleeping, scattered around the fire pit haphazardly. There was little warmth emanating from the fire, but the air was thick and humid. It wasn't like the cool nights in winter — hardly cold — but a fire was always welcome.

The sky was gray and puffy, like someone had laid a blanket of dirty cotton in between the earth and the blueness of yesterday. There was a hint of rain in the air, a refreshing fragrance that offered no immediate threat. A steady breeze shimmered through the trees, just enough to caress the back of Josiah's neck and let him know it was there.

Scrap lay sleeping on the ground on the other side of the fire pit. Josiah hoped the trouble between them had passed. It seemed to have after they'd had their talk and gone for supper. It had been late when they'd returned to their spot, after a little entertainment and baths, and it had felt like nothing had happened. But if anybody knew how Scrap held a grudge, it was Josiah. He would be watchful of it in the days to come.

He carefully put a few fresh logs on the coals, and they started to smoke right away. After washing his face with water from his canteen and relieving himself, Josiah saw no need to wait. He grabbed up Juan Carlos's saddlebag and headed dutifully to McNelly's tent.

The canvas tent glowed from the inside out, but the flap was pinned shut. Josiah stopped, and thought about going back to the camp. But he stood fast. He wanted to put yesterday behind him with McNelly, as much as he did with Scrap.

A shadow passed the flap from inside the

tent, allowing Josiah to relax, seeing that McNelly was present, and up and about. He tapped on the canvas. "Excuse me, Captain, it's Sergeant Wolfe. Doc Tinker said I was to see you first thing this morning."

McNelly coughed three times consecutively. "Well, come in then," he said with a gasp.

Josiah drew in a deep breath, squared his shoulders, glanced up at the cloudy, gray sky, and made his way inside the tent.

Captain McNelly was dressed and looked ready for the day. Fresh pomade glistened in his hair, and his clothes were free of mud and blood. Any sign of battle had been washed away from him, as well. He stood at the planning table, looking down at a map. "What is that?" he asked, looking up, catching sight of the saddlebag.

"It was Juan Carlos's. There are contents in it that are quite valuable," Josiah answered. He stood stiffly just inside the flap. "I didn't want to leave it unattended, and thought you should be made aware of the contents."

"The man's personal belongings are of little concern to me."

"I understand, Captain."

"Are you saying that there are thieves among us, Wolfe?" McNelly's lungs rattled so loud that the sound echoed off the tent walls.

"No, no, I just wouldn't want to take a chance, sir. I'm not accusing anyone of anything."

McNelly nodded. "All right then." He eyed Josiah from head to toe, then sat down in the chair that faced the table. "Relax, Wolfe, this is not an inquisition or trial for your life, or freedom. You've been through those, and should recognize that this meeting offers little in the way of unwarranted consequences."

"The previous day's events leave me little to relax about, sir."

"I understand. All I need you to do is recount the incident as you saw it."

Josiah knew that Scrap had talked to McNelly already — but he wasn't sure what was said between them, whether Scrap's version had been filtered through anger and vengeance, or truth. "Juan Carlos's death?"

McNelly nodded. "Howerson's death seems explainable. Mind you, I am in need of details, only to send in a report to General Steele and the governor. They need to be made aware of the losses we encountered in this fight. What they do with the information is out of my control, though I do have some influence over it, as you well know."

"It was a victory," Josiah said.

"Indeed. The shipment of stolen cattle to Cuba was stopped, and the vessel destroyed, thanks to you and Ranger Elliot. But Cortina is still a free man, walking this earth, plotting, I assume, to regain what he has lost. So, the victory falls short of our intent. There will be another fight, another day when we will face Cortina. The war is not over."

Josiah let the word "war" fully settle before he spoke. He was starting to believe that there was always going to be a war of some kind to fight in. "I apologize for the loss, and my behavior toward Ranger Elliot, sir. I have apologized to him directly, and gratefully, he has accepted it like a gentleman."

"Your actions were unbecoming a man in a leadership role, Wolfe, there is no question about that. I witnessed the act itself, but lack the knowledge of what prompted such an outburst. I have known you to be both friends as well as comrades. Your partnership with Ranger Elliot has appeared strong, which is why I pair you together as frequently as I do. I was surprised, but not shocked. Hardly so. Youth compares to idiocy in such a way no mirror is needed."

"I hope you will continue to see Elliot and myself as partners, sir."

"Perhaps. It will depend on Elliot's desires, as well, but I doubt he will argue with any assignment from me. My need of your services will continue, I suppose, as long as that is what you want."

"I beg your pardon?"

"It is up to you to continue on as a Ranger. There is no enlistment here."

"Oh, I see. I have not considered leaving the Rangers, sir. Though I was concerned about your position on my continued presence."

"We have had this discussion before, Wolfe, been in situations even more dire than this. I expect you to continue riding with us, simple as that. Could what happened to Juan Carlos have been prevented?"

"I think so, but improperly, if I had allowed Ranger Elliot to shoot the man when he first stepped foot on the beach."

"And Juan Carlos walked up to the man freely, knowing full well that he was the enemy?"

"Yes. It was too late to back away once the man produced the knife. He took Juan Carlos by surprise."

"It was his error, not yours," McNelly said, his voice cold and hard. "A man of his experience should have known better than to trust a rat."

"But . . ."

"There are no buts, Wolfe. The only mistake you made was striking Ranger Elliot, and even that seems like a stretch. Something tells me he deserved it."

"I'm not sure of that," Josiah said.

"This wasn't your first battle, Wolfe."

"Hardly."

"Exactly my point. It wasn't Elliot's either. He was in Lost Valley, and there have been some other scuffles since, but he's still green behind the ears. Emotions run high. The boy lacks the knowledge to know when to keep his mouth shut — but he's a fine marksman. Grade A as far as that goes. A remarkable talent. We went to extra lengths to free him when he got himself in that trouble in Austin, and now he's learned a lesson. Let's hope it sticks."

"It won't happen again."

"I wouldn't go that far," McNelly said. He stood up and faced Josiah. "Now, about Juan Carlos. He was a good man. A better spy than most, and one of the most private men I have ever met. But still, I am well aware of his personal connection to Captain Fikes. Hank made me aware of that relationship a long time ago. It is why I have instructed Doc Tinker to preserve the body. It needs to be dispatched to Austin if I am to understand correctly? That is where his family resides?"

Josiah nodded yes. "He said he wanted to ride alongside his brother again. I assumed he meant he wished to be buried there. There were no instructions in his satchel. Just papers and currency that require the attention of his surviving kin."

"Pearl?"

"Yes."

More silence followed. McNelly knew Pearl Fikes, and he also knew, thanks to the newspaper in Austin, of Josiah's entanglement with her. What the captain didn't know was that Pearl had severed the relationship between them recently.

"Well, then, this currency you speak of, this money of Juan Carlos's, it is of a substantial amount, I assume?" Captain McNelly asked.

"Yes. Enough to make an honest man reconsider his morals for a moment, and a dishonest man to salivate at the possibilities the money would afford."

"I understand." McNelly rubbed his chin with his index finger. "Then you will need an escort to ride along with you on your return."

"I'm sorry?"

"An escort. You'll be taking Juan Carlos's body back to Austin, and all things considered, I think it would be best if you shared that journey with Ranger Elliot."

CHAPTER 48

The freshly built coffin sat squarely in the back of the wagon. Where the milled wood came from was lost to Josiah, but he knew there were more than a fair share of carpenters among the boys, so its construction was no mystery. Like the formaldehyde, the wood had probably been brought along in case something happened to McNelly or one of the other officers in the company. The logistical effort to stop Cortina was far more complex than Josiah knew, but was obvious from the size, and scope, of the Ranger camp.

It was early afternoon, and the gray, puffy sky had yet to change. It didn't look like it was going to anytime soon. Rain had yet to show itself, and it didn't look like they would be riding into a storm, or any foul weather. At least, Josiah hoped not. The dry ground turned to impassable mud, almost instantly, with little more than a cloudburst.

That would slow, or stop, the journey entirely.

Clipper was tied to the back of the wagon, and Josiah was packed, ready to go, with the reins in his hands.

The wagon was well stocked with enough supplies for the journey, but there wasn't enough room in the bed for two coffins. Pip Howerson was to be buried not far from where he fell, on higher ground. Word, of course, would be sent to his kin, and his grave marked simply with a white wood cross. Like a lot of simple foot soldiers' graves, time would wash away any evidence of its existence, but Josiah wouldn't forget Pip, or his amazing horse.

Juan Carlos's saddlebag was behind Josiah, not far out of reach, and locked in an ammunition box. Captain McNelly had decided that the shaggy black horse should stay behind at the camp. It probably wouldn't have survived the long trip back to Austin in the shape it was in and would only have served to slow them down.

Scrap sat comfortably on Missy, next to the wagon. He'd had no objections to the trip. He seemed eager to be away from the coast and, surprisingly, from the promise of more battles with Cortina. He'd calmed down around Josiah, but held little reserve for any of the boys stupid enough to make a comment about his black eye. Josiah had to stop him from fighting three separate times as they prepared to leave.

"This feels a bit familiar, don't it, Wolfe?" Scrap said.

"It does," Josiah said. "I was thinking about that trip once Captain McNelly told me what he wanted from us. I started to object, but realized the honor he bestowed on us by asking us to take Juan Carlos back to his family. On one hand, I'm sure it wouldn't matter to Juan Carlos where he was laid to rest. Anywhere on the trail, in Texas, was his home. But I think laying him next to his brother is more than fitting, and an effort I'm willing to see through. I know he would have done the same for me."

Josiah and Scrap had both been charged with returning Captain Fikes's body to Austin when he'd been killed by the outlaw Charlie Langdon's gang. It had been at the start of the Frontier Battalion, and it seemed like ages ago, but, in truth, only a few years had passed between that journey and this one. A lot had happened since then.

It was on that trip that Josiah and Scrap had begun to form their friendship, as it was, and when Josiah had met Pearl, the captain's daughter and Juan Carlos's niece, upon their arrival in Austin. Just the memories of it all were enough to muddle Josiah's emotions, especially considering that now they had to fulfill the same duty with Juan Carlos's body.

Josiah was glad that Scrap had agreed to come along; he had seen it fitting to both the present and the past. There was no one else Josiah would have wanted to make the trip with, but he would have done it regardless.

The trip would be long, and there would be plenty of time for reflection along the way. Still, the sadness of the past days weighed on Josiah's shoulders, slumped them a bit.

"Well, at least we have a coffin from the start this time around," Scrap said. "Won't have to battle the stink and flies much."

Josiah cast a furtive look toward Scrap, but said nothing. McNelly was approaching, and besides, Scrap was just being Scrap. There was no changing that.

"I see you're packed and ready to venture out," McNelly said.

Lieutenant Robinson was a few feet behind the captain and stopped in McNelly's shadow. Robinson said nothing, just stood stoically, with a look of disapproval plastered on his face.

"We are," Josiah said.

McNelly reach up and handed Josiah a bundle of letters. "Please deliver these to General Steele. He will know what to do with those that do not concern him."

Josiah took the letters and immediately swung around, snapped open the lock to the ammunition box, and put them in with Juan Carlos's satchel. "I will do that," he said. "Is there anything else, Captain?"

McNelly nodded yes. "Tom Darkson's been notified that he is riding along with you two. He's on the perimeter, keeping watch, and will join you when you pass. The value of your cargo may draw attention from Cortina, his bandits, or other wayfarers along the way. I doubt you'll have trouble with the Apache, but you never know. It's imperative that you reach Austin safely, and as soon as possible. I thought Darkson would be a worthy addition to your charge."

"I'll keep an eye out," Josiah answered. "There was a lone rider come to see me off after you and the company left me there to bring back Juan Carlos. I couldn't get a clear sight of the man, but I figured it was a scout come to see the damage done to the plan, or it was Cortina himself. But he was gone before I could get a shot off." He watched McNelly process the information, and waited for a response. When none came, Josiah continued, "And thank you for sending Darkson along with us. I know you need every man here to finish the fight with Cortina."

"I am counting on your return, and reinforcements from the other companies, if General Steele sees fit to send them along. Otherwise, we will do the best we can with what we have," Captain McNelly said. He looked away from Josiah and settled his gaze on Scrap. "You keep a sharp eye out, too, Elliot. If there was a scout, then you'll be in danger the whole way."

"No worry there, Captain."

"Well then," McNelly said, "be off with you now. Have a safe journey." He coughed then — so deeply the power of it bent him over. Robinson was at the captain's side in two shakes, guiding him back toward his tent.

Josiah nodded with concern but knew there was nothing he could do about the captain's consumptive fit. He flipped the reins and headed the wagon slowly out of the Ranger camp — without fanfare, or much attention from the other boys at all.

Tom Darkson sat on his horse, a paint gelding that was more brown than white, at the top of a hill, waiting for Josiah and Scrap to arrive. Once they met up, Darkson pulled up alongside the wagon and tipped his well-worn black felt Stetson to Josiah, offering a silent hello.

"Nothing I could see for miles," Darkson said. "Ain't seen hide nor hair of no Mexicans or Apache. I think we sent 'em runnin' back to their holes."

"Just because you can't see them doesn't mean they're not there," Josiah said. "We didn't kill every man that's loyal to Cortina. There's still eyes about that answer to him. This is a long ride. You ready for that?"

"Sure am. I ain't been up Austin way in a coon's age. Last time I was there, I was punchin' longhorns on the way to Dallas. I got to tell you, I don't miss those days. I'll take my forty a month with the Rangers, and be glad to do whatever the captain says, just like you fellas." Darkson glanced back at the coffin, then to Josiah. "Can't you cover that up with a blanket or somethin'? Who wants to see a reminder of a dead man every step of the way?"

"It might ward off some trouble," Josiah said.

"Never thought of that," Darkson replied, nodding his head as a flash of recognition crossed his face. "That's a good idea."

"Wolfe has those every once in a while," Scrap said. He was on the other side of the wagon, keeping pace. "You got enough supplies to make the trip?"

Darkson eyed Scrap curiously and shrugged his shoulders. "Enough is enough, I 'spect. We can all split off and share huntin' duties, unless you want to take that on, Elliot."

"Sharin's just fine with me. It's the cookin' I can do without."

Josiah chuckled — he'd eaten Scrap's cooking. The boy could burn water and make a rabbit taste like jerky without trying. It was nice to ease into the trip with some decent conversation and, better yet, to have Tom Darkson along. "How's those ribs holding up? Doc Tinker tell you what to do?"

"Still pretty durn sore, I'll tell you. But I'll be fine. I think that's one of the reasons the captain sent me along. I ain't much good to him other than standin' watch or pickin' up duty at the camp. I can ride, but the pain tires me some. I'll be fine, though. Doc just said to keep wrapped tight, that's all. Not much else I could do to heal but give it time. That's all he said. Give it time."

"Like the rest of us," Josiah said. He had the scabs on his face from the scattershot wound, and the gunshot wound on his shoulder. Scrap had his black eye and damaged ego. Along with Darkson's broken ribs, they were a broken trio, hobbling north toward the promised land of home, bearing a dead body, bad news, and wealth of an unimaginable amount, at least to Josiah, to an unsuspecting woman.

CHAPTER 49

Josiah stopped the wagon at the crossroad that led to Arroyo.

The ride had been silent and calm, with Tom Darkson leading the way and Scrap bringing up the rear. Nothing had changed in the sky, hidden by the persistent gray blanket of clouds. The change in weather had been a nice reprieve from the beating sun of the last few days, and there was a coolness to the air, offering some much needed comfort.

It would take Josiah a while to adjust to the wagon's seat instead of a saddle, but the hardest part of the journey — starting — was behind them all. There was no lightness in any of their moods. Their cargo and purpose prevented that. Still, it felt as if the farther away from camp they got, the more comfortable the idea of the trip became.

Scrap stopped a couple of horse-lengths behind Josiah, keeping quiet, eyeing the road to Arroyo with disdain. It would have served Josiah to feel the same way, but he didn't, couldn't find it in himself to feel anything but a moment of desire and regret.

Tom Darkson doubled back and came to an easy stop next to the wagon. "Somethin' the matter, Wolfe?"

Josiah shook his head no. "Everything's fine, Tom. Don't you worry."

"Then why we stoppin'?" Darkson asked. He eased his hand down to his sidearm, a Colt Peacemaker, the same model as Josiah's, even newer, with nary a scratch on the grips.

"Just thinking some things through. Give me a minute. We'll be on our way shortly," Josiah said. "There's no threat, so you can relax those fingers."

Tom Darkson started to say something, then obviously thought better of it because of the serious look on Josiah's face. He spun his horse around and galloped about fifty yards up the road that led to Austin, and stopped. His head darting about like one of those ground owls', on the lookout for anything that might attack.

Josiah sighed. There was no way he could explain to Darkson the choices he was faced with. Fact was, he didn't want to. He didn't even want to face the decisions himself, but he knew he had to.

What he faced was simple, really. He could ride into Arroyo and do his best to sweep Francesca off her feet, and never leave. It would be easy enough to send for Lyle and all of his earthly belongings, pull up stakes in the capital city, and plant new roots in the desolation of Arroyo. If Ofelia chose to come, that would be fine. But she was free to go on with her life if Arroyo didn't appeal to her. The move to Austin had been a big enough upheaval for her; expecting her to follow him to South Texas so soon would be a bit much to ask.

Josiah considered that, and then the idea progressed further — if he were a dishonest man, knowing full well that there was no accounting of Juan Carlos's entire wealth, he knew he could live comfortably for a long time. Pearl would never be the wiser about her inheritance and the amazing fortune that her uncle had amassed and carried with him. She would never know what was to come to her from her uncle's death. Josiah could feel the letter from Pearl stuffed in his pocket — it felt like fire to his heart as he thought about deceiving her.

And then he considered the manner of Juan Carlos's death, matched as it would be with Josiah's sudden wealth if he chose to carry out the scheme. Some people might eventually construe that the death was purposeful, that Josiah had set Juan Carlos up to die so he could get access to his money.

The farther away from the truth the tale got, the more it could grow, and Josiah could easily find himself on the wrong side of the law. He'd be more than a thief — especially with his history of violence taken into consideration — he'd be a greedy, murdering outlaw.

Josiah sighed again and focused on the distant buildings at the end of the road. He could not bring more trouble to Francesca than he already had. Her heart was tender, and needful, as it was.

Truth was, Josiah didn't feel any love for her. Just desire. Just the want of her body next to his in a more acceptable location. His needs were carnal and natural, but hardly worth changing his life for, or tossing his morals to the wind. He'd known that before he stopped the wagon, but he also knew he would have to make the choice one last time.

Francesca was a beautiful woman, hard to resist, easy on the eyes, but even if he did love her, he didn't know if it would be enough to overcome what the world would inflict on them, what with him being Anglo and her a Mexican. Life would be made ugly for them both, but even more so for Lyle.

And that was the stopping point, that and the idea of taking something that didn't belong to him. No matter how he felt about being spurned by Pearl, putting Lyle into a situation that could lead to trouble, or worse, and being a dishonest man just didn't sit well with Josiah. No matter the beauty of a woman, Mexican or otherwise, and the amount of money at hand. Nothing was free, and Josiah knew that wasn't going to change now. He'd pay a hefty price for the theft of Juan Carlos's fortune, and the love of a brown-skinned woman. But the decisions were separate, not dependent on each other. Still, it was also one big decision, and there was no question which one Josiah had to make.

Regretfully, he flipped the reins to the horse and urged it to move on as quickly as it could.

A cloud of dust kicked up behind him, rising on the steady breeze, trailing into the sky and obscuring anything behind that might be worth a second look. Scrap pushed Missy into a hard run, passing Josiah without saying a word, catching up with Darkson, then running faster still, until he, too, was almost out of sight.

CHAPTER 50

Night fell comfortably around the three men in a shallow limestone canyon. The place was foreign to all three of them, but the look of it had appealed to them. There was a stream cutting through the land, offering a decent spot for watering, resting the horses and themselves. Wildlife seemed plentiful. The surrounding trees were full of birds, the chatter only quieting briefly as the trio of Rangers set up camp. A few squirrels scolded them for interrupting their tranquility.

Scrap had gone out and shot two skinny jackrabbits. Both had been cleaned and stuffed on a makeshift spit and were now cooking over a healthy fire. Mesquite smoke streamed upward into the sky, filling the air with the smell of cooking meat, and the comfort of camp.

The clouds had started to break up, previewing a starry black sky. The promise of rain throughout the day had never been fulfilled, which was just as well as far as Josiah was concerned. All that remained of the day's weather was the steady breeze, pushing up from the south, bringing a slight taste of ocean salt to the tongue.

They were still close to the edge of land and the beginning of the ocean, but by late tomorrow, they would be far enough away from it for it to be just a memory, out of range of the senses. Whether that memory would be bad or good was yet to be determined, but Josiah was leaning toward bad.

He would never forget Juan Carlos falling to the sand, with the sound of the waves crashing behind him so loudly that the surrounding screams, yells, and gunshots could hardly be heard. There was no way he would find joy in remembering the ocean. Not now. Maybe not ever.

"I think when we get to San Antonio, I'm gonna get me a bath, sleep in a nice soft feather bed at the Menger Hotel, and chase me down some fine soiled dove for a little entertainment," Tom Darkson said. He was sitting next to Josiah, watching the jackrabbits roast over the fire. The skin was getting crispy, and occasionally, a bit of fat would drip into the flames, causing them to flare up.

Scrap was on the other side of the fire, smoking a quirlie, paying neither man any mind at all. He was quiet, more so than usual, but Josiah knew that wouldn't last. Something would get in Scrap's craw, and he'd go off on some sort of rant. Or out of the blue, he'd start talking endlessly about nothing at all, just to hear his own voice. Tom Darkson was like that, too. Only not as quiet and brooding as Scrap. Still, he was turning out to be a decent traveling companion, and Josiah was glad for his presence on the trip.

"We're not stopping in San Antonio," Josiah said.

"What do you mean we're not stopping?"

"Exactly what I said. I don't care what Doc Tinker did to preserve that body, you think it's going to last forever?"

Darkson shrugged his shoulders, then looked deep into the fire. "I don't care to think about such things."

"None of us do," Josiah said. "But it's a fact of life. We need to get that body to Austin and in the ground as soon as we can." He titled his head to the south.

"What's the matter?" Darkson asked.

Scrap stood up, staring off in the same direction that Josiah was listening. He'd heard something that alarmed him, too.

A coyote howled not far off in the distance. It yipped three times, grew silent, then yipped three more times.

"Sounds odd, Wolfe," Scrap said. "A little too close for my liking."

"Mine, too." Josiah nodded as he stood up and glanced over to Clipper. The horse was tethered to a line between two cottonwoods with the other two horses. All of the gear had been removed from their backs, including the scabbards that held the rifles. At the moment, Josiah cursed himself for getting too comfortable too quick.

"Scrap, grab your rifle and scout the north. Darkson, you need to dash the fire. Don't kill the coals just yet, in case I'm wrong," Josiah ordered.

"Wrong about what?" Darkson asked, the color of his face growing pale, even in the bright firelight.

"Apache, you idiot," Scrap said. "Me and Wolfe both have crossed paths with 'em comin' and goin' this close to Mexico. Or it could be some of Cortina's men, tracking after us for a dose of revenge."

"Oh," Darkson said. "What do I do if it is Apache, after I put the fire out?"

"Shoot first and ask questions later," Josiah said.

■ ■ ■ ■

The blackness of night was like a heavy veil away from the campfire. Josiah crawled on his belly to the top of the limestone embankment that overlooked the canyon they had taken refuge in. It was difficult to see very far. He had barely seen the patch of prickly pear, coming up the game trail that led to the top. He'd hoped not to disturb a rattlesnake, or a nest of scorpions on the way, too.

The coyote had gone silent. Just the three calls, followed by three more. Josiah had learned the hard way not to trust his ears, especially when it came to the Apache or Mexicans. They favored raiding camps at night. The Indians were ruthless fighters, and though he doubted they would find much value in Juan Carlos's papers, the gold coins would be enough to justify the attack. Cortina's men would be after a bounty of a different kind.

The dead body, on the other hand, might be enough to ward off the Apache. Regardless of their reputation, Josiah had never heard of any Indian that favored being around dead bodies. There was a good chance that if they had been scouted, the coffin had been a bad sign, sending the Apache on their way, into the night, searching for something else to attack and steal.

The vista that stretched out in front of Josiah was amazing, even in the darkness. The land toward Austin grew flat, but Josiah knew that wouldn't last. There were more canyons to the south of San Antonio, and the hill country to the north of it. Luckily, the trails through both were reasonably easy to traverse with a wagon — unless it rained.

Josiah brought to his eye the spyglass that he'd carried with him and scanned the outlying land. He saw nothing moving. Not man or beast. He hadn't really expected to. Apache and coyotes both seemed to have some kind of magical control over the shadows of night. Still, he had hoped for some kind of sign to prove himself right, or allow him to relax.

After several long minutes, he withdrew the spyglass and collapsed it back down, then made his way back down the embankment the same way he'd come up — on his belly.

Trusting his eyes, and taking his sight for granted, had been stupid. McNelly had warned him of the Apache's existence in these parts, and he knew of it himself — just like he knew that Cortina might well be on the lookout for revenge, like Scrap had said. Still, he had lit a blazing fire and set to cooking like he was in the big Ranger camp, protected by the presence of men just like himself and an armed perimeter to keep them all safe.

If it had just been a coyote he'd heard, this would be a lesson quickly learned. A reminder that they were in the wilds of South Texas with no protection but their wits and the guns they carried. There was no one near to come to their rescue.

The trip down the limestone embankment was easier than getting up it. Knowing where the holes and prickly pear were helped Josiah navigate it easily.

Once at the base, he stood up and came face-to-face with the barrel of a gun. He had to blink to make sure it wasn't Darkson or Scrap mistaking him for an intruder. It wasn't. There was no mistaking that the man was a Mexican. And that could only mean that he was one of Cortina's men or a threat of some kind; perhaps the lone rider Josiah had spied on the hill after the company had gone back to camp after the battle. Josiah's mouth went dry. For all he knew, the man could be Cortina himself.

"One move, señor, and you are a dead man. And do not think to call out for your *amigos,* do you understand?"

A cold chill traveled up Josiah's spine. The man had not shot, had not taken the opportunity to kill him when he easily could have. "Who are you?" Josiah asked.

"It makes no difference," the Mexican said. He was nearly as tall as Josiah, and he had obviously been riding for days without a bath. He smelled like a dead possum that had been baking in the sun. "Cortina wishes to kill you himself." He pressed the gun, an older Colt, but still a viable gun, against Josiah's forehead. "Now, when I say so, turn around, and don't make a sound. *Entiendes? Understand?"*

"My boys will come looking for me."

"We will be long gone. Now, turn around slowly." The Mexican pulled the gun away cautiously. The sight of it almost disappeared completely in the darkness of the night.

Josiah knew the farther away from camp he was, the greater chance that he would die, either by Cortina's hand or his captor's. He had no choice but to fight, with the hope that Scrap and Darkson would come to his rescue.

Instead of turning, Josiah stood still, refused the order.

"I said move, now!" The Mexican pushed

him in the chest with his other hand, and with as much quickness as Josiah could muster, he grabbed the man's wrist, pulled it toward him, bringing the man's chin directly into contact with his rising elbow. The Mexican screamed out, and the old Colt tumbled from his grasp, landing on the ground, just out of his reach. But Josiah wasn't done. He brought his knee up, catching the man's groin with enough force to knock the lungs out of a longhorn. The Mexican screamed and tumbled backward.

Josiah didn't hesitate. He pulled his gun and fired without thinking of the consequences, unloading all six shots on the Mexican. There was enough information to know what to do. Shoot first and ask questions later; follow his own advice. Only Josiah knew the most important answer. Cortina was coming for him. The day would come when they would face each other, but as far as Josiah was concerned, today was not that day. Scrap and Tom Darkson came running, coming to a stop next to Josiah as he kneeled down and began to strip the dead Mexican of his knives and bullets.

"Hot damn, Wolfe," Tom Darkson said, "what the heck happened?"

"He was waiting for me, looking to take to me to Cortina."

"Looks like you sent him to hell," Scrap said.

Josiah shrugged. "Just saved my own skin."

"Cortina ain't gonna give up," Darkson said.

"He will someday," Josiah said. "Either him and me will face down, or something else will stop the man. He can't dodge every bullet that comes his way. But we need to keep a sharper eye out. This might have been the man I saw on the hill, following after us, or there might be more, set on stopping us from reaching Austin to finish the mission McNelly assigned us."

Both Scrap and Darkson nodded in agreement.

"You gonna bury him?" Scrap asked.

Josiah shook his head no. "The coyotes can have him."

CHAPTER 51

Morning came and went without incident, or the sound of another coyote yip. For all Josiah knew, it could have actually been one of the animals. But he still wasn't sure the Mexican was on his own.

He would be on the lookout for any sign that they were being tracked. If there were any Apache, too, which was always a worry in this country, then they would wait until the most opportune time to attack — and if that happened, Josiah was determined to be prepared. As much as possible, anyway. The three men combined, injured and fatigued as they all were, probably equaled one good man — against countless Apache, or more of Cortina's men. It would hardly be a fair fight, if another one came their way.

Scrap came off watch as the blazing red sun poked up over the horizon. The relief of weather from the day before was not going to be an ongoing gift. It was already growing warm and humid, and without any sign of clouds, the coming day would surely be a scorcher.

After a decent breakfast of hard biscuits, bacon, and coffee, supplied for the trip by Captain McNelly, the three men packed up silently and continued on toward San Antonio.

As with any long journey, they were falling into a routine. Tom Darkson took the lead without orders, and Scrap hung back, trailing behind the wagon about fifty yards. Josiah was as comfortable as he was going to be driving the wagon. He was determined to hold the reins of responsibility for Juan Carlos's body for as long as he could. There might be some point, though, when he would consider trading off with Scrap, putting his tired butt in the comfort of a saddle.

The only one of them who seemed to mind the arrangement was Clipper. The Appaloosa was none too happy about being tied behind the wagon, forced to tag along instead of ride at a hearty pace. Occasionally the horse would try to stop, or pull back with a whinny and a snort. A couple of times along the way, when they were stopped to water the horses and themselves, Clipper tried to kick Josiah. He just avoided the cross Appaloosa as much as possible, and tried to understand that being tied, instead of running free, would put any creature in a bad mood.

There was little to do on the trip other than keep an eye out for the Apache or Cortina's men. Any traveler was suspect when it came right down to it. But there were very few of them. Towns were sparse, too, and when the three men came across them, they just passed through. The coffin garnered some curiosity, but Josiah was accustomed to that. He'd experienced the same kind of scrutiny when he'd taken Captain Fikes back to Austin.

This trip didn't feel the same. Tom Darkson's presence changed things. But so did the fact that Captain Fikes had been murdered, and his killer had been on the loose during the entire trip back to Austin.

Josiah had plenty to be concerned about. Not Charlie Langdon or his gang, though. And hopefully the farther away from the Gulf of Mexico they got, the less he would have to worry about Juan Cortina.

He pushed on at the thought of his own safety, urging the nameless horse who pulled the wagon to speed up and get them out of range even quicker.

Much to Tom Darkson's disappointment,

they did not stop in San Antonio for the night. There would be no hot bath in the Menger, or some sordid connection made with a soiled dove. Darkson would have to restrain himself until they arrived in Austin. What he did then was up to him. Instead, they stopped briefly at a mercantile, stocked up on some coffee, which was the only supply they were running short on, and then stopped at the telegraph office to check and see if there were any messages. There weren't any.

Five days into the trip, they had not seen one Apache or a Mexican set on revenge. Any threat from the raid on Cortina seemed to have been left behind . . . the only thing remaining was the scars they all carried, and the cargo in the back of the wagon.

It was good to see the familiarity of the Hill Country as they made their way north of San Antonio. It was a trip Josiah had made more than once, so he knew the good places to stop, where to hunt, and what to expect.

New Braunfels, or Neu-Braunfels as the Germans called it and originally named it, was where they had stopped with Captain Fikes, where they had found an undertaker who deposited the body in a coffin. There would be no need for such a thing on this trip. But he might stop and pay his respects. It would be nice to see a new face.

Scrap and Tom Darkson seemed to have run out of things to talk about. The campfires in the evenings were quiet, almost despondent. Neither of them carried, or played, a musical instrument. There was just storytelling, and that had fallen flat from the lack of natural talent or lack of resources, because they, neither one, had a clue how to talk about anything other than themselves. The quiet was not necessarily objectionable to Josiah, but the trip had been long, and his own ailments and silent thinking had started to wear on him.

The undertaker in New Braunfels had moved on, and the marshal of the town had died suddenly, just sitting at his desk one day. According to the new marshal, a young man with a limp, not much older than Scrap, named Lester Wilson, the previous marshal just keeled over his plate of beans one evening and that was that.

Tom Darkson, of course, was hopeful of spending enough time in the town to seek a moment of female companionship, but not knowing anyone in New Braunfels left Josiah a little cold and anxious to get back on the trail north. Darkson took the lead in a huff, but Josiah didn't mind. He could almost smell Austin in the air.

San Marcos came and went, and there was little traffic to contend with, no heavy cattle drives pushing up to Dallas, or farther, to Abilene, so the driving was easy enough, especially on the parched trail. It had sprinkled a few times along the way, but there had been no rain to speak of. The land needed it, and so did the streams, but there was still green in the grasses and water in the creeks. That wouldn't last long though. A drought was settling in.

Scrap seemed a little anxious the final morning out. They had packed their gear but were in the process of clearing camp when Josiah noticed. "You all right, Elliot?" he asked.

"I'm fine." Scrap kicked dirt over the waning coals of the fire.

"You sure don't act fine," Josiah said.

Tom Darkson had learned to give Scrap a wide swath when he was in a mood. They'd almost come to blows a couple of times on the trip, but had backed off on their own, without any interference from Josiah. Tom stood next to his horse, waiting for the signal to mount.

"Guess I ain't lookin' forward to bein' back in Austin. I like bein' away."

Josiah glanced to the north quickly. There

was nothing but open country for as far as the eye could see, but he knew they were close. "I like it, too. But there's people for us both to see while we're there."

"Not me," Scrap said.

Josiah started to say something but noticed Scrap staring angrily at Tom Darkson. He knew then that he would have to have a talk with him, and warn him not to go to Blanche Dumont's house — or mention an intended visit to the soiled doves there, in front of Scrap. The last thing the boy needed to hear was that Darkson had taken up with Myra Lynn for an hour. There'd be a fight for sure.

"Well," Josiah said, "maybe you'll change your mind."

"I doubt it," Scrap answered. "I sure do doubt it."

CHAPTER 52

Austin rose up in the distance as if an image deep out of Josiah's memory had come to life.

There had been times on the trip south when he was certain that he would never see the city again. That his death was as certain as the coffin that sat securely bound in the back of the wagon. But that had not happened. Josiah had survived. Not only the scouting trip to Arroyo, the battle with Cortina's men, but the fight with the lone Mexican on the journey back, as well.

Josiah stopped the wagon and waited for Scrap to catch up with him. "Let's ride in together, Elliot."

"Suits me." Scrap whistled, causing Tom Darkson to come to a stop and look back. Scrap motioned for him to stop, and he did.

Darkson waited for them to catch up, then the three of them headed north down a slight valley and across the slow-running

Colorado River.

Surprisingly, the hustle and bustle of Congress Avenue, once they made it there, was music to Josiah's ears.

The sun was shining brightly, as expected on a late-June morning in the heart of Texas. The heat of the day had not fully set in, but it almost certainly would — there wasn't a cloud in the sky. Summer droned on, but the air was comfortable, with the wind easing down from the northwest, instead of flowing up from the south. Now that the city was a reality, the ocean, from where the wind usually came, was only a memory, best to be forgotten. If that were possible.

The business of the capital city was in full swing. Wagons and horses clogged the dry, dusty street. People walked three abreast on the boardwalk, coming and going from restaurants, shops, and lawyers' offices. A Butterfield stagecoach sat waiting in front of a hotel, and deep in the distance, a train whistled as it rumbled out of Austin, heading west for the Arizona Territory.

Scrap rode on the left side of the wagon, while Darkson took up the right. They kept an easy, even trot, and both men sat up straight in their saddles and kept their faces free of emotion. They were stoic and proud, yet respectful to the cargo they were escorting.

Josiah maintained the same posture, well aware that the coffin would draw attention the moment they'd headed up Congress Avenue.

He had thought about riding into town under the cover of darkness, knowing with certainty that he was recognizable, his face known by a lot of folks in Austin, and not held in high regard. The fact that he was carting home another dead man would set tongues a-wagging. His past reputation as a killer would be revisited. He was sure of it. But he knew that there was no avoiding the eventual outcome. It didn't matter whether he came into town in the dark or the light of day, he would have to answer some painful questions . . . at least from Pearl. He tried not to care what the rest of the city thought, but it was impossible not to when it affected those that he loved as well as himself.

"Where we headin'?" Tom Darkson asked.

"I figure the best thing we can do is take the coffin to the undertaker's, then you'll be free to go about your business," Josiah said.

Scrap cast Darkson a slight look, then glanced down the street. His gaze settled on the capitol building. It's dome glimmered like it was a temple. And maybe it was, to democracy, but no God that Josiah knew of walked its halls. He was glad of that for the moment.

Darkson nodded. "That's a fine plan. But what comes after that? We're still Rangers, ain't we?"

"Sure we are," Josiah said. "I've got some letters to deliver to General Steele. I'm sure he'll have orders for us, whether McNelly included them or not. You just need to let me know where to find you. We'll be back in the saddle, one way or another. This isn't the end of anything other than Juan Carlos's journey to the grave next to his brother."

"I don't know much about Austin," Darkson said.

Scrap cleared his throat. "There's a workingman's hotel just around the corner from the livery where Wolfe keeps his horse. I'll bunk there. Why don't you, too, so it's easy for Wolfe to find us when we head back to the boys?"

"If that's what we do," Josiah said.

"Why wouldn't it be?" Scrap said.

"I don't know what McNelly or Steele has in mind for us."

"I ain't gonna be a spy again, Wolfe. Look what happened to us this time. You barely

431

made it out alive."

"It's duty, Scrap."

"I ain't enlisted in nothin'. You can't desert from the Rangers. You just quit."

"You're free to walk away anytime," Josiah said.

Scrap shrugged, and silently agreed with Josiah. At least that was what Josiah thought his silence meant.

"That workingman's hotel?" Darkson interrupted. "They got a bath?"

"No," Scrap said. "But there's a barber, and a bathhouse around the corner."

Tom Darkson smiled broadly. "Good, I'll be needin' both."

It was Josiah's turn to toss a silent glance. He'd had a talk with Darkson about Scrap's sister, so there was no misunderstanding. Josiah wanted to be free of conflict between the two boys, drop the coffin off at the undertaker, seek out Pearl, and then head home to see his son, Lyle, before making his way to General Steele's office.

As it turned out, he didn't have to wait too long to find Pearl Fikes.

He had just crossed the intersection of Congress and Pecan, when he looked up to see her walking out of the Sampson & Hendrik's Dry Goods store, arm in arm with Rory Farnsworth.

432

CHAPTER 53

Pearl Fikes recognized Josiah almost at the same moment he spotted her. She stopped dead in her tracks, her face draining pale as a sheet instantly. Rory Farnsworth, the sheriff of Travis County, which encompassed all of Austin, had kept on walking a step or two, until he felt the obvious tug and turned around toward Pearl to see what the problem was. His happy-go-lucky casual expression faded away just as quickly as Pearl's had when his gaze landed on Josiah, driving a wagon into town with a coffin loaded in the back.

Josiah brought the single horse pulling the wagon to a stop in the middle of Congress Avenue. The street was arid, and just braking kicked up a poof of dust. He could taste nothing but dirt, and oddly he was glad for it since it washed away the distaste in his mouth that had erupted upon seeing Pearl with Rory Farnsworth. He was immediately angry, jealous, and after a long breath, not surprised at all by the pairing.

There was little time to consider any other emotions. Rory Farnsworth broke away from Pearl, and marched directly to the side of the wagon.

"What is the meaning of this, Wolfe?"

Farnsworth was shorter than Josiah, and he stood dressed in his dandiest clothes, out and about courting as he was. He looked more like a Yankee carpetbagger than a Texas sheriff. The recent business with his father, a banker, who had been found guilty of murdering four soiled doves, had obviously not affected his financial standing or position in society. If it had, he wasn't showing it.

The sheriff sported a finely waxed mustache and wore a black bowler hat that matched the color of his fancy suit. The silver star on his chest remained highly polished and properly positioned, offering no clue to any shame, or lack of authority, that he might have carried.

Scrap and Tom Darkson stopped alongside the wagon, but both of them held silent, instinctively leaving Josiah to the business of handling the sheriff.

"This doesn't concern you, Rory," Josiah said, through gritted teeth. "Unless you've found yourself in a new profession as an undertaker," he added with a penetrating glare.

Without thinking, Farnsworth thrust his chest out and boosted his chin at the sky. "I am still the sheriff of this county, thank you very much. Now, tell me, what is this coffin you carry, and who occupies it?"

"A dead body, Rory. What the hell do you think I'm carting around, a treasure box full of gold?"

"There's no cause to get snide with me."

Josiah broke his gaze with the sheriff and looked past him, to Pearl. She looked mortified and terrified at the same time. If that were possible. "I think there is plenty of reason to be snide, Rory. Plenty . . ."

Farnsworth looked over his shoulder, then back to Josiah just as quickly. "Your connection, and business, with Miss Fikes has come to an end from what I understand."

Josiah sighed. "Not quite yet, Rory. I come to town bearing bad news."

He hadn't taken his eyes off Pearl. She was as beautiful as ever. She was dressed in clothes Josiah had seen before, when she had worn them on an outing to the riverside on a lazy Sunday afternoon — not too long ago. Though it seemed forever since he had been in her company.

Pearl had long flowing locks of blond hair that cascaded over her shoulders, and she was wearing a boater hat with blue satin ribbons flowing off the back. The ribbons matched the color of her dress that highlighted her hourglass figure perfectly. Josiah knew from experience that her undergarments only accented a nearly perfectly shaped body — she needed little help from tight bindings. She had on her best kid-and-cloth shoes, but they were starting to show some wear. All of her clothes were worn, though from a distance she looked like the proper belle of the ball that she had been in the past. Since her father's death, when her fortunes had changed dramatically, the local dressmaker would not even extend her a line of credit.

Pearl slowly walked toward the wagon. Her fingers were trembling. Sweat was forming on her brow. She looked extremely uncomfortable, like she was weakening from some unseen sickness.

There was no wind, and the heat of the day seemed to press in around them from all sides. People walking the boardwalk and driving the street, whether in buggies or on horses, had started to slow, noticing the coffin and the presence of the sheriff.

"Josiah," Pearl whispered, looking to the

ground as she stopped next to Farnsworth. They were touching elbows. "What pray tell have you brought to Austin?" Her voice was weak, trembling to match her fingers. "I have seen you driving a similar task, and my life has not been the same since."

Josiah drew in a deep breath. "I'm afraid this time is no different, Pearl. It is Juan Carlos I have brought home to bury. I'm sorry, your uncle is dead."

Pearl gasped, whimpered, brought her hand to her forehead, and promptly fainted. Luckily, Rory Farnsworth looked to have experience for such moments and caught her handily, embracing her like he'd been waiting for such a moment to prove his worth and value.

CHAPTER 54

After seeing to Pearl, then standing back and letting Farnsworth see her safely to a bench that sat in front of Sampson & Hendrik's, Josiah instructed Scrap and Tom Darkson to take the wagon to the undertaker.

Scrap hesitated. "What then?"

"Take the horses to the livery like I said. If I'm not there shortly, go ahead and get yourself settled in. I'll be at my house in a little while. This won't take long, and besides," Josiah said, "I'm anxious to see Lyle now that I'm back in Austin. I keep looking for him and Ofelia."

"I bet you are," Scrap said. The condescending tone Scrap usually took toward Ofelia was not evident in his voice. He almost sounded respectful.

"I am." Josiah stared at the boy's black eye. It had fully blossomed over the trip back to Austin. It looked as if a fading

438

purple chrysanthemum was stuck on his face. "I'm glad to be back in Austin."

"Home?" Scrap said.

"This city's never much felt like home to me, and Cortina knows to find me here, now." Josiah looked over his shoulder at Pearl. Farnsworth was fanning her with his handkerchief, whispering words Josiah couldn't hear. He rolled his eyes and then turned back to Scrap. "Go on now, I got some business to tend to before I'm free to do as I please."

Scrap nodded, climbed aboard the wagon, and grabbed up the reins. Before he could say anything, or get completely settled, Josiah put his hand up, stopping him from going on any farther.

"Hold on," Josiah said. He walked around to the back of the wagon, climbed up gently, and made his way to the ammunition box, trying not to touch the coffin — but that was impossible. He opened the box and grabbed up Juan Carlos's satchel with the letters in it. "All right," he said, climbing down. "You and Darkson take care to stay out of trouble, and I'll meet up with you later."

Scrap nodded, and so did Darkson. The boy had a confused look on his face; he had no idea what was going on, what the past and present circumstances meant to the sheriff, Pearl, or Josiah, but Scrap sure did.

Darkson plodded off alongside the wagon without offering any words — like a good solider should.

Josiah stood and watched them disappear around the corner, then turned his attention back to Pearl and Rory Farnsworth.

He stepped up on the boardwalk and stared the sheriff directly in the eye. "Can we go to your office, Rory? I'd like to finish up some business with Miss Fikes, if you don't mind. There's too many ears and eyes about in the open, and what I have to say is not knowledge I want gossiped about or passed on around town."

Farnsworth looked to Pearl for approval. She wiped the sweat from her forehead and nodded silently. "That would be fine, Josiah. Tell me, though, did Juan Carlos die a hero?"

The question surprised Josiah. "Yes," he said, softly, after thinking about his answer. "He died protecting me, Scrap, and the rest of the boys."

"So the Rangers have taken another man I loved?"

"I suppose so. Yes, they have," Josiah said.

The inside of Rory Farnsworth's office was

cool and comfortable. The walls were made of whitewashed stone and beaded with perspiration. A fan circled overhead, offering a nice reprieve from outside. Two simple chairs sat in front of the ornately carved desk that Farnsworth usually sat behind, and one wall was lined with locked cabinets full of rifles, guns, and ammunition.

The most noticeable thing, at least for Josiah, was the bare spot on the wall where a picture once hung. The whitewash around it was fresher, whiter, suggesting the picture had been removed recently.

Farnsworth noticed Josiah looking at the spot where the picture of the sheriff's father had once hung. "That newspaperman of yours is set on seeing my father hang."

"Paul Hoagland is not a friend, but he's not an enemy, either," Josiah said. He pulled out one of the chairs for Pearl to sit in.

"You could have fooled me," Farnsworth said. "I've moved my father to Tarrant County until the next trial convenes. Three down. One to go."

"I'm sure you'll be glad when this is all over with, Rory," Josiah said, respectfully. He felt some sadness for the man. Being the sheriff and having your father being tried as a murderer had to be difficult.

"Out of sight, out of mind. You know how

that goes."

"Yes, I'm well aware of the strategy."

Pearl exhaled slightly, drawing Farnsworth's attention to her. "Can I get you a glass of water, Pearl?"

"Please," she answered.

Josiah had remained standing. "If you could give us a few minutes in private, Rory, I would appreciate it. What I have to share with Pearl will not take long, then I'd like to see my son."

Pearl cast Josiah a quick, disturbed glance, then looked away. "We'll be fine, Rory. Josiah Wolfe is an honorable man. You know that."

"If you insist," Farnsworth nodded.

Pearl nodded, and the sheriff turned, exited the office, and closed the door behind him with more than a gentle pull.

Josiah ignored Farnsworth's annoyed exit and put the satchel on the desk in front of Pearl. "Really, Pearl, Rory Farnsworth? You broke off our courting to take up with him?"

"It's not like that, Josiah. That didn't come about until after I had sent you that letter."

"I have to believe that, don't I?"

"It makes no difference to me what you believe," Pearl said. "And besides, why not Rory Farnsworth? We have a lot in common. The places we once ventured no longer welcome us. We have fallen from grace according to polite society. Me for my mother's instability and poor financial dealings and Rory for his father's misdeeds. He is the only man in this city who has shown me any decency at all."

"Murders. His father murdered those girls. They were not misdeeds."

"Call them what you want. Rory has been around me most all of my life, but we have never gotten to know each other very well. The turn of events brought us closer together. But if Juan Carlos's death does not demonstrate what I meant in that letter, then nothing will. I could not bear to wait for your body to be paraded into town, dead from a Ranger's mission like my father and uncle. It is even more apparent now, at least to me, that I made the right decision. No matter how much I loved you, I could not send you off and then wait for you to be killed. And I will not expect you to change. You walk the streets in Austin like they are ill-fitting clothes. You do not belong here, Josiah. We could never be happy."

"It wouldn't matter who you were with," Josiah whispered. He didn't finish the sentence. But he continued the thought silently to himself: *I would not be able to bear seeing you on the arm of another man.* He knew then that she was right, and what he had to do once he got the matters at hand settled.

"I beg your pardon?" Pearl said. She looked away from Josiah to the satchel.

He ignored her question. Their relationship was over. It had been the moment the letter arrived in camp, and most definitely soon after, the first time he laid eyes on Francesca. "That was Juan Carlos's. I took the liberty of going through it. It seems," Josiah said, picking up the satchel and handing it to Pearl, "that you're now a very wealthy woman."

Pearl accepted the satchel. "I'm sorry?"

"There are gold coins, deeds, bank notes, and more documents that I don't understand. But it seems to me that when you add them all together, your days of pursuing an education to become a schoolteacher are over if you want them to be. I'm sure once the ears belonging to high society hear of this, they will welcome you back with open arms."

"That sounded spiteful, Josiah."

He didn't offer to defend himself. "I'm sorry, Pearl, for what happened to Juan Carlos. He was a good friend to me, and I will mourn his death for the rest of my life." He started to head for the door.

Pearl stood up, clutching the satchel

tightly, with tears growing in her eyes. Josiah couldn't tell if they were from happiness or sadness. "And we are done? Just like that? There's no hope for us now? This money could change your life, too."

"Money suddenly changed your heart?" Josiah scowled.

Pearl just glared at Josiah, all of her beauty gone for him. She looked like nothing more than the gossiping, heartless women she proclaimed to hate.

Josiah stopped at the door. "You're best off to stay with Rory. He'll know how to navigate the streets of Austin alongside you and get you where you want to go."

"Where are you going, Josiah? What's going to happen to you?"

"I'm going home, Pearl," he said, opening the door, coming face-to-face with Rory Farnsworth. "I'm going home."

EPILOGUE

There was very little furniture to load up, but the wagon was full of all the belongings that Josiah had brought with him to Austin. He sat with the reins in his hands, with Lyle next to him, and Ofelia, happily on the other side of the little boy.

Clipper had been relegated to the rear of the wagon again and remained aloof, and annoyed, at the prospect of being pulled somewhere else — instead of having the lead, and the freedom of his head going whichever direction he wanted.

A crate full of chickens sat in the back of the wagon, and they clucked nervously, as Josiah prepared to leave.

Scrap stood next to the wagon, staring at the ground. "You really think this is a good idea, Wolfe?"

"I told you after Juan Carlos's funeral that this was what I thought was best, not just for me, but for Lyle and Ofelia. We need to go home, to Seerville, where we belong. This city is only going to get bigger and louder. It sets my teeth astride now. I can never relax. I miss the piney woods, the places I know. I came here looking for a new life, but I was running away from the pain of my old life, too. None of that seems to matter now. It would just be too hard to live here for the rest of my life. Seems there's bad memories everywhere I turn, and I might as well be in the comfort of familiarity and a slower pace, if that's truly the case. Besides, I want to know my family's safe from the likes of Cortina and his men. It'll be easier in Seerville than here to see to that."

"I understand," Scrap said. "But we got orders to return to the company once we're all healed up. McNelly needs us to fight on against Cortina."

"I said nothing about leaving the Rangers, Scrap. Where'd you get that fool idea?"

"I don't know. I just figured you was done with everything."

"No, I'm going home and get settled. Once this shoulder is better, then I'll ride back south and join up with McNelly. He's a fine captain. You'll be fine here with Darkson, I 'spect."

Scrap scrunched his shoulders. "He's not actin' like them broken ribs hurt him much.

He's carousin' around like a tomcat, and that just leads to trouble, if you ask me. At least it did for me."

Josiah smiled as Lyle squirmed next to him. "Let's go, Papa," the little boy said.

Josiah peered around Lyle and said to Ofelia, "We have everything, right?"

She nodded. "*Sí,* Señor Josiah. I have double-checked and double-checked. I do not believe I have even left one speck of dust for the next peoples to come."

"Well, that's it then," Josiah said. "You know, Elliot, you can always come with us. There's a tack room in the barn. We can put a bed in it. There's room for you in Seerville. There's not much to carouse there."

"I don't want to be a bother," Scrap said.

"Where else are you going to go? Your Aunt Callie's in Dallas? It's almost as far a ride to Seerville."

"No, I don't want to impose on you. I'll stay here, and figure things out for myself."

"All right, suit yourself, but you're always welcome."

"Thanks, Wolfe, that means a lot."

Josiah nodded. "Well, we're going to go. I'll see you down the trail, I suppose."

"I hope so," Scrap said. "I sure hope so."

With that, Josiah flipped the reins, and the

horse that had brought them from the Arroyo Colorado headed out, kicking up a bit of dust, pulling the wagon down the street in no hurry, but obviously glad, like Josiah, to be leaving the city.

Lyle stood up and started waving to Scrap. "Bye-bye, Mr. Scrap. Bye-bye, Mr. Scrap," he yelled.

Josiah was tempted to look back, hoping all along that Scrap had changed his mind and was trailing after them, but he didn't. He just kept his eyes forward, looking straight ahead, watching happily, as Austin slowly disappeared behind him.

ABOUT THE AUTHOR

Larry D. Sweazy (www.larrydsweazy.com) won the WWA Spur Award for Best Short Fiction in 2005, and the 2011 and the 2012 Will Rogers Medallion Award for Western Fiction for novels in the Josiah Wolfe, Texas Ranger series — *The Scorpion Trail* (Berkley, 2010) and *The Cougar's Prey* (Berkley, 2011). He was nominated for a Derringer Award by the Short Mystery Fiction Society in 2007 and was a finalist in the Best Books of Indiana literary competition in 2010 for *The Rattlesnake Season* (Berkley, 2009). Larry won the Best Books of Indiana literary competition in 2011 with *The Scorpion Trail* (Berkley, 2010), making the novel the first Western to ever win the award. Larry is also the author of a modern-day thriller, *The Devil's Bone* (Five Star, 2012). He has also written, and published, more than fifty nonfiction articles and short stories, which have appeared in *Ellery*

Queen's Mystery Magazine; The Adventure of the Missing Detective: And 25 of the Year's Finest Crime and Mystery Stories; Boys' Life; Hardboiled; Amazon Shorts; and several other publications and anthologies. He is a member of MWA (Mystery Writers of America), WWA (Western Writers of America), and WF (Western Fictioneers).

He lives in Indiana, with his wife, Rose; two dogs, Rhodesian ridgebacks, Brodi and Sunny; and a black cat, Nigel.

We hope you have enjoyed this Large Print book. All our Thorndike, Wheeler, and Kennebec Large Print titles are designed for easy reading, and all our books are made to last. Other Thorndike Press Large Print books are available at your library, through selected bookstores, or directly from us.

For information about titles, please call:
(800) 223-1244

or visit our website at:
http://gale.cengage.com/thorndike

To share your comments, please write:

Publisher
Thorndike Press
10 Water St., Suite 310
Waterville, ME 04901